Most people had family to turn to

But Anna had no idea where she really belonged. The Skwars and Burics had helped raise her, but they were bonded to their own families. She was bonded to no one.

The only thing saving her sanity was the possibility that she'd been kidnapped by Antonin Buric. Ever since her talk with Mr. Markham, she'd been imagining the family she'd been born into.

She had blue eyes—did her parents have blue eyes, too? Anna was a natural blonde. She stood taller and had a more slender build than the women at Skwars farm.

Was her mother tall, or did her height come from her father? How many brothers and sisters did she have— or was she an only child? Was Anna the oldest? The youngest?

What was her real name? Was she of English or Scottish stock? Maybe Scandinavian?

The questions went on and on....

Dear Reader,

My house is only five minutes away from the home of Elizabeth Smart, the teen who was abducted in the middle of the night in June of 2002, and was miraculously returned to her family a year later.

During this time, all of Salt Lake City went into mourning. Yellow ribbons were tied on trees and school fences throughout the valley. A pilot friend of mine and his wife went on many searches during his free time, looking for her.

Young women and couples I knew combed the hills and canyons behind the Smart home looking for any trace of her. Volunteers by the thousands were busy putting up flyers in every conceivable place to make people aware.

Night after night my family and I, along with millions of families throughout Utah, the U.S. and overseas, prayed for that girl, for that family. The goodness of people united in a worthy cause was awesome to behold. To see Elizabeth returned to a family that never lost faith filled every heart with joy.

It is because of her story I was inspired to write these two Harlequin Superromance novels—*Somebody's Daughter* (February 2005) and *The Daughter's Return* (June 2005). Enjoy.

Rebecca Winters

P.S. If you have access to the Internet, please check out my Web site at www.rebeccawinters-author.com.

The Daughter's Return
Rebecca Winters

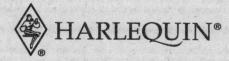

HARLEQUIN®

TORONTO • NEW YORK • LONDON
AMSTERDAM • PARIS • SYDNEY • HAMBURG
STOCKHOLM • ATHENS • TOKYO • MILAN • MADRID
PRAGUE • WARSAW • BUDAPEST • AUCKLAND

ISBN 0-373-71282-0

THE DAUGHTER'S RETURN

Books by Rebecca Winters

HARLEQUIN SUPERROMANCE

Don't miss any of our special offers. Write to us at the following address for information on our newest releases.

Harlequin Reader Service
U.S.: 3010 Walden Ave., P.O. Box 1325, Buffalo, NY 14269
Canadian: P.O. Box 609, Fort Erie, Ont. L2A 5X3

CHAPTER ONE

Bethesda Naval Hospital Grounds, Maryland
July 1

THROUGH HIS SUNGLASSES, Jake Halsey saw his CIA superior, Dan Ellerby, coming from a long way off. Even if Dan didn't walk with a slight limp, his seersucker shirt would have branded him. He swore by them in the humidity. Jake wouldn't be caught dead in one.

The shirt reminded him of the old men who sat around on their porches in Jacksonville, Florida, where he grew up. They wore seersucker and those big white pants pulled up around their ribs with a wide belt while they watched the world go by.

Though Jake was almost thirty-five years of age, he might as well have been an old buzzard like them, waiting to die. That's the way he'd been feeling for months.

Eager for this meeting that would end his exile, Jake's long, powerful legs picked up speed as he hurried toward the man who'd been his boss for the past nine years.

They met beneath a towering oak and shook hands, but Jake could tell immediately something was wrong. He pushed his shades on his head to get a better look.

The other man's countenance remained serious. In an instant, Jake's skin went clammy. His saliva seemed to dry up.

"It's good to see you, Dan."

"You're looking fine, Jake."

"But—"

"I didn't like your latest evaluation."

Jake shot him a hardened glance. "Then you know what you can do about it. Forget you saw it and let me go back to work."

"Can't do that, Jake. You know why."

"I won't be anybody's liability. Just leave me alone to do my own thing."

"You know that's not possible. What if you get into a situation you can't physically get out of—someone's going to come to the rescue. You could both be killed."

"So because of a shoulder replacement, I'm all washed up, is that it?"

"You still have fifteen percent disability. It's too much."

"That's a bunch of BS and you know it. For one thing, I'm right-handed and my right shoulder's fine. The other one will get better with time and therapy."

"Shall I tell you what else the doc said?" Dan kept on talking without acknowledging Jake's comment. "You have difficulty getting to sleep and staying asleep. When you do, the nightmares come. Since the explosion you've fallen into a deeper depression but still deny suicidal impulses."

"Who in the hell wouldn't be suicidal after being moved from one hospital to another and then being laid up here for the last five months?"

Dan squinted at him. "After your last covert operation, it's a miracle you're alive. I know you want to get back out there and do some damage, but I can't let you."

"Then it's a damn shame I've been taking up bed space here." He turned on his heel and headed toward the hospital.

"Hold on, Jake. I didn't come to give you your walking papers. Anything but. There's another assignment waiting for you when you've healed."

Jake paused midstride and turned around. "A job shuffling papers isn't what I had in mind."

"Me, either. Just hear me out. Until you're better and I can brief you about it, I've managed to arrange something for you while you're biding your time."

Because it was his boss pleading with him, Jake felt obliged to listen. Dan had forgiven him for a lot of unorthodox things he'd pulled in the past. He supposed this was payback time.

"Go ahead."

"I'm placing you on medical leave. You need a year to prove you're a hundred percent, but I can't give you that much time without raising too many questions from the higher ups. So it'll be six months."

Jake's head reared. "Six months?" He'd rot in that amount of time.

"It'll be a desk job, but not with the CIA. By then if you've improved enough to pass the physical fitness test, I'll send you back out."

They stared hard at each other. Jake knew Dan was once again sticking his neck out for him. He should be kissing the other man's feet.

"Thanks," he whispered.

"I'm on your side, Jake. Tomorrow you'll leave the hospital and be flown on a military transport to Hill Air Force Base outside Salt Lake City, Utah."

Jake frowned. His first instinct was to ask why Dan hadn't found him a position near the ocean. Pacific or Atlantic. It didn't matter as long as it was within sight of water.

"What's in Salt Lake?

"You mean you've never been there?"

"Afraid not. It's one of those places you fly over on your way to California."

"Exactly. Salt Lake means anonymity, the perfect cover for you while you're on the mend. The city happens to be the world's greatest repository for genealogical records. The famous Family History Center in downtown Salt Lake links people from every country around the globe to their ancestors. Genealogists assemble there by the thousands. They need translators for that kind of work. With your knowledge of Czech and Polish, it's a job right up your alley, yet no one would think to look for you in such a benign environment.

"You'll be given a car. There's an apartment close by. A hospital you can walk to. It has the latest techniques in therapy following a shoulder injury like yours where damage from shrapnel was the cause."

Dan went on. "Before you tell me you'll expire if you're landlocked, I have something important to tell you. It'll explain why I want you to blend in with the sand and salt of the desert."

His choice of words caused Jake to freeze.

"In the last few days it's come to light one of the men in your section is a double agent. He was behind several 'supposed' accidents, including the explosion that took out two of our best men and almost got you killed."

They'd been set up?

"The three of you were earmarked for assassination, but by some miracle, you survived." His boss took a deep breath. "You couldn't have prevented it," he said in a quiet voice.

Adrenaline shot through Jake's system. "Who's the mole?"

"I can't tell you that yet, but knowing you couldn't possibly have been responsible for their deaths should help you sleep better nights."

Hearing those words brought Jake exquisite relief. He'd headed that particular operation. He'd relived the explosion a thousand times, wondering what he'd done to make everything go wrong.

It appeared Dan knew him a lot better than Jake had given him credit for. The man had just removed an untenable burden.

"Do me one more favor? Get me to Prague? I need to see Kamila before I fly to Salt Lake."

Dan's expression didn't change, but his hesitation made Jake nervous as hell. "I knew you would ask, and I'd like to do it, but your cover's been blown. We haven't spent the better part of a year bringing you back to life only to let you be a walking target inside the Czech border now."

"What else haven't you told me?"

Dan pursed his lips. "Your father's wife disappeared soon after he was buried."

"And you never told me?"

His father had died of complications following an infection in his chest. Jake had gotten to Prague in time to say goodbye to his dad and help his stepmother bury him, but he hadn't been able to get back there since.

"By the time our operatives learned of her disappearance, you were deep undercover. Then came the explosion that almost wiped you out. With you barely hanging on, it wasn't the right time to be giving you bad news about your stepmother."

Dear Lord. "There's been no trace of her?"

"Afraid not. The company where she worked launched an investigation. One of our agents told us the police have been looking into the matter, but you know how far down their list of priorities that goes."

Jake knew exactly how missing persons cases were handled. Anyone over eighteen was an adult and capable of coming and going without permission. After fifteen months, the case would have been shoved into a box and forgotten. That was true in any country, including the Czech Republic.

Since the Velvet Revolution in 1989, the country had transformed itself into a Western-oriented market economy. More than eighty percent of their enterprises were in private hands. With that kind of major improvement, the Florida-based manufacturing firm his father worked for had expanded their toiletries branch overseas to include Prague.

But the old secret police still operated the same as before. Things weren't that different throughout the former Eastern Bloc. The KGB might operate under another name, yet it continued to flourish.

Jake's hard-muscled frame broke out in a cold sweat to think his work in the CIA might have been responsible for Kamila's disappearance.

His job had been to track the sale of Czech munitions to countries supporting terrorist groups in exchange for oil. Once discovered, he blew up the munitions while ground support from special forces took out the enemy, who used and guarded the stockpiles. His work had taken him around the globe. The horrific planned accident that almost cost him his life had happened in the Middle East.

"You've got to help me get to Prague, Dan. I know my dad's old haunts and friends. People who might be reluctant to talk to anyone else will talk to me."

"Can't risk it, Jake. I've had operatives looking for her ever since she didn't show up for work. I swear you'll hear news the minute I'm given any information on her."

Jake covered his face with his hand. By now those monsters could have done anything to his stepmother. If she was being held somewhere and tortured because of him…

Claremont, California
July 29

THE GUESTS CLUSTERED around the bottom of the staircase at the Talbots' Spanish mission-styled home, waiting for the beaming bride to toss the bouquet over her shoulder. Melissa Kit Aldridge Talbot McFarland looked beautiful.

She shot Maggie McFarland a wicked glance before starting the countdown.

"Whoever catches this is going to be the next bride, so watch out! One! Two! Three! Here it comes!"

A dozen pairs of female hands reached up to grab it, but when Kit threw the bouquet, it sailed high over everyone's head. As if it were a heat-seeking missile, it came straight for Maggie, who, at five feet nine inches, stood a little taller than the other hopefuls.

She'd been an easy mark for her new sister-in-law. In order not to hurt Kit's feelings, she had no choice but to pluck it out of the air and pretend to be overjoyed.

What nobody knew was that Maggie had never been hopeful in the marriage department. In fact, *hopeful* was the wrong word. Maggie had never aspired to marriage, period. She was thirty years old, free as the clouds where she loved to fly, and she ran a thriving law practice.

But she adored her brother Cord, who badly needed to be married to the right woman. Kit was made for him. Theirs was one of those marriages you knew had been made in heaven.

Please, God. Let it last forever. Don't let something ghastly happen to destroy their happiness.

"Come on, Maggie. We're driving the lovebirds to the hotel. Let's slip out the back way to the car before the mob descends."

Steven Talbot, Kit's twenty-five-year-old brother, grasped her hand and pulled her along, bouquet and all. They darted through the house and out the back door off the kitchen into the soft, balmy night air.

Over the last six weeks, while prewedding parties

had been going on both in Salt Lake City, Utah, and Claremont, California, the two of them had become good friends. Whenever the families got together, he naturally gravitated to her because he was starting his third year of law school at UCLA in Los Angeles at the end of August.

With his dark brown hair and blue eyes, he looked so much like Kit, whom Maggie loved, it was almost like being with her twin. Steven shared Kit's zest for life.

She hurried toward his parents' car with him. Once they were inside, he turned to her. "Quick, while we're alone, how about staying on for a while? We can drive to Laguna, spend a few days at our beach house."

"That sounds tempting, but I've got clients, plus foundation business to see about."

"You work too hard."

If he was trying to make her feel guilty, it had the opposite effect. "I like work."

"Everyone needs time off, Maggie."

"I'm afraid I'm one of those people who has such a hard time trying to enjoy a vacation, I need one after it's over."

He burst into laughter. "You mean to tell me you wouldn't like a day to lie on the sand with nothing more to do than listen to the surf?"

"It would be pure torture."

After a sustained silence he said, "You meant that, didn't you?"

She watched the guests start to pour out the front door of the house. The newlyweds would to be coming out any minute now. "My mind won't shut off, Steve."

"Because of your sister?"

"It started out that way. I was four when Kathryn was abducted from the house. Though I wasn't old enough to comprehend everything, I knew something terrible had happened to make my parents and brothers so grief stricken. As I grew older, I learned their grief was shared by thousands of parents and families who also had missing children."

He grimaced. "When Kit was stolen from Mom by that bank robber, neither David or I were even born yet. I'm afraid my parents' pain didn't impact me the same way."

"You mean you didn't feel compelled to spend your whole life looking for Kit?"

Steven pounded the steering wheel with the palm of his hand a couple of times. "Something like that."

"Your mom was lucky to get pregnant right away after the horror your parents had to live through. No doubt being able to dote on you made a huge difference in their ability to recover as well as they did."

"You're right."

"Then your brother came along. Your folks were so busy raising you both, they were able to detach themselves from the worst of their pain. Unfortunately Kathryn was Mom's last baby because the doctor advised her not to get pregnant again due to her high blood pressure. I'm afraid her arms have always felt empty."

Steve sobered and shook his head. "It's incredible the same thing happened to both our families. I've noticed how your mom clings to you. Mine would like to cling to Kit, but she can't."

Maggie thought Kit's brother was a shrewd observer

of human nature. "Your sister is torn, too, Steve. The last thing she wants is to live away from your family now that she's found you. I know Cord will make sure she gets down here a lot."

"He's a remarkable man. Besides making her insanely happy, I don't know too many men who would dedicate their lives to running a shelter. Most men with his resources wouldn't be satisfied to give all their money away to help others. In fact, your whole family's involvement in the foundation makes me feel guilty."

"Every situation is different, Steve. My family had the money and the means. They realized their social and political prominence could make a difference, which was why they were driven to start the Kathryn McFarland Foundation. My brothers and I were swept into it without realizing what had happened to us. Their guilt that they hadn't heard the kidnapper come in, plus my desire to make our parents smile again, pretty well set us up to be as involved as Mom and Dad."

"Thank God for your family, Maggie! The foundation's Web site helped bring Kit home to my parents. They're so happy, they're not the same people anymore."

"Neither is Cord. Kit has changed his world. It's like he's been released from a prison. He laughs and smiles like he never did before. I hardly recognize my brother these days."

"I could wish the same thing would happen to your family," Steve whispered.

"After a miracle like yours, it has given our family renewed hope that Kathryn's alive and out there somewhere." Maggie looked out the car windows before continuing in a soft voice. "You know it was Frankie Burke, the man Kit thought was her father, who finally cracked enough to help solve *your* sister's case and unite her with your family." She turned to face him.

"Even though he's in prison serving time for armed robbery, he refuses to talk about *my* sister's disappearance, but he knows the truth behind it. I won't rest until we get answers from him."

"Let me help."

"Keep praying for us, Steve."

"I'd like to do more than that. I heard you telling Dad you were going to go to Lompoc prison and talk to Frankie. How about letting me come along for support?"

"I've got some research to do first. By then you'll be in classes."

"Right now class seems very far away. Since our family has been united with Kit, we're all having trouble wanting to do anything but be together. It's been a nonstop party. But it's about to end."

"That's why I fly. It keeps me focused."

"You know what I mean."

"Of course I do, so I've got an idea. How would you like to move to Salt Lake for fall semester and clerk for me?"

Steven's head swiveled around. He looked like a man in shock. "You're serious?"

"Absolutely. I've been thinking of asking you since I heard your specific area of study was contract law. If you're anticipating a specialization in debtor's rights, then my office is a good place to start."

Not only would Steve make a great addition to her office, she knew how important it was for Kit to have someone in her own birth family around. It would give the McFarlands and the Talbots a sense of continuity they all needed.

"I could take classes at the U law school while I'm there…."

Maggie could hear his intelligent mind turning everything over. "Kit will be at the U finishing up her last year. You guys could see a lot of each other. It would be fun."

"If I thought it were possible…"

"It is. You've been to my penthouse with your family. Two floors down there's a great furnished apartment like mine ready to move into. It has enough rooms to hold your whole family when they want to come for visits."

"I couldn't afford it."

"Since I own the building, I'm sure you and I could negotiate a price within your law clerk's budget."

"Maggie—"

"Best of all it's only a two-minute walk to the cottage where Kit and Cord will be living during the week. I often eat lunch with him. On the weekends they'll stay at his house in Alta Canyon. The whole situation's perfect."

"Too perfect. Something's wrong with it."

Maggie laughed softy. "Maybe after a while it will seem like too much togetherness and you'll be thrilled to get back to California. But my offer is sincere. Why don't you come to Salt Lake in a few days and visit the law school, take a look around my office and the empty apartment, see what you think."

Though Maggie had loved all the wedding festivities, she was glad it was over. After the honeymooners returned from Europe in a few weeks, there would be another big reception at the McFarland home in Salt Lake. Then everyone would be getting back to their busy lives and she could once again concentrate on finding out what happened to Kathryn.

None of the family had ever stopped looking for Maggie's sister. They never would. *Maggie never would.* Since a miracle had happened to unite Kit with her real family after twenty-six years, Maggie was on fire with renewed hope that the McFarland family could experience a similar miracle.

"I think you and your family are the most generous, extraordinary human beings I've ever known. It's probably the reason Kit fell in love with your brother on sight," Steve murmured in a husky tone. "You're all made of the same great stuff."

Before Maggie could respond to such a touching compliment, the newlyweds were climbing into the back seat of the car.

She looked over her shoulder at them. Talk about two radiant lovers...

Skwars Farm, Wisconsin
July 30

THE SMALL LIVING ROOM of the tiny farmhouse looked larger with a fresh coat of pale yellow paint. Anna looked around, satisfied with her handiwork. Time to wash the roller brush and pan, then go home.

After putting in a full day's work at the farm bakery before coming over here to paint, she was exhausted. Bed was sounding better and better.

She started for the kitchen, but stopped when she glimpsed Nelly and Miki through the doorway. They were getting married next week, and would be living in this little farmhouse. The two of them were so wrapped up in each other, they'd forgotten anyone else was around. Anna experienced bittersweet pain just watching them.

Though she was thrilled for her cousin, it meant Anna was losing the closest thing she had to a sister. With Nelly moving out of her parents' home where Anna had been living for the past two years, she felt her world crumbling.

Not wanting to disturb them, she put the pan and roller on the floor against the wall and quietly let herself out the front door into the warm, humid night. Her house was a half mile down the road. Anna started walking toward it.

All of the lush farmland and buildings she could see in every direction belonged to the Skwars' descendents and their progeny. There were thirty farmhouses, large and small, plus different outbuildings and shops dotting the landscape. The earliest ones dated back a hundred years when the first Skwars immigrant from Czechoslovakia settled here.

It was after 11:00 p.m., but she felt no fear being alone. Everyone was a relative. They were a tightly knit group who watched out for each other. That sense of community kept generations of Skwarses together. Today their thriving fruit-farm enterprise was renowned throughout the state of Wisconsin. Yet it had never felt like home to Anna.

She'd lived here all her life. First with Olga, the niece of Anna's great-grandmother. When the old woman's health had failed, Anna had been passed around among the different family members.

Two years ago, she'd been rotated to Josef and Milena's house. They had five children, the oldest of whom was Nelly. Anna had always liked Nelly, who was close to her age. Sharing the same bedroom, working in the bakery together, they'd become great friends.

But those days were over. After the wedding, Nelly would be helping her husband to get ready for the harvest.

With Olga long since dead, and her favorite cousin married, Anna knew she couldn't live here any longer. Unlike her relatives who were satisfied to stay on the farm all their lives, something inside her yearned for a new experience. She had her dreams, but she felt as if they were unlikely to become reality. Seeing Nelly in Miki's arms tonight had jolted her in ways that left her aching and feeling empty inside.

She could have been married by now. Two different guys with no imagination from neighboring farms would have loved to join the Skwars dynasty. But the thought of spending the rest of her life with either of them brought her no joy.

When she entered the house, Nelly's father was just starting up the stairs.

"Josef?" Though he was a cousin who was a generation older than herself, he was like an uncle of sorts. Of all the family members she'd lived with, he was her favorite. "Do you think Milena would mind if I talked to you for a few minutes?"

"Of course not. She's already gone up to bed. Where's Nelly?"

"Still out with Miki."

He grinned. "That was a foolish question, wasn't it? Come in the parlor." He opened the door for her. After she passed through, he asked, "How's the painting coming?"

"It's done."

"I'm sure they appreciated your help."

"I was happy to do it."

He sat down in one of the wingback chairs and indicated the couch for her. She sank down on the end of it. "What's going on? You look like you've lost your best friend."

"I have."

His gaze studied her features for a minute. "You're talking about Nelly."

She nodded.

"My Nelly will only be a five-minute walk down the road."

"It's not the same as having her here and you know it."

Josef sat forward. "You've never been happy here, have you?"

"Out of all the family members I've lived with, I've enjoyed being in your home the most."

"That's nice to hear, but it's not exactly what I meant. I see something in your eyes that's always looking beyond the mark."

He understood a lot.

"I've got to do something with my life, Josef."

"You mean college."

"Yes."

"If that's what you want to do, then the family will get together to help you, but there's just one problem."

"What is it?"

He stared at her for a long moment. "When Olga brought you and Great-aunt Marie to the farm, you were a baby with no papers."

"Papers?"

"You had no birth certificate. No christening record. Nothing."

Anna blinked. "But you *have* to have a birth certificate to do anything. To go to school, to get married—"

"Exactly. Olga couldn't believe your mother and father would simply leave you to your great-grandmother's care without giving her some kind of documentation. After you arrived here, I understand the family searched for your parents to no avail.

"When Olga wanted to go to the authorities about it, Marie wouldn't hear of it because she was so certain your parents would make contact. Before she left New York, she left a forwarding address and phone number with all her friends so your father and mother would know where to find the two of you.

"I'm afraid the months stretched into years while she waited in vain for some word from them. According to Olga, Marie was adamant about saying nothing to the authorities. She was so positive they'd come, and Great-uncle Jainos backed her up.

"In the meantime, the family protected you by keeping you with us and giving you jobs where you didn't need a social-security number. I didn't know about the missing documentation until you came to stay with Milena and me. Julia's the one who told me something should be done to get you legalized.

"We were waiting to see if you would accept Robert's proposal before we brought up the subject. But since that didn't happen, and you want to go to college, then it's time to do something about your situation. You need to consult a good attorney. The family will pay for it."

Anna was in shock.

Her thoughts flew back over the years. As certain incidents came to mind, she realized how well the family had shielded her. She particularly remembered the time she'd wanted to get a driver's license, and the family had told her to wait until she could afford to buy her own car. They'd let her drive around the farm, but not out on the highways.

"What kind of an attorney should I see?"

"Julia has some ideas. Why don't you talk to my sister in the morning. She's the one who knows the most about your situation. I'm sure she'll be able to help you."

Devastated, Anna got up from the couch to leave the room. He followed after her.

When they reached the bottom of the stairs, he said, "Don't hate the family too much, Anna. Everyone has wanted to honor Marie's plea to leave this situation alone in the hope that your parents would come for you."

"But they didn't! They never wanted me!"

He put a hand on her shoulder and squeezed gently. "I'm so sorry. There's something wrong with parents who abandon a little baby. Deep down I know Great-aunt Marie must have been ashamed to think she had two grandsons who turned out to be—" He stopped himself.

"Go ahead and say it, Josef! It would only be what I'm thinking." Tears gushed down her hot cheeks.

"No. I'm not going to do that. They couldn't have been all bad, otherwise your mother and father wouldn't have given birth to a wonderful daughter like you. I've told you before that I love you, Anna. We all do."

"I love you, too," she said in a quiet voice before racing up the stairs where she could give vent to her grief.

CHAPTER TWO

Salt Lake City, Utah
August 6

NINE DAYS IN A ROW above one hundred degrees, and another one hundred–plus day predicted for today. It was a dry heat, but still nothing compared to the oven of the Middle East at its worst.

By seven, Jake had finished his early morning run up City Creek Canyon behind the State Capitol. His spacious furnished apartment was one of five ideally located in an old Tudor-style mansion on the hill running up to the Capitol where there was a superb view of the city.

The landlord indicated the tenants kept to themselves. Everyone had a different schedule. He wasn't more specific than that. That suited Jake just fine.

He hadn't expected to like living in Utah, but the many scenic canyons and rugged mountains rising from the valley floor caused him to change his mind.

Quite a few people enjoyed jogging at the same time of morning. He'd met several women who gave out signals they'd like to get to know him better. So far he wasn't interested and only smiled at them without slow-ing down. With less than five months to go before he was back on the job, he'd made the decision not to get involved with anyone.

Out in the field, the women agents he dated knew the score. If they had expectations for something lasting, they kept it to themselves. Out here, he didn't want to have to explain himself, so it was better to leave well enough alone.

Most weeknights he cooked his own meals and read until late. Occasionally, he took in a movie downtown. On the weekends he drove to the mountains to camp out and fish.

Since Dan had told him he wasn't responsible for leading his team to their deaths, he'd been sleeping better nights.

He could only recall one nightmare that had brought him out of a deep sleep. It had happened the first week of his arrival. This time it hadn't been about the mission that had turned into a tragedy. He'd dreamed Kamila was being tortured.

The doctor in charge of his physical therapy at North Avenues Hospital urged him to stay away from all alcohol, coffee, tea and tobacco as a way of keeping fit and warding off bad dreams.

Since Jake had taken his advice, he was beginning to have a sense of well-being he hadn't experienced in years. Though he was living a spartan existence, he liked the feeling.

If the worry over his stepmother hadn't been eating at him, he probably wouldn't have been as restless at his sedentary day job. So far he hadn't been presented with anything to really challenge his mind. But there was one plus to the job. His five co-workers, all married and older than he was, were nice people who for the most part minded their own business.

Once showered and shaved, Jake ate breakfast, then headed for work with a bottle of freezing-cold citrus Gatorade.

The Eagle Gate Genealogical Firm was located on the ground floor of an apartment building at the bottom of the hill. It was a two-minute walk from his own apartment.

"Morning, Jake."

He shut the front door. "How are you, Wendell?"

"Couldn't be better," the owner said, his head already buried in a census book. "Some new disks came in for you to transcribe. Late nineteenth–century names. I've put everything on your desk."

"Thanks."

Wendell, whose expertise was the U.S. and British Isles, manned the front desk located on one side of the room. He helped people who wanted to trace their lineage back across the water to England, Ireland and Scotland.

The opposite side of the room had been set up as a reception area. Jake walked past him to reach his own small room down the hall where the offices were located.

At present, the firm specialized in Western and Eastern European genealogy. Since Jake's arrival to help with the Czech, Polish and Slovak research, it had eased up the heavy workload for Lara, who could now concentrate fully on Russian searches.

Arnie, a Dane, ran the Scandinavian department. Simone, who spoke Italian, French and Spanish, headed up the Romance languages research. Gunter worked on Swiss, German and Austrian genealogies.

Jake admired their collective expertise. They adored their work helping people research a family name to its roots. Genealogy was more than a job to them. Once you got hooked, you couldn't stop. In the future, the CIA would be able to hire all of them for intelligence-gathering purposes.

His office was mostly desk with a couple of chairs for clients. No window. But the blessed cool of good air-conditioning made it a welcoming place.

Lara loved gardening so she supplied him with two pots of pink and purple petunias to keep his space from being completely colorless. Simone steeped herself in clutter and couldn't understand why he didn't have one family picture displayed.

He had a lot of mementos in storage in Florida, including pictures, but they had to remain there while he worked undercover with the CIA. Jake had no plans to retire.

To satisfy everyone's curiosity, he'd told the staff his belongings hadn't caught up to him since his move from San Diego where he'd been brought up in a Czech household. No one suspected his cover story about being a detective wasn't on the level. Simone took pity on him and hung two large posters on his walls, one of Prague, the other of Warsaw.

After switching on his radio to a classical-music station, he booted up the computer and began reading in Czech off the first disk. It contained names from a cemetery in Bohemia, or precisely, from the village of Oujezdec, in the town of Kutna Hora in County Caslav.

The cemetery can be reached by turning directly off the public road east of the town with access open to all via a continuous masonry wall and locking gate. The cemetery is about 0.06 hectares. Twenty to one hundred stones, most in original location, date from 1880s.

This cemetery has special sections with no detail given. Marble, granite, limestone and sandstone are finely smoothed and inscribed. Some tombstones have iron decorations or lettering and portraits on the stones.

Jake scanned the first set of names: Hurtoovi, Hurtowvi, Markvicka, Metivelski.

Slowly and meticulously he began converting the information to English. He added notes that names like Hurtoovi or Hurtowvi were probably changed to Hurt once the person arrived in America.

As soon as the translated information was put on a new disk, he would file it in the main computer database. Professional and nonprofessional genealogists around the world could access it through the Family History Link.

Every time he wrote down a head-of-family name, it prompted him to ponder that person's life. He or she was precious to someone who lived a hundred, maybe two hundred years later, depending on the date.

Until Dan had made arrangements for him to work undercover here, Jake had never given a great deal of thought to tracing one's ancestry. As far as he knew, his own forebearers were English.

Wendell glommed on to that bit of news and insisted on researching one of his grandparents' lines for him. So far he'd found out Jake had a great-great-grandmother, Lilley Bowen. Lo and behold, she was a Scot!

Jake hadn't realized he had any Scottish blood in him. He'd thought himself of pure English stock.

Lilley's family had moved from Scotland to Ulster in Ireland before emigrating to Virginia. Later on, the family relocated to Florida, and eventually Jake's mother, Jane Bowen, was born.

Knowing he had Scottish blood in him, Jake had told Wendell he'd pay him to do more searches on his family lines when he had the time. That was three weeks ago.

When Wendell came into Jake's office two hours later, he wondered if his boss had made another surprising find and couldn't wait to inform him.

"I've got a new client for you. Do you have time to see her now?"

"Of course."

"I'll bring her back and introduce you."

The bulk of Jake's work was transcription. He didn't get a lot of clients. When he did, they were usually retired people who finally had the time to search for their roots. Still, this interruption made a change in his daily routine, which was normally pretty quiet.

After finishing off his Gatorade, he saved everything to the hard drive, then opened a new client file to take down information. Footsteps in the hall prompted him to get to his feet.

To his astonishment, a striking blonde who was probably in her late twenties stood in the doorway of his office. With those long, shapely legs she had to be five-eight, five-nine.

She wore a two-piece cotton suit in a light blue color that matched her dark-lashed eyes. Her chin-length hair, a blend of cream and dark honey, framed an oval face. With that wide mouth and high cheekbones, she was a total knockout. The kind of woman he hadn't come across in years.

Damn if he didn't find himself looking for a wedding ring on her left hand.

Double damn if he didn't notice her fingers and wrists were bare of jewelry except for a gold watch.

Wendell was all smiles. "Jake Halsey? I'd like you to meet Margaret McFarland."

They both said, "How do you do," at the same time.

Wendell chuckled. "She's ex–U.S. Senator Reed McFarland's daughter and is probably as prominent. But in case you—"

"I know his name very well," Jake interrupted. "I understand he chose not to run for a fifth term because of personal reasons."

"That's right," she said without making any additional explanation. With those two words, Jake got the feeling she was a private person who'd learned to deal with her father's fame a long time ago.

Senator McFarland from Utah had sat on the intelligence committee for three terms. It represented about the same amount of time Jake had been working for the CIA.

The senator had been one of the men most open to breaking down the barriers between the different intelligence-gathering agencies in order to share information. Jake had always admired him for his firm stance on that issue.

What would his daughter be wanting from a Czech genealogist?

"Please have a seat, Ms. McFarland."

Hoping Wendell would take the hint and leave, Jake walked back around his desk and sat down in the swivel chair.

"Did you know her great-great-great-grandfather was John McFarland, Utah's Copper King? He was the son of Scotch-Irish immigrants, just like you, Jake."

"Is that right?"

"Yes, and he ended up making millions."

"*Not* like me."

Jake's quip produced a faint smile on her lips, which he reciprocated. Their eyes locked while Wendell said, "The mansion he had built in Salt Lake is only six blocks up the street on South Temple. It's the showplace of the whole valley."

"I've seen it," Jake murmured, still looking at the composed woman seated across from him. "It's magnificent. So are the grounds."

"Ms. McFarland's brother has turned it into a women's homeless shelter called Renaissance House."

"That's very commendable." Jake meant it.

Wendell must have finally realized his presence wasn't needed. "Yes, well, I'll leave you two alone to get on with business." He went out the door and shut it behind him.

"What can I do for you, Ms. McFarland?"

She sat opposite him with her elegant legs crossed. He forced himself to concentrate on her expressive features, which was no penance at all. If the flush on her skin was anything to go by, she'd been out in the hot sun for a little while. Jake could swear she didn't wear makeup except for lipstick the color of a red-gold peach.

"I need help tracking down any information you can find on a Franz Buric from New York City. He's in a California prison right now doing time for armed robbery."

"Spell that name for me."

When she did, he started typing the information.

"He would have been fifteen years old thirty-three years ago, the time of his first arrest. According to the information I have on him, he was living with his Czech grandmother."

"Do you have her name?"

"No. That's what I'm hoping you can find, along with the names of his parents and any relatives. I'm willing to pay you three times the amount you charge to get this information for me as soon as possible."

While he was reacting to the genuine tremor in her voice, she cried, "I can imagine how that sounded. Please don't think I go around throwing money at people to get what I want. It's just that in this case—"

"You're desperate?" he supplied the words.

Her complexion lost some of its color. At the same time her eyes had grown suspiciously bright. "Yes," she whispered.

"What aren't you telling me?"

He expected her to pretend she didn't know what he was talking about. Instead she surprised him.

"A lot."

Just as Jake had thought.

"You've got me so intrigued, I couldn't care less about the extra money, which I wouldn't accept under any circumstances. If you'll give me a number where I can reach you, I'll call you as soon as I've made a search."

"Thank you."

She reached in her purse and pulled out a brochure. Across the top she wrote a phone number, then handed it to him. "When you find any information, please don't hesitate to call me no matter the hour."

As she got up from the chair to leave, his gaze followed her willowy figure out the door. She left the delicate scent of flowers in her wake, bringing his senses alive. He reached for the brochure and lounged back in the chair to read it.

Welcome to the Kathryn McFarland
National Foundation
Located in the McFarland Plaza on South Temple
in Salt Lake City, Utah.
This Web site is updated daily

May 3 marks the twenty-sixth anniversary of the abduction of our fourth child, Kathryn McFarland, from the McFarland home in Salt Lake City, Utah. Born April 2, she'd only been a month old at the time she was taken.

Jake let out a groan.

Soon after the kidnapping and community search, the Kathryn McFarland Foundation was founded and now honors Kathryn's memory by finding missing children and preventing them from going missing in the first place.

When Kathryn was kidnapped, our community and many others joined together to help us find her because there was an immediate recognition that she was everyone's child and that we are all in this together.

Child abductions across our nation since its early beginnings have highlighted the need for legislation to enhance our ability to protect our children from predators of all types. When a child is kidnapped, time is of the essence.

All too often it is only a matter of hours before a kidnapper commits an act of violence against the child. That is why we're pleased that the U.S. Senate has acted to pass legislation creating a national AMBER Alert system, which galvanizes entire communities to assist law enforcement in the timely search for and safe return of child victims.

Since its inception the foundation has assisted approximately 17,000 families, as well as law enforcement agencies in their searches. We have seen over 85% of those children returned home safely. This is what continues to give us hope.

Please help us to keep all our children safe.
The Reed McFarland Family

Jake's eyes darted to their family picture, which included Reed McFarland, his wife Ellen, a son Richard, a son Benjamin and daughter Margaret.

A very attractive family, all of whom ran the foundation.

Our hotline phone is manned twenty-four hours, 365 days a year. To report a missing child and ask

for support, call 1-800-KATHRYN. Volunteers welcome. Foundation headquarters are open Monday
through Saturday year round from 8:00 a.m. to
8:00 p.m. (Christmas Day and New Year's Day ex-
cepted).

On the reverse side of the brochure was a list of
things parents could do to cut down the risk of their
child being kidnapped.

After Jake had devoured the information, he sat there
staring blindly into space.

Margaret McFarland was on a mission to find the
predator who'd abducted her baby sister. Jake didn't
need a crystal ball to know Franz Buric was their family's number-one lead in an unsolved case.

Ever since Dan had told him his stepmother was
missing, Jake had been in agony because there wasn't
anything he could do to find her until he could get to
Prague. But there was a lot he could do to assist this
woman in her search.

Why it had taken twenty-six years for Ms. McFarland to come up with the name Buric was a mystery that
wanted solving.

Without hesitation he pulled out his cell phone. Franz
Buric was in prison, which meant he probably had an
extensive police record. Jake was anxious to learn the
details. Dan had contacts in high places. It was time to
call in a few favors.

As his superior had said, he had a job for Jake that
was right up his alley. For the first time since arriving
in Salt Lake, he was beginning to believe it. The sooner

Jake obtained the information Ms. McFarland wanted, the sooner he would have the legitimate right to set up an appointment with her to discuss everything. They *were* going to discuss everything, face-to-face.

His biggest problem was that he might break his own rule and call her anyway because he couldn't help himself.

It shouldn't have surprised him Wendell appeared at the door a few minutes later. "How did it go?"

If curiosity killed the cat, Wendell would have been dead years ago. Jake lifted his head. "She's asked me to research a Czech name in New York City."

Wendell scratched his balding head. "I didn't know the senator had Czech ancestry. Fascinating! Make it your top priority. You can finish transcribing those disks later."

Less than an hour had passed before Dan called back to give him the phone number of an agent at headquarters in New York, who'd be able to get him the pertinent information on Buric.

Not wanting to waste any time, Jake walked over to Wendell's office and asked, "Do you have a recent New York telephone directory?"

"Coming right up."

Wendell quickly went in search of the requested item. Jake had barely returned to his own office when his boss walked in with the directory.

"What name are we looking for?"

Jake smiled to himself. "Franz Buric."

It was obvious Wendell was thrilled to have the senator's daughter for a client. But his excitement wasn't about money—otherwise he wouldn't be in this business. Wendell had the true genealogist's lust for the hunt. Jake could identify with that.

Though their careers were poles apart, deep down they hunted for information and wouldn't stop until they'd found what they were looking for. In Jake's case, the intelligence he'd been after on his last mission had caused him to walk into a booby trap that claimed lives.

Wendell had chosen the safer course. Because of that choice, look who'd walked into the office a little while ago—

Jake was still reeling.

He could tell himself it was because he hadn't been with a woman for a long time. But that wasn't strictly true. There'd been a couple of nurses in the last year who'd wanted to get into a permanent relationship. Both were good looking, intelligent, but neither one of them had inspired him to let go of his deceased wife's memory.

"I've only found one Buric in the whole directory," Wendell exclaimed, bringing Jake back to the present. "Initial *F*. Maybe we've gotten lucky. Go ahead and call. I'll dictate the number. It's a two-one-two area code."

Wendell's impulsive nature reminded Jake of his own. He reached for the receiver and pressed the digits. It rang six times. Jake was about to hang up when a male voice answered. *"Dobry den."*

Good. He spoke Czech.

"Dobre jitro," Jake responded in kind. After telling him his name was Bedrich Veverka, a genealogist re-

searching a family line, he explained he was looking for a Franz Buric.

"Prominte." Sorry, the voice on the other end said.

Jake listened as the man named Frantisek told him he didn't know another Buric in New York, let alone someone named Franz. His people were from Tabor. He was an only child and had emigrated to the U.S. after he'd lost both parents.

But Frantisek was happy to give him the names of his parents and grandparents. He also promised to notify Jake by e-mail if he learned anything about the man named Franz.

They exchanged e-mail addresses. Before they hung up, Jake gave him his cell-phone number and told him to call collect if he happened on to a vital piece of information.

Jake shot Wendell a glance before telling him what he'd learned. "He'll contact me if he discovers anything."

"It's a start." Wendell stood up and reached for the directory. "Wish I could stay in here, but I've got a client waiting. Keep me posted."

"I will. Thanks for your help, Wendell."

"You bet."

Deciding to skip lunch, Jake spent the rest of the day researching the surname Buric in Czechoslovakia from the records already in the database. Long before it was called the Czech Republic, he found lists of them between 1700 and 1800, mostly from Susice, Tabor and Zhor.

After that date, he found other lists simply stating Bohemia as their origin. Those Burics who'd emigrated to the U.S. settled in Iowa, Illinois, Minnesota and Wisconsin, with the latter having the largest percentage of settlers. Everything he could find he put in Ms. McFarland's file. He noticed no Burics had settled in New York.

With only one Buric in the most recent New York City telephone directory, Jake had to conclude many of the early Buric immigrants had turned to farming as soon as they arrived.

So what had Franz Buric been doing in New York City with his Czech grandmother? Why hadn't she ended up on a farm? Had her grandson come from the old country to live with her and gain citizenship? Or had he been born in the States? Where were his parents? Who were they?

There were too many questions for which Jake wanted the answers now.

And you know why, Halsey. So you'd better plan a full evening to keep your thoughts occupied or you're not going to make it.

He e-mailed the New York Bureau of Vital Statistics for a birth record anywhere in the state of New York on a Franz Buric. Just in case Ms. McFarland was off on the man's age, he instructed the person in vital records to check on a male born any time between forty-five and fifty years ago.

Having done all he could for now, he finished taking the information off the disk he'd been working on earlier. The next set of names and dates came up on the screen: Bucek, Buric, Dozbaba, Molan.

Buric.

Vojtech Buric, born 1871. Married Anna Molan, 1896, in Kutna Hora. Children: Katrina, born 1898, Jan, born 1900, Oujezdec.

Quickly Jake put the information in Ms. McFarland's file, then finished transcribing the disk.

On his way out of the office, he waved to Arnie who was still on the phone. Everyone else had gone home, and no wonder. It was ten after six.

Jake locked the front door behind him with every intention of heading straight for his apartment. But some inner force compelled him to walk to the corner. He found his legs striding up South Temple toward the Mc-Farland Plaza he'd passed many times since coming to Salt Lake.

The knowledge of Kathryn's abduction increased his anxiety over Kamila's disappearance. Both weighed heavily on his mind. He hardly noticed the intense heat rising from the pavement.

In the plaza courtyard, he paused to study the sculpture of a mother with a baby in her arms. He'd stopped once before to admire the moving work of art. But since Ms. McFarland's visit to the office, it held brand-new significance for him. The plaque read Blessed Are The Children.

His throat swelled.

People were coming and going from the complex as he approached the main doors. Once inside the lobby, he couldn't miss a whole room to the left, open wide to the public. Running above the opening from one end to the other were giant screens, the kind at airports.

But instead of arrival and departure times, these flashed the names of kidnapped children with the time and date of their abduction. While he and several others stood there reading them, new names kept popping up at the top.

Those names meant some family's agony was just beginning. The sight of them was gut-wrenching. He heard the woman behind him groan.

Suddenly a voice sounded over a loudspeaker. "Welcome to the Kathryn McFarland Foundation. Take the time to come in and learn how to help us fight crime so the next kidnapping won't be your child."

There was a wide-screen television in the middle of the entry flashing pictures of the children named on the screens above. Like everyone else who passed, Jake stood there mesmerized and appalled.

So many children missing…

Obviously there were other businesses on the ground floor of the plaza, but Jake noticed that most people took the time to go inside the foundation room. He was no exception.

It was like being in a library, but all the information had to do with educating the public about abductions. Volunteers manned the various displays to answer questions.

One station dealt with ways to fight Internet crime. The statistics on the amount of teens who disappeared after an Internet encounter were staggering.

Another area explained that most kidnappings were done by someone the child knew. Literature and videos were available to instruct the whole family.

In one corner, a display had been set up to show how

to proof your home against break-ins and violent abductions from total strangers. Jake watched the video that showed the wrong and right way to secure windows and doors.

He picked up one of the pamphlets put out by the local police department. The McFarlands hadn't left a stone unturned.

According to the brochure Ms. McFarland had given him, the foundation had assisted in over 17,000 recoveries. Thousands and thousands of grateful parents were indebted to the remarkable McFarland family for their tireless effort and generosity. Yet they still hadn't been able to find their own child.

Out of the corner of his eye, Jake glimpsed a volunteer seated at a desk behind the counter. Without conscious thought, he approached her.

"Good evening," she said. "We're glad you took the time to come in. Is there something special I can do for you?"

"I hope so. I'd like to volunteer my services."

She flashed him a bright smile. "That's wonderful. We always need help. Here." She handed him a clipboard with an application and a pen.

"Go ahead and fill it out. The people who run the foundation meet on Saturdays and they'll review your application."

Saturday…that was the day after tomorrow.

"If everything's in order, you'll receive a phone call asking you to come in and meet with them for an interview."

The McFarlands ran a tight ship. Everything he

learned about them increased his admiration. The fact that he might have to wait until next week for an answer was his problem, not theirs.

He filled in all the blanks, putting in Wendell's name for a reference. In case Ms. McFarland felt inclined to contact him personally, he wrote down his work and cell-phone number.

Obviously they needed people who could go out on searches, people who would help feed volunteers who assembled to help find an abductee.

He checked all the boxes. Under preferences, Jake indicated he would like to answer the hotline several times a week during the dead hours of the night. Why not? On Saturdays he was available to work on the foundation floor in any capacity they wanted.

"Here you go."

The woman glanced at his application, then lifted her eyes to him. "On behalf of the McFarland family, I want to thank you very much for your willingness to help, Mr. Halsey."

He nodded. "How long have you worked here?"

"Six months. My neighbor's little boy was kidnapped. But thanks to the AMBER Alert, the kidnapper was caught on the freeway. Billy was returned to his parents. It's all because of Senator McFarland's insistence in getting that bill passed. I figure I need to do my part."

Jake thought of his stepmother. Only God knew what had happened to her, but one thing was certain. There was no foundation with volunteers out looking for her. No AMBER Alert. Until he could find a way to get over to Prague undetected, he would have to live with this feeling of helplessness.

"I feel the same way. Thank you for your time."

As he turned away from the counter and passed one of the displays, his attention was diverted by the tall beauty in pale blue who swept past the television screen at the entrance in a great hurry. He'd know those long, gorgeous legs anywhere.

With his eyes riveted, he followed her progress to the volunteer counter, which she slipped behind. Jake was in no hurry to leave. He observed the two women chatting for a few minutes. Then the one who'd taken his application left the room. Apparently her shift was over.

He glanced at his watch. Ten after seven. Jake had a hunch Ms. McFarland was late. A smile broke the corner of his mouth. It was nice to know she had a foible or two.

CHAPTER THREE

MAGGIE WHIPPED OUT her cell phone. "Hi, Mom."

"Darling—why aren't you here? We've put off dinner waiting for you!"

"I'm sorry. Cheryl's husband had a business dinner he wanted her to attend with him. No one else could cover for her at the last minute. You and Dad go ahead without me. I have to stay at the foundation and close up."

"Not again. This isn't right, darling. You haven't even had time to eat."

Maggie closed her eyes for a moment. "Mom—I haven't had to fill in for anyone in a long time. It's all right. I grabbed a bite in the cafeteria after I left my office."

The quiet on the other end spoke volumes. "We'll expect you for dinner tomorrow night."

"I can't. Steve's flying up from California for a few days. After I pick him up at the airport we're going straight to my office. Maybe on Sunday we can all get together."

"He can do that when he comes for Cord's wedding reception on the seventeenth."

"Steven will be too busy with the reception then. Right now's a good time to look into the law-school program here."

"He's too young for you, darling."

"Not necessarily, but just so you know, we're not interested in each other that way. Listen Mom, someone's at the desk. I've got to go."

"You always have to go."

"Talk to you later. Love you."

"I love you, too."

Maggie clicked off, but the greeting died in her throat when she discovered who was standing on the other side of the counter.

It was absurd, of course, but when she'd been introduced to him this morning, she'd had the impression he could be quite formidable.

That impression was still with her and growing stronger by the second. Seeing him up close, she picked out the faint scar over one eyelid, the little pucker at the left side of his mouth that hinted of rough play.

Jake Halsey was tall like her brothers, but much more hard-muscled and fit. With those solid features and firm jaw, she found him too rugged to be considered handsome. But he had an indefinable quality that transcended the physical; something that made him stand out from the many attractive men she'd known, setting him apart.

Startling black hair and lashes brought out the deep blue of his eyes. They were studying her so intently, she felt exposed…vulnerable. In fact she was helpless to ward off the curl of warmth that swept up through her body to her face.

Though he was dressed in a civilized sport shirt and chinos, he reminded her of a military man. He didn't fit her idea of what a genealogist should look like, an older man like the owner of the Eagle Gate firm. Not this…this…

"I read the brochure you left, and decided to volunteer," he said in his low, masculine voice, breaking the mysterious tension between them.

No, not mysterious. Maggie knew exactly what she sensed. It was called chemistry. She'd experienced various degrees of it before, mostly in high school, a time of life when hormones raged and emotions ran high.

Jake Halsey was no teenager. He was a full-blooded male in his midthirties. Her instincts told her he was a man who'd probably seen and done things she didn't want to know about. Because she was in the legal profession, she'd learned how to size up a client, though in this case she'd gone to *him* for help. Everything about him shouted caution, dependability and determination.

"We always need volunteers, Mr. Halsey. I'll give you an application to fill out."

"I've already turned it in."

Maggie's gaze slid to the box designated for collected applications. She reached for the paper on top of the pile, hoping her curiosity about him wasn't blatantly obvious. Who was she kidding?

He lived near the Capitol. She recognized the address. "How do you like living in the old Jordan mansion?"

She felt his scrutiny. "How do you know about that?"

"I serve on the historic register committee. We helped save that one. Thomas Jordan was a railroad magnate. One of your neighbors is the architect who converted the rooms into apartments."

"He did a good job. I like mine."

"After working in that cubbyhole all day, I would imagine the spaciousness and high ceilings have great appeal."

"You imagine right."

Something was wrong here. She was the one doing all the talking. It was totally unlike her.

"According to the application, you moved to Salt Lake five weeks ago. Before the foundation committee can make a decision, we need to know if your move is permanent."

"No, it's not. I'll be leaving in January. Does that disqualify me?"

Maggie shouldn't have been disappointed by his direct answer. What on earth was wrong with her?

"Of course not. But some jobs take more training than others. The hotline for instance."

He shifted his weight. "I can understand why you wouldn't want to invest the time training someone who's temporary."

Now she felt terrible. "It's the lifeline of the foundation. We've been lucky enough to find psychologists who know how to talk to frantic parents."

He cocked his head. "Well, you already know I'm no psychologist. I can see by this impressive place that the McFarland family knows firsthand the best methods to help people who are going through this agony. It only makes sense you'd want the most qualified people available. I have nothing but respect for you."

She felt his sincerity clear through to her bones. "My parents have done what any family would do if they had the means."

"That's not true and you know it." His reply held a note of conviction.

Clearing her throat she said, "I wish there were a floor job available, but I'm afraid they're filled for the time being. We have other needs though."

"What's the most important one?"

"People who can go out on a search at a moment's notice."

"Then I'm your man."

Her pulse quickened. "What about your job at the genealogy firm?"

"It's like housework."

"What do you mean?"

"You can do it at any time because it's always there waiting for you."

Maggie smiled. "You mean you and your wife don't share equally in the duties?" She didn't see a ring, but she still wanted a definitive answer to that crucial question before any more time passed.

"At one time we did, but after she was killed in an accident, I've had to bungle along."

He'd been married. She'd wanted to know.

"I'm sorry for your loss. Is that why you moved here from San Diego?"

"No. She died nine years ago. I came to Salt Lake for medical treatment."

Every revelation he made about himself surprised her. "Are you ill?"

"I was injured on the job and had to get a shoulder replacement."

Before she could stop herself, Maggie looked to his

broad shoulders. His amazing physique gave no hint of what he'd been through.

"I take it you weren't doing genealogy."

His sudden smile rocked her world. "I'm a detective who walked into a trap I had no way of avoiding." She knew it! The man lived dangerously. "After the accident, I woke up in the hospital. They sent me here for special therapy."

"North Avenues Hospital?"

He nodded, drawing her attention to his short-cropped black hair. If it were longer, she had an idea it would curl.

When she could gather her wits she said, "It has one of the best orthopedic departments in the country."

"Let's pray that's true. They won't let me back on the force unless I'm a hundred percent."

She needed to stop staring at him. "So what is a detective doing in a genealogy firm?"

"I needed a desk job that would challenge my brain. Since I grew up in a Czech household, and the department calls me in to translate when they need to interrogate a Czech-speaking suspect, it seemed a logical choice."

"Then you're not a real genealogist," she murmured mostly to herself, but he heard her.

"No, but don't let that worry you."

"Did I say it did?"

"You didn't have to. The disappointment is emblazoned on your face. If it's any consolation, I've discovered that genealogy is a giant clue game, not unlike my career job. You get hunches and you go with them. If I get stuck, I'm surrounded by experts. Give me some time and I'll find the information you're looking for."

"I'm sure you will."

The tension between them crackled.

"What reason do you have to believe this Franz Buric is the one who abducted your sister?"

Maggie sucked in a breath. He'd made the obvious connection between her request for information on Buric and Kathryn's abduction. Then again, not everyone read the brochure she automatically handed out to every person she met.

"We think he did it, but he's not talking."

"Which prison is he in?"

"Lompoc Penitentiary."

He cocked his head. "Closer to my neck of the woods."

"Yes."

"Excuse me?" A patron was standing at the counter.

Maggie couldn't believe she'd been so lost in the conversation she'd forgotten where she was.

"I'm sorry. I didn't see you standing there. What can I do for you?"

"I'm Helen Marsh, the owner of the Marsh Day Care Center. We run a summer program for elementary-age children whose parents work. I'd like to set up a time when one of your people could come and talk to the children, teach them how to take the proper precautions."

"Of course."

"I'll call you the second I have information," Jake said before leaving.

"Please do," she said to his retreating back, experiencing the oddest sense of loss as he disappeared.

PLEASE DO.

Those words reverberated in his head as he walked out of the plaza and across the courtyard.

He could have pushed her to meet him after she closed up, but some instinct told him to proceed carefully with her. Finding answers to her sister's abduction was Ms. McFarland's whole raison d'être. She'd spent a lifetime on her quest.

If she'd been married, and was now divorced, it was probably because her husband couldn't bear not to come first. Yet in his gut, Jake believed she'd never married. She had an untouched quality about her. Still, he supposed he could be wrong.

But he wasn't wrong about his hunch that until her sister's kidnapping case was solved, she would never allow herself to let go and just enjoy being with him. Since he'd made up his mind he wanted a personal, intimate relationship with her, he would focus on helping her learn the truth about her sister's whereabouts as soon as possible. So, he made a new rule for himself. No contact until he could give her information…unless she called him to go out on a search.

Filled with a different kind of energy than he'd felt in years, he started jogging down the street and around the corner. Before he knew it, he was home, unable to recall the faces of people or the scenery on his way up the hill.

Hungrier than he'd been in a long time, he fixed a big dinner. Much as he would have liked a beer, he used restraint and didn't get in his car to go to the store. Since meeting Ms. McFarland, *restraint* was going to be the key word.

While he was watching the ten o'clock news, his cell phone rang. The possibility that she might be calling him already made his pulse race. He picked it up from the coffee table and checked the ID. Out of area.

After grinding his teeth, he clicked on and said hello.

"It's Lewis."

Jake shot to his feet when he heard the agent's voice. "What have you got?"

"Plenty. Buric's locked up in the Lompoc pen." Jake already knew that. "He's forty-eight years old. His first arrest was at fifteen. He was part of a gang in the Bronx. The crimes he has committed stretch from New York to California. A half-dozen aliases.

"When told he was going to get life for abducting the McFarland baby, he denied having anything to do with it. Through a plea bargain that would cut two years off his armed-robbery sentence, he confessed to the Talbot baby abduction."

Another kidnapping? "Did he kill the baby?"

"No. Melissa Talbot was found alive in Venice Beach, California, under the name Kit Burke, and is now united with her birth parents who live in Claremont, California. Dr. and Mrs. Talbot.

"That case was very bizarre. Kit was raised by a woman named Rena Harris who'd supposedly been married to a Frankie Burke—one of Buric's aliases. According to Kit, he ran off when she was just a child. Rena raised Kit as her daughter. When she became very sick, she made a deathbed confession. She told Kit the McFarlands in Salt Lake were her real parents, and made her promise to go to them and let them know she was alive.

"After Rena died and it was confirmed her DNA didn't match Kit's, she went to Salt Lake to find out if her mother had told her the truth. But it turns out her DNA didn't match the McFarlands, either. The investigation led back to Frankie Burke.

"His DNA proved he wasn't Kit's birth father, but out of fear he'd rot in prison for the McFarland abduction, he finally confessed he was the one who'd kidnapped Kit from Mrs. Talbot during a bank robbery. It's one of the damnedest twists I ever heard of.

"I spoke with an Agent Kelly out in California. The FBI is actively investigating Buric in the hope he can solve some other kidnapping cases, including the abduction of Kathryn McFarland. There's an obvious connection to Frankie since Rena Harris was either his wife or girlfriend, and she believed Kit was the McFarlands' daughter."

Jake rubbed the back of his neck with his right hand. "Sounds like Buric was involved in a baby-smuggling ring."

"Could be."

"Or he was a serial kidnapper acting on his own," Jake theorized. "Maybe he made enough on ransom money to keep him alive until he turned to other forms of crime."

"There was never a ransom note for either the Talbot or McFarland babies."

No ransom notes? "So how come the Talbot baby lived?" He said this more to himself than the other man.

"Agent Kelly has been asking the same question. Buric told him to look up an old newspaper story about a kidnapping in Rosemead, California, twenty-six years ago. That's what led to the reunion of Kit, otherwise known as Melissa, to her birth parents. Mrs. Talbot identified Buric as the man who'd held a knife on her during the bank-robbery getaway and abducted her baby."

Jake was taking all of this in. "Obviously something went wrong and he didn't have a chance to kill the baby."

"That's my take on it."

"What work records did Agent Kelly find on Buric?"

"He did laundry in various hotels across the country for temporary periods. But talking with the employers hasn't given the agent a lead on the McFarland kidnapping."

"Buric only worked in hotels?"

"I think so."

Jake frowned. "Unless he used an alias that hasn't turned up yet and went to work on a ship…"

There was always laundry personnel on a ship. Jake's stint in the navy reminded him Buric might have signed on to a tanker or even a cruise ship for that kind of job. It was safe work. Offshore, a man could hide for years….

"I've faxed all of Agent Kelly's information to the number you gave me, Jake."

"Could you give me his phone number?"

"Sure."

Jake wrote it down. "Thanks, Lewis. You've given me something to chew on."

"You're welcome."

"I owe you."

"Forget it. I owe Dan, so we're even. Call me again if you need anything else."

After they hung up, Jake phoned Agent Kelly. It was

ten o'clock in California. This was too important to wait until morning.

A man's work record was like a paper trail. It could lead nowhere. Then again, it might lead to an important clue.

Racine, Wisconsin
August 7

"HOW DO YOU DO, Ms. Buric. Please sit down."

"Thank you for fitting me in so fast."

Anna took a seat opposite the desk of the immigration attorney. Anxiety caused her heart to race.

"My secretary told me it was an emergency. I see your address is Skwars Farm near Caledonia."

"Yes."

"It's a wonderful place Every fall my wife and I drive there to buy apples and those wonderful Czech wedding pastries."

"You mean *kilaches,*" she said with a nod. "I bake them fresh every day."

"Well, they're mouthwatering. My compliments."

"Thank you."

"What can I do for you?"

She took a deep breath. "My cousin Julia Skwars suggested you might be the person who could help me, Mr. Markham. Have you ever had a client come to you who couldn't prove who she was?"

The middle-aged lawyer studied her for a moment. "Yes. But with research, the necessary documentation finally came to light."

"In my case, I'm afraid there isn't any. The family

I've been living with all my life hasn't been able to come up with a birth certificate or a hospital record. All they can tell me is what they heard from their parents who heard it from their parents."

Frowning, Mr. Markham reached for his yellow legal pad to take notes. "Let's start at the beginning. Tell me what you *do* know about yourself."

"For as long as I can remember I've lived at Skwars Farm. It's a huge family business started by my great-grandmother's brother, Jainos Skwars. When he came to America from Czechoslovakia and became a naturalized citizen, he settled in Wisconsin so he could farm. Then he sent for his wife and two children.

"They came with his sister Marie Skwars, my great-grandmother. But she married a man from New York City named Jan Buric, an engraver, and remained in New York where they became naturalized citizens.

"According to the family history, two of their children went to the Wisconsin farm one summer for a vacation. They ended up staying there to farm along with their cousins.

"Their third child, Vaclav, helped my great-grandfather, Jan Buric. When he passed away, Vaclav stayed in New York to run the family engraving business. He married a woman named Anna Ludmilla. The two of them died in a car accident, leaving two young sons, Franz and Antonin."

The attorney kept on writing.

"My great-grandmother Marie ended up taking care of her grandsons, but Franz and Antonin got into a lot of trouble and ran away. She never saw Franz again, but Antonin showed up several years later with a wife, Leah, and a two-month old baby, Anna. I was that child.

"From what I understand, he asked my great-grand-mother if Leah and I could stay with her while he went job hunting. It might take a week before he returned. Apparently she said it would be all right. A few days later Leah went out to get more milk for me and never came back.

"At that point my great-grandmother wrote her brother Jainos in Wisconsin and told him what had happened. He was ailing, so he sent his daughter Olga and her husband to come and get me and my great-grand-mother. We ended up at the farm. Both Marie and Jainos died within a year of each other. I don't remember them, of course.

"It's Olga who was the closest thing to a grandmother to me. But she died, too. She has eleven brothers and sisters. Between them and my great-grandmother's two children, who bought farmland next to them, I ended up with dozens of aunts and uncles and over a hundred cousins. They all helped raise me while we worked the farm."

He stopped writing and looked up. "How old are you?"

"Because Olga remembered the year she went to New York with her husband to get me, I have to be twenty-six."

"How have you lived all this time without a social-security number?"

"I never had a problem or was aware I had a problem because I worked in the farm bakery during high school where I didn't need one."

"Who claims you on their income tax?"

"No one."

"What about a driver's license?"

"I don't have one."

"What about a bank account?"

"I never needed one. I work in the family business. I know how much is in my savings. When I want money, I ask my Uncle Petr and he gives me cash for what I want."

He sat forward. "Has your family prevented you from talking to the authorities about your problem?"

"Not at all. My cousin Josef was the one who urged me to seek out an attorney. It was his sister Julia who gave me your name for a reference."

Anna related what Josef had told her last night. "They've always been fair and kind to me, Mr. Markham. Deep down everyone believes my father wasn't a good man, but they would never say it to my face.

"They've tried to shield me by not talking about him or my mother and the way they abandoned me. Like my great-grandmother, I think there's a part of them that hoped my parents would seek me out. Certainly I did."

"So what has changed for you?"

"Nelly, my favorite cousin who has shared the same bedroom with me for the last two years, is getting married next week. She's the only reason I hung on as long as I did. With her gone, I don't want to stay on the farm. What I'd like to do is go to college, but I can't do anything without a birth certificate."

He stared at her for a long moment. "You have a real problem, all right. What troubles me are the people who were supposedly your parents. After what you've told me, I've got a lot of questions."

"So do I," she whispered. "Early this morning I put in an inquiry to the New York Bureau of Vital Statistics to see if there are marriage records on my parents, and a birth record on me.

"The family says they've never been able to get this information, but after what I learned last night, I had to try again. The thing is, after my talk with Josef, I've decided I could have been born anywhere."

Mr. Markham shifted in his leather chair. "If your father was a drifter, it might account for the reason he left you with his grandmother. Perhaps he and your mother planned to join up later, perhaps not."

"It's hard to imagine parents doing that to their child, but I know it's happened to other people." Anna looked at the floor.

"More often than you would think. If he was in a lot of trouble as you've indicated, it's my guess he was on the run with the woman who could have been his wife or a girlfriend. A baby would have held them up, so he turned to his grandmother before disappearing."

"I'm wondering if he went back to the Czech Republic where he couldn't be traced."

"It's possible, but not likely."

"Why not?" This was all very confusing for Anna.

"For one thing, American citizenship is a precious commodity. For another, if he was in trouble with the law, he would want to avoid any entanglements, especially with the immigration authorities.

"My guess is that if he's still alive, he's probably operating under an alias somewhere in the U.S. in case he didn't want the family to find him. You said he had a brother who was in trouble and disappeared, too. Maybe they moved around together."

"I have no idea."

"What was his brother's name again?"

"Franz."

He adjusted his glasses. "Do you know the date you and your great-grandmother left for Wisconsin?"

"Olga said she and her husband came for us around the first of July. It had to be then, before the main harvest started."

"So if you were with your great-grandmother a month or so, you would have been around three months old by the time you arrived at the farm?"

"Something like that. What are you thinking?"

"Several things. Maybe you weren't his baby. Maybe you were kidnapped and the woman was his accomplice."

She shivered. "I've thought of that. I never told anyone this before, but I don't really resemble any of my family, young or old."

After her comment he said, "There's another possibility."

"What?"

"About twenty-five or -six years ago there was an illegal baby-adoption ring operating in New York City. Before it was closed down and arrests were made, it was discovered they'd brought in over a hundred Czech mothers with newborns.

"They came in via Canada where immigration laws were lax. Those children were adopted by wealthy couples from all over the nation willing to pay as much as fifty thousand dollars for a white baby. The adoptive parents were told they had to pay extra for the nannies who brought the children from Czechoslovakia. In reality those women were the mothers wanting asylum and willing to give up their babies for enough money to survive here."

"You think Leah was one of those women?" Anna cried softly.

"It's just a theory, but not an implausible one."

"Then maybe Antonin wasn't my father. Maybe my birth father could still be in the Czech Republic!"

"Maybe. But at this point you have no way of knowing the men she'd been with. Your birth father might have been another nationality altogether.

"If the man you thought was your father had been involved in this adoption ring, he could have used his grandmother's home for a holding tank until the adoptive parents came through with the money."

"But something went wrong?" Anna hadn't realized she'd said this aloud.

He nodded. "When he didn't come back, the woman panicked and fled, leaving you behind. But let's assume for the moment your great-grandmother believed you were her flesh and blood and had no idea he'd lied to her about the baby's paternity. Naturally, she kept you and did the best she could for you."

"If that's the case, how am I ever going to prove who I am?"

"Don't worry. Wherever the true answer lies, be assured I'm going to help you get legal. Give me a week to work on this and then I'll contact you. Let me have a phone number and address."

Once Anna had given him the information, she said, "I don't have a lot of money. The best I can do is pay you on a monthly basis. Will that be all right?"

"Certainly. To be honest, my biggest concern is helping you be able to join the world so you can go to college or do anything else you want."

He smiled as he said it, but it didn't reach his eyes. "Because of a force beyond your control, you've been obliged to live a very different life."

"If by that you mean I wasn't raised by my birth parents, then you're right. But Olga loved me, and the others have been nice, kind people to me. They'd do anything for anybody because it's in their nature. Every time I think about that, I'm thankful for the life I do have."

After a long silence he said, "You're a remarkable woman, Ms. Buric, and a strong one. I'll do everything I can to help you."

"Thank you very much."

She turned to leave but he called her back.

"Do you have a picture of yourself with you?"

"No, but I'll bring one to you tomorrow when I come to town with Nelly to do some shopping."

"It would help if you brought all pictures of you, and any of Franz, Antonin, your grandparents and great-grandparents. The FBI will be interested in anything you can contribute to help them solve your case."

"The FBI?"

"Yes. They're the people who can find the answers, given time."

"My relatives won't get into trouble, will they?"

"I doubt it, but the authorities will be making a visit to your uncle Petr since he's the one paying you from the family business. I have no idea what will happen from there."

She had to trust him. "Don't let them come until Nelly's wedding is over."

"When is it?"

"August twelfth."

"I'll see what I can do."

"Thank you for seeing me. I'll be by again tomorrow with everything I can gather."

"Good." He got up from his desk and walked her to the door.

Anna felt his eyes on her back as she walked down the hall past the receptionist. She had an idea he believed she'd been sold through that baby ring or kidnapped. She believed the same thing. At this point she had little hope she would ever be united with her birth parents.

CHAPTER FOUR

Salt Lake City
August 9

"...AND IN THIS CASE," Maggie said as she put another legal brief in front of Steve, "I asked the court to strip off the wholly unsecured fourth lien. Because the creditor failed to appear, I filed a default judgment."

"How did that go?"

"The bankruptcy court denied the motion based on the Nobelman case. I filed an appeal and I'm waiting for the bankruptcy appellate panel to reverse the court's holding."

"Which they should do because the bankruptcy code's antimodification provision doesn't protect secured credits holding completely unsecured claims."

"That's ten cases you already have a grasp on. I'm impressed, Steve. But I'm going to ask you one more time. Is this what you want to do? Move to Salt Lake and clerk for me?"

"Come on, Maggie," he half laughed as he spoke. "You know the answer to that."

"The dean of the law school was impressed with you, and he's not easily impressed."

"No." Steve shook his head. "He was bowled over because it's *the* Margaret McFarland who is offering me the plum clerking job in the state."

"Don't sell yourself short. Your grades are outstanding. How do you like the condo after sleeping there for two nights?"

"It's a lot more than I need."

"That's not what I asked."

"You never let up!" He laughed again. "Who wouldn't love a place like that?"

"But traditional decor's not your style."

His smile faded to be replaced by a much more serious look. "Actually it is. Everything here is so much my style, I'm nervous."

"Why?"

"It all seems too easy, too wonderful."

"I think I heard a yes in there somewhere."

Steve's eyes had grown suspiciously bright. "You heard it, all right."

"Then we have a deal?" She put out her hand.

He gripped it hard. "I don't know how to thank you, Maggie."

It was her turn to chuckle. "You shouldn't have let me hear that. It can get crazy around here, especially when I'm gone on foundation business. At times I'll probably lean on you too much."

"I want to learn all I can."

"You've already proved that. Since you still have the key to the condo, you keep it." She rummaged in her desk drawer. "Here's a key to the office door. You can move in whenever you like."

He put it in his pocket. "I'll drive up in a few days and get settled before the reception. That way the family can stay with me."

"Perfect. Now I'd better get you to the airport."

Steve checked his watch. "You're right. Four o'clock already. What's the traffic going to be like?"

They both got up from the table and started out of the room.

"No problem. It's Sunday. I'll get you to the terminal within twenty minutes."

"That's what I love about Salt Lake."

"Wait till you're stuck on I-15 at four-thirty in the afternoon on a weekday. You'll think you're back in L.A."

He grabbed the suitcase he'd left near the front doors of the law firm and followed her down to the underground parking lot. Once they were seated in the car and she'd turned on the air-conditioning, they drove out and headed for North Temple, which would take them directly to the airport.

She turned on State Street. Jake Halsey lived on the hill a little farther up.

Considering that the heat had spiked to 102 today, it was absurd to think he might be taking a walk until much later in the evening. Yet she found herself looking for his hard-muscled frame. He would definitely stand out from the other people milling around downtown.

Her mind was still on Jake when they reached the entrance to the airport. As if thinking about him had conjured him up, her cell phone rang. With her heart racing, she glanced at the caller ID. It was ridiculous how disappointed she felt when she didn't see his name.

"Hi, Mom," she said after clicking on.

"Has Steven left yet?"

"Almost. I'm driving toward the Delta terminal right now."

"Let me talk to him, will you, dear?"

"Just a minute." She handed him the phone. "Mom wants to tell you something."

"Hello, Ellen."

A few seconds of silence passed before Maggie heard him say, "You're welcome. After that delicious meal, I wish I'd been able to give you a lot more than a box of candy."

There was another pause, then he said, "Yes. I made the decision a few minutes ago, but I'm still in shock. Here's hoping your daughter doesn't live to regret it."

Maggie pulled up to the curb.

"The family will be staying with me at the condo. Mom will call you the second they arrive. See you again soon. Here's Maggie."

She took the phone from him. "Mom? Got to go. I'll call you later."

"Come on up to the house after you drop him off. I want to hear everything."

I know. "We'll see. Bye for now."

Steve turned to her. "You've got a great mom. She told me I could eat dinner with her and Reed every night while I worked for you."

"She means it, too," Maggie murmured. "But of course you're not going to take her up on it or your life won't be your own. Trust me on this one."

He sobered. "I do."

"Don't get me wrong. I adore her, but she's needy. Now that Kit and your family have come into her life, she'll want to mother you, so be careful."

"Maggie! Don't worry. I know exactly what's going on here. I lived with a needy mom, too, and recognize all the symptoms. Thanks for giving me the opportunity of a lifetime."

That was what was so nice about Steve. He *did* understand. "California's loss is my gain."

He kissed her cheek, then got out of the car. After pulling his suitcase from the back seat, he waved to her before disappearing inside the terminal.

A lot of cars had let off passengers at the same time. She waited for the next car to leave her room to break in, but the Chevy Tahoe came right up alongside her and stopped.

The driver's rudeness prompted her to flash him an irritated glance. He was wearing sunglasses, but she recognized him immediately.

Jake. Suddenly her heart rate took off like a rocket.

He was alone. When she noticed the front passenger window go down, she lowered the window on her side.

"Ms. McFarland?"

"Hello!"

"By coincidence I just came from Express Air to pick up a package and saw you driving the loop. Since I planned to phone you the minute I got home, I decided to catch up with you instead. As long as you're here and your boyfriend's gone, why don't we go someplace where we can talk. I have information."

Her first thought was to tell him he'd gotten the

wrong idea about Steve, but this wasn't the place to carry on a private conversation. "I'll meet you at the Red Iguana. It's—"

"I know where it is. I like Mexican food, too."

He drove off. To her surprise, the car behind him left a space so she could pull away from the curb. She gave the other woman a friendly wave and followed Jake.

The drive to the restaurant took less than ten minutes. As he left his car and came around to escort her inside, she noticed he wore khaki cargo pants and a white T-shirt. Both items of clothing molded to his well-defined chest and body. She'd never met a more "male" male in her life.

He asked the waiter to show them to the overflow room off the main dining area, which was darker and less crowded. Within seconds they were seated at a corner table with a basket of warm, homemade chips and salsa.

The waiter handed them menus. "Would you like to order drinks first, then decide on your meal?"

"I won't be eating, but I'd like a virgin strawberry daiquiri, please."

"I'll have the same," Jake stated. He handed back the menus. "You didn't want something stronger, Ms. Mc-Farland?" he said to her after the waiter had left.

"Please call me Maggie."

"If you'll call me Jake."

She nodded. "To answer your question, I don't drink except for the rare occasion."

"Now that I'm in physical therapy, I've sworn off alcohol myself. You're not hungry for something besides chips?"

"No. I ate earlier with the man you saw getting out of my car. He's my new law clerk."

"Law clerk—you're an attorney?"

"Yes. Bankruptcy and family law. My firm is located on the ground floor of the plaza across from the foundation."

He shoved his sunglasses on top of his head. His eyes looked almost navy in the dim light. "You're full of surprises."

"We worked at my office all day and ordered in a big lunch."

"Do you always get kissed by your latest law clerk?"

"Only if he's my brother-in-law."

When Jake suddenly smiled, she smiled back.

"His name is Steve Talbot. His sister Melissa was kidnapped twenty-six years ago, almost at the same time as my sister. Our family's search ended up in her being united with her birth family. It's been a time of joy for them."

After a pause Jake said, "Kit Talbot?"

She blinked. "Yes. She married my brother, Cord. How do you know *her* name?"

Jake whistled. "I've learned a lot in the last couple of days."

By now her adrenaline had kicked in for another reason besides the thrill of seeing him again. "Did you find any Buric relatives living in New York?"

The waiter served them their drinks. After he left, Jake took hold of the glass stem, but he didn't drink yet. "Not in New York."

"What do you mean?"

'Through my various sources I've discovered Franz Buric has a brother named Antonin Buric. He's the elder brother by two years."

She was stunned. "How did you come across that information? Agent Simpson, the FBI agent working with our family, never said anything about that."

"In my line of work the rule of thumb is to find out if the person you're searching for has ever been in trouble with the law."

"But she already did a background check."

"Sometimes it takes another person to think of another angle to get at the truth. I happened to get lucky."

"Where does this brother live?" Maggie asked. "I want to know anything he can tell us about Frankie."

Jake was slow to respond. "That's not possible yet because no one knows where he is. His police record is as long as Franz's. Over the years this man has been operating under half a dozen aliases, too."

Maggie remembered the day Agent Simpson gave her, Kit and Cord the list of Frankie's fake names. "They're a real pair." Her voice trembled.

He nodded. "Between the Burics' many crime sprees, they've worked mostly in various hotel laundries across the country, including one in Venice Beach, California."

"Venice Beach… Then Kit's mother told her the truth when she said she'd met Frankie at a hotel doing laundry."

Jake swallowed part of his drink. "The pieces are starting to fit together. Tell me about Kit's mother."

"Rena Harris was an alcoholic from Venice Beach who raised Kit alone after Frankie abandoned them. She did housecleaning, but when she met Frankie, she was working for a hotel doing laundry. Kit thought Frankie was her father, but now we know differently. Before Rena died of a diseased liver, she told Kit to go to Salt Lake where she would find the McFarlands, her birth parents.

"After the funeral, Kit came to Salt Lake, not knowing what to think. She met Cord first and they fell in love before she realised he might be her brother. Until it was determined that she wasn't a member of our family, the situation was very painful, to say the least. But that's all over now and they're happily married.

"Naturally Kit still can't understand why Rena lied to her for years about being her mother. We all have questions we'd like to ask Rena, but that isn't possible. Only Frankie can give our family information about Kathryn, but he's not talking,"

Jake studied her intently. "Three months before your sister was kidnapped, both brothers were working in laundry on a Cunard cruise ship traveling from San Pedro, California, to Acapulco and back.

"According to the personnel records while they were onboard, they were known as Tom and Mickey Franks. Their last name sent up a red flag. Agent Kelly checked out the pictures on their work applications. They matched other mug shots of the Buric brothers."

Maggie had just started to take another sip, but at that revelation the drink slipped from her fingers. Fortunately the glass didn't break and she was quick enough to keep most of the slush from spilling.

Jake's right hand moved like quicksilver to clean up the excess with a napkin. "What did I say to cause that reaction?" he asked in a voice of barely suppressed urgency.

"My parents—they went on a New Year's cruise to Mexico three months before Kathryn was born. Daddy hoped it would help Mother to relax and bring down her blood pressure, which had started to elevate late in her pregnancy. He wanted her to rest and keep her legs up. Do you know the exact dates?"

"December twenty-ninth to January ninth." When he mentioned the year, she gasped.

"That's the year Kathryn was stolen. I'll check with Mom and Dad on the dates, but we have to be talking about the same cruise. My grandparents tended us while they were gone.

"Of course I don't remember any of it, but I've always heard the story about Mom when she came home and her blood pressure was worse. The doctor ordered her to bed until Kathryn was born so her toxemia wouldn't get any worse."

Jake's well-shaped brows formed a black bar. "If you can verify the dates and the specific ship, then there's no doubt the Buric brothers heard talk that the multimillionaire Reed McFarland and his pregnant wife from Salt Lake were onboard. I would presume that had to be the moment the men decided to target your parents."

His eyes held a faraway look. "It was a premeditated kidnapping thought out in elaborate detail. They would have had to get to Salt Lake earlier than the abduction and study the lay of the land weeks before they struck."

"The thought of two predators casing my family's home sickens me."

Jake's expression hardened. "They only worked for that cruise line for one sailing. Then they collected their pay packets and didn't show up for work again.

"If you think about it, Kit Talbot's abduction took place on April eighteenth, less than a month before your sister was stolen on May third. They must have run out of money and decided to rob the bank in Rosemead to fund their activities."

Maggie couldn't keep up with his brilliant reasoning. "I still find all of it unbelievable."

"The criminal mind is a dark place," he murmured. "According to the newspaper, it sounded as if Frankie, who held Kit's birth mother at knifepoint, snatched the baby on the impulse of the moment. Yet it hardly makes sense when they were already planning to steal your parents' baby after she was born," he said more to himself than to her.

Maggie shivered again. "They might have been stalking the Talbots, too. But they couldn't have known what moment she would choose to go to the bank unless they had sophisticated electronic surveillance equipment and listening devices."

He shook his head. "Since neither family ever received a ransom note, it sounds like the Buric brothers could have been part of a well-organized illegal baby-adoption ring."

Maggie stared at him. "What if they kidnapped a lot of babies?"

Their gazes held. "It's entirely possible. Twenty-six years ago one white baby could bring payoffs from thirty to fifty thousand dollars. For a bunch of criminals like the Buric boys, that was big money back then."

"What they did was inhuman."

He eyed her with compassion. "Let's pray it's true."

"Why do you say that?" she whispered.

"Though Kit wasn't adopted, for which reason we don't know yet, she *is* alive and has been united with her family. That means there's a good chance your sister was adopted."

Tears prickled behind Maggie's eyelids. "I've always believed she's alive somewhere."

He finished off the rest of his drink. "Given time, we'll find her."

We?

Who *was* this man who'd found out Franz Buric had a brother Antonin, that they'd operated under different aliases aboard a ship? How had Jake come up with this kind of information when it had eluded the FBI for twenty-six years?

Why did he care about what had happened to Kathryn, to her family? He was on medical leave from the police force doing work as a genealogist. This wasn't his problem.

On top of everything she knew about him so far, he hadn't said, "if Kathryn's alive," like so many of the media people prefaced their statements. That alone raised her trust level to an unprecedented high.

"Before I allow myself to become too optimistic—" *before my attraction to you becomes too obvious* "—I need to talk to my parents about that cruise. If you'll excuse me, I'm going to go talk to them now."

"The sooner you give me that information, the sooner I can do more searches."

She nodded. "I'll find a way to get the information without them becoming suspicious. Mom especially will be better off not knowing about this development, or she'll brood. That's when her depression gets worse and it drags Dad down."

He sat back in his chair. "Your parents have been through enough grief in their lives. For now I think you're wise to keep this information to yourself." He pulled some bills from his wallet and laid them on the table. "I'll walk you out."

Quite apart from her excitement that he might have discovered the most vital piece of evidence in her sister's case, she had a growing awareness of him as a flesh-and-blood man.

With the slightest contact of their bodies accidentally brushing against each other, feelings of desire whipped up inside her like wind fanning sparks to flame.

Maggie averted her eyes so he couldn't read her thoughts. "Thank you for the drink," she said after he'd helped her into her car. "Once I've talked to my parents, I'll call you."

"You've got my cell-phone number. If I'm not able to answer, leave the message on my voice mail and I'll get back to you."

She nodded to him before driving off.

It shouldn't have upset her that he didn't even mention trying to meet up with her later. He obviously wasn't interested in her that way. After the many men who'd thrown themselves at her over the years, why was it she wanted this particular man to pursue her?

You know why, Maggie McFarland, and you're a fool.

JAKE WITHDREW THE infrared goggles from the packing box. For dual use, with a twist of the eyepiece, they could change from day to night vision. State-of-the-art issue. Without their ability to pick up the heat and shape of moving targets, his life would have been snuffed out long ago.

He had called Dan earlier to thank him for the package. There was still no news of Kamila's whereabouts. More than ever, he was thankful for Maggie McFarland's entry into his life. Her presence was already helping him push his own family's nightmare to the back of his mind while he dealt with something where it might be possible to make an immediate, positive difference.

To test out his new toy, he opened the doors to the terrace, which had an eastern exposure, and made a slow sweep of the foothills with the day-vision adjustment. Superman himself would be amazed by what he could see through these.

Jake intended to be prepared for his volunteer job should he be called to go out on a search. When everyone else had to quit at dark, he could keep on going.

That was if he survived the foundation's scrutiny and was allowed to help. If he could get Maggie in his corner, then it was a fait accompli.

In his mind's eye, he could see her driving off in her Ford Excursion. It hadn't been hard to let her go, not when he knew he'd be hearing from her before the evening was out. He was counting on it. In fact, he was counting on a lot more than that.

Today she'd been wearing a silky cream dress, tailored and very chic. But in truth, her height and the way she moved through a room would make her look elegant in anything. He pictured her in cutoffs. With her slender curves and those legs that went on forever...

She'd gone into bankruptcy law. He hadn't known she was an attorney. That came as an interesting surprise, though her specialty didn't. The whole McFarland clan was dedicated to helping others deal with their losses whether they be physical, mental or financial.

Tragically, no one had been able to restore their daughter and sister to them. Not yet anyway.

Jake couldn't comprehend such a loss. The closest he'd come to an understanding of what that would be like was the news his stepmother had never showed up for work after his father's funeral.

Realizing that thinking about Kamila would get him nowhere, he went back inside. Aware he was still thirsty, he pulled a cold root beer from the fridge. As he shut the fridge door, his cell phone rang.

Maggie? His heart responded with a violent kick. But when he reached for it, the screen said out of area. Maybe it was Dan calling back.

"Hello?"

"I have a collect call for a Mr. Bedrich Veverka. Will you accept the charges?"

Jake knew exactly who was calling. "Yes."

"Very well. Go ahead, sir."

"Mr. Veverka? Is that you?" a male voice asked in Czech.

The pulse at Jake's temple started to throb. "Yes, Mr. Buric," he answered back in kind. "You must have important news."

"I don't know, but maybe this will help. I drive a taxi.

Today while I was in the Bronx waiting for a fare to come out, I noticed a sign in front of a small construction site. It said the old Buric Engravers building had been torn down. Soon a new Erskins bookstore would be going up. I couldn't believe I saw my name, especially when you just called me about it the other day."

Jake couldn't believe it, either. The probability of his seeing the sign was highly unlikely. He hurried over to his desk. "Can you give me the address?"

"Near the corner of Boston Road and East 163rd Street in the South Bronx."

"I'm writing it down. This could be the link to something very important. Thank you, Mr. Buric."

"You're welcome. Glad to be of help."

Why was it always Sunday night when you suddenly decided you wanted to reach someone in the business world?

First thing in the morning, Jake would start calling a bunch of engraving companies in the Bronx. Someone had to know of the now-defunct Buric company.

With his body charged, he couldn't sit still. Without hesitation, he pocketed his cell phone and jogged down the hill to the genealogy firm. After grabbing the New York City yellow pages out of Wendell's office, Jake retired to his own.

In the process of compiling numbers from the list of engravers in and around the Bronx, his cell phone rang. The caller-ID screen said unavailable, but it could be Maggie.

He clicked on. "Hello?"

"Mr. Halsey?"

Jake didn't recognize the man's voice. "Yes?"

"Reed McFarland here."

Now that he thought about it, Jake recognized the ex-senator's voice from his interviews with the media. It meant Maggie had already talked to her parents.

"It's a privilege to speak with you, sir."

"The privilege is mine, believe me. My daughter has told me all about you."

Whatever happened to her plan not to give herself away?

"A little while ago the subject of the Mexican cruise my wife and I took before Kathryn was born came up in the conversation. I sensed Maggie had a definite reason for bringing it up, particularly as she asked if I remembered the dates and the name of the cruise line.

"When I confronted her, she admitted going to the Eagle Gate Genealogical Firm to do some investigating on her own. That led to a full disclosure of the facts."

Maggie's father didn't pull any punches. It's what made him a great congressman and no doubt an exceptional parent.

"Your detective work is brilliant, Mr. Halsey. Ellen and I were on the same cruise ship as the Buric brothers. If it isn't an imposition, could you drive up to our house in Federal Heights? Maggie has gone over to my son's place to bring her mother home. We both want to hear this information from you in person."

The muscles relaxed around Jake's chest. "Give me the exact address and I'll be there within a half hour."

"Excellent."

After they hung up, Jake folded the list of numbers and put it in his pocket. Once he'd returned the directory to its rightful place, he took off for his apartment and showered.

With a change of clothes to a sport shirt and trousers, he was ready. On his way out the door, he grabbed the keys and headed for his car.

If Maggie McFarland didn't like things getting this personal this fast, then it was too bad. Her father had just given his permission for Jake to be in their lives.

Mr. McFarland had carried a great load on his shoulders and in his heart for many years. When Jake thought about it, he imagined Maggie's father would love to do something proactive for a change where his daughter's kidnapping was concerned. It was Maggie's mother who sounded fragile.

Energized by this much progress, Jake drove faster than usual up B Street to Eleventh Avenue, where he turned east. It would lead to Federal Heights. From Wendell, who was a talking encyclopedia, he'd learned this was an old area of Salt Lake where some of the most classic homes had been built.

The McFarlands had carved out their own little society with the McFarland Plaza, the shelter, and their homes all within a radius of several blocks to a few miles.

He had to slow down once he left the boulevard. Soon he was making his way beneath a canopy of trees. As he rounded the corner, he saw the old, huge, Tudor-style home high up on the wooded property just as Mr. McFarland had described.

The house of half timber, half fieldstone had been built in a magnificent asymmetrical design with cross gables and dormers.

Jake parked at the bottom of the hill. After getting out of the car, he started climbing up the drive. It lined the lush, grassy slope. The landscape looked unreal, it was so green and perfect. He couldn't help but marvel over the immaculate flower beds alive with masses of white and purple petunias.

From the top of the hill, he gazed over the grounds, thinking he'd never seen anything so beautiful. That was until a certain dark blond woman emerged from the recessed doorway to greet him.

The twilight brought out the creamy tone of her skin. There was the slightest overlay of pink on her cheeks, due to the heat. The combination made his breath grow ragged. For the first time in his life, Jake understood the expression "she looked good enough to eat."

"Dad figured out what I was trying to do," Maggie explained in a slightly breathless voice. "I hope you don't mind that he wanted to talk to you tonight."

"Not at all. Your parents deserve to know what's going on. It's always better if there aren't any secrets, even if they're kept for the best of reasons." If lightning struck him just then, he wouldn't have been surprised.

"Come in. Mom and Dad are waiting for you."

He followed her through the beamed foyer with its extended ceilings to a small, cozy sitting room.

"Mr. Halsey—" Maggie's trim, brunette mother rushed to welcome him. Her husband was right behind her.

She couldn't be more than five-three or -four. Maggie had inherited her mother's classic features, but in most other ways, including her light blue eyes, she resembled her father.

The ex-senator was a tall man with grayish blond hair. He had the look of a statesman. Both were very attractive people.

"I'm honored to meet you, Mrs. McFarland." They shook hands.

"Call me Ellen, please. This is my husband, Reed."

"Thanks for coming over tonight, Jake," he said, extending his hand. "You don't mind if I call you that, do you?"

"I'd rather you did," he said, aware of Maggie's eyes watching him. He liked that. He had plans to become the major focus of her attention before long.

The older man smiled. "Good. Let's all sit down."

He indicated the wingback chair for Jake, which was next to the couch where the McFarlands took their place. Maggie found an upholstered chair on the other side of the coffee table.

"You have a magnificent home. The grounds are breathtaking."

"Thank you. We've been killing ourselves off to get ready for a wedding reception we're giving here on the seventeenth, " Reed exclaimed.

"Who's getting married?"

"Our son Cord recently married in California. They're on their honeymoon. When they get back to Salt Lake, we're hosting a reception for them. But let's not talk about that right now."

Jake's breathing slowly returned to normal. For just

a moment he'd wondered if Maggie had failed to inform
him of a piece of information vital to his existence.

"Maggie tells us you're a detective from California
who came up here for treatment at North Avenues Hospital. We understand you're working at the Eagle Gate
Genealogical Firm while you convalesce."

"That's right."

"We're overjoyed to think you've uncovered such
astounding information about the kidnappers of our darling daughter. Tell us the details."

After Jake had related everything, the silence that followed was broken by Reed McFarland's sobs.

Jake felt the older man's grief to his bones.

"Do you really have proof those two brothers were
aboard our cruise ship?" Ellen cried.

"I was sent a fax with the documentation. I'll bring
it by tomorrow," Jake answered quietly.

"All this time—who would have dreamed any human
being could think up such a monstrous plan."

The pain in her voice, her tear-soaked eyes brought
a hard lump to Jake's throat. He looked to Maggie. This
family had been suffering for too many years.

CHAPTER FIVE

MAGGIE HAD BEEN AFRAID this would be too emotional an experience for her mother when they still didn't have answers yet. Somehow she hadn't counted on her father losing control in front of company. He'd always been so strong. To watch her mom try to comfort her dad by throwing her arms around him was a revelation.

Jake could have no idea Maggie had never witnessed her dad this broken up before. She'd wondered how he'd managed to keep his anguish under control all these years. Now it came pouring out. Her heart ached for the suffering he could no longer hide.

Their family had concentrated so hard on easing their mother's pain. But who had ever eased their father's?

With her hand still on her dad's shoulder, Maggie's mother turned to Jake. "From the captain to the maid who did up our room each day, everyone made such an embarrassing fuss over me on the ship. Your theory that the housekeeping staff gossiped and word spread to those two horrible men working in the laundry makes perfect sense.

"It means they came to Salt Lake and devised a way to break into the mansion. They must have been watching us for days and knew our exact schedule, when we would be the most vulnerable. Having come home from the hospital with Kathryn, I wasn't aware of anything but her and our other children."

"None of us was that vigilant," Maggie's father spoke at last. He wiped his eyes with his fingers. "We were too excited with our newest little addition."

"You were preyed upon," Jake declared. "As I told Maggie, it's my belief the kidnappers were paid a good sum of money to steal your baby so she could be sold through an illegal adoption. I believe Kathryn is alive."

"We do, too!" Maggie's parents declared at the same time.

Jake nodded. "I'm going to do everything in my power, use all my contacts who are working with the FBI, to try to find her."

Her mother shook her head incredulously. "It's a miracle you came to Salt Lake."

"The miracle is that your daughter chose the genealogical firm where I work to begin her own search."

Maggie's mom looked at her. "What made you go there instead of the Family History Center, darling?"

She cleared her throat. "Because it's small. I didn't want a lot of people to know what I was doing, especially the media. Even after all these years, they still love to print upsetting things about Kathryn and our family. With the Eagle Gate Firm only a two-minute walk from my office, it seemed like the best idea."

"Thank God for you, honey!" her father exclaimed.

"Jake's the one to thank for everything."

"These are early days yet," Jake inserted. "Before I

leave, I'd like to inform you of an additional piece of information I learned about after meeting with Maggie earlier."

"What is it?" her father asked before she could.

In a matter of minutes Jake explained about Frantisek Buric. The New York cab driver's sharp observation had led Jake to the trail of a Buric who'd once owned an engraving business in the Bronx.

On his feet now, Jake said, "What I'm hoping is that someone will know if that Buric is the one we're looking for, particularly the grandmother in question. If she's still living, it's possible she knows the whereabouts of Antonin. Since Franz refuses to talk, she could shed a whole new light on this case."

Maggie's father got up from the couch. "Jake? We want you to know how indebted we are to you for everything you're doing. Whatever you need, be it money or anything else, you've got it."

"Thank you. I'll keep that in mind."

"Please don't go yet," Maggie's mother pleaded with him. "We haven't even offered you a drink."

"Thank you, but it's getting late. I promise to keep you informed of any new developments."

"I'll see you to the door, Jake." Maggie jumped up from the chair.

As it turned out, the whole family walked to the front of the house with him. With her father's arms around her and her mom, Maggie couldn't very well break away to run down to the bottom of the drive where Jake had parked his car. Much as she wanted to, it would be a dead giveaway that she saw him in more than a professional light.

"Good night," he said to all of them. Maggie's eyes met his for a brief moment. It was too dark to read his expression. "I'll be in touch."

When? Maggie's heart cried.

After he'd gone and they'd walked back in the house, Maggie said, "Did I tell you he made an application to be a volunteer at the foundation?"

"What a fantastic man," her mom murmured.

Fantastic was right. In every conceivable way. But Maggie had a disturbing feeling that an unattached man so focused on work was still in love with the memory of his deceased wife. That was the hardest kind of obstacle for another woman to overcome.

Her dad nodded. "If I didn't know better, I'd think he was an angel sent down to help us. The kind on that TV series you enjoy, Ellen."

Maggie's parents were looking at Jake through blinders. Who could blame them? But she knew he was no angel. More than ever, Maggie was convinced the arresting Jake Halsey was dangerous and full of secrets.

No police detective, however high in rank or experience, could have so much information at his fingertips this fast and easily. Even Maggie, with all her pull as an attorney and clout as a McFarland, could never produce the leads he'd uncovered so quickly and so precisely.

MORNING COULDN'T COME soon enough for Jake.

The night had been endless, all because he'd been forced to say good-night to Maggie before he was ready. But he hadn't dared linger at her parents' home.

Unable to lie there any longer, he rolled out of bed

at six and took off on his usual run up City Creek Canyon. When he returned to his apartment, his adrenaline was still surging.

In his gut, he knew Maggie hadn't wanted him to leave. He could swear she felt an attraction to him on a deeper level than she was willing to admit. The chemistry was there. His own radar was never wrong about something that crucial to his happiness.

Though he still held to his original feeling that Maggie would never be heart-whole until her sister's case was solved, he planned to make her more aware of him before the day was out.

After a shower, he got ready for work and went in early to start making calls to New York. Whether he hit pay dirt or not, he would visit Maggie's law firm afterward and give her an update. Anything to be with her again.

Two hours later, he'd gone halfway through the list of New York engravers without success. Their businesses were too new to remember the former company.

When his cell phone rang, he clicked on without even looking at the caller ID. It was the receptionist at the hospital. She asked him to come in for therapy in the afternoon because the doctor was going to be gone on Tuesday.

Jake said he'd be there, and hung up.

Wendell popped in several times to know how the search for Ms. McFarland was progressing. Simone stopped in to give him some marzipan candy a family member had sent to her from France.

When Lara came in to water his flowers, he decided he wasn't getting anything done. Why not leave the office and surprise Maggie with an unscheduled visit?

Among other things, he'd been wanting to see her office ever since he'd found out she was an attorney.

Ten minutes later, he entered the double doors of her inner sanctum and approached the middle-aged receptionist. "I'm Jake Halsey from the Eagle Gate Genealogical Firm. Ms. McFarland asked me to come by when I had information for her."

"I'm sorry, Mr. Halsey, but she just left on foundation business."

Jake struggled to hide his disappointment. "How long before she's back?"

"She has a two o'clock meeting with a client, if that helps."

Maggie McFarland was a driven woman. But as long as no man had a claim on her, Jake could live with it.

"Tell her I dropped by will you?"

"Of course."

He stopped in the plaza cafeteria for a sandwich before returning to his office. The rest of the day, Jake continued to make phone calls without hearing back from Maggie.

Frustrated, he checked his watch. It was ten to three. His therapy session started at three-thirty.

Two more phone calls to go.

"Lofgren's Engraving."

Jake identified himself and the reason for his call.

"Just a moment please. I'll see if the senior Mr. Lofgren's still here."

It was closing time in New York. If Jake's efforts didn't produce results, he would have to attack his problem a different way tomorrow.

"Hello," came the voice of a man who had to be in his late seventies or even eighties. "I hear you're trying to locate Buric Engravers. It was bought out years ago by Fetzer Stationers. I believe the original building has been torn down."

Stationers!

"Thank you, Mr. Lofgren. You've been very helpful."

In the next instant Jake called New York information for the number, but when he tried to reach Fetzer's, their voice mail had been turned on.

There was always tomorrow.

By the time he'd returned to his apartment after his therapy, Maggie still hadn't called. It looked like it was going to be another long night.

Skwars Farm
August 11

ANNA HAD JUST TAKEN the last tray of *kolaches* from the bottom shelf of the oven when Julia entered the bakery kitchen and walked over to her.

"Those two men from the FBI who interviewed Petr the other day are out in front wanting to talk to you. I told them to sit down at one of the tables."

Since their first visit to the farm, Anna had expected they'd be by again to see her, but today wasn't the best time. Nelly's wedding was tomorrow. Milena was coming by in a few minutes to take her and some other cousins to Caledonia where they were going to decorate the church.

"I'll be right there."

After putting the pastry on a cooling rack, Anna washed her hands, removed her apron and walked through to the front of the bakery. She spotted the men immediately.

They were dressed in lightweight business suits and ties. Julia had served them something to eat. Anna wove her way through the other tables toward them.

"Hello. I'm Anna Buric."

They both stood up and introduced themselves as Agents Davis and Polk. "If you don't mind, we'd like to talk to you for a minute. This won't take long," said Agent Davis.

After they were all seated, she said, "I don't know what more I can tell you than I told Mr. Markham."

"We're not here to ask more questions. We came to give you something important."

She looked from one man to the other. "I don't understand."

"We've been working hard with your attorney to solve the mystery of your past. No answers have emerged yet, but we've issued you a temporary social-security number so you can get on with your plans to go to college, buy a car, get a new job, open a bank account. Whatever."

They presented her with a card. She looked at it in disbelief, then her gaze flicked back to them.

"That's your passport to the future. Don't lose it."

"I never expected to receive this so soon!"

Both men smiled. The one on her left said, "Mr. Markham thought you might like this present so you can enjoy your cousin's wedding tomorrow."

The other agent nodded. "All we ask is that you check in with us once a week and keep us alerted of any change in your address." He handed her another card with their names and phone numbers.

"Do you have any theories about what happened to my mother and father?"

Agent Davis's expression sobered. "We know nothing about your mother. The man purported to be your father, Antonin Buric, a man who would be fifty years old today, has a record of criminal activity stretching back to his teens. At this point in time we have no idea where he is, or even if he's alive."

A criminal.

Anna had discussed that possibility with Mr. Markham, but it didn't make it any easier to hear.

"It's our opinion he's not your birth father. Mr. Markham suggested he might have been part of an illegal baby-adoption ring having to do with Czech mothers that was in operation years ago. But we've looked into the court records on all the arrests made at the time. There's no evidence to indicate Antonin Buric or his brother Franz had any connection to it."

"So you think I could have been kidnapped."

Agent Polk slowly nodded. "It's only a hunch, but it's a strong one."

"I'm inclined to believe the same thing," the other agent asserted.

Anna started to get excited. "Then my real parents could be looking for me—"

"If you were abducted, then there's no question about it. We've worked with other parents who even after decades have passed are desperate to find their stolen children. They never stop hoping and praying for a miracle."

"We haven't ruled out the possibility that Antonin could have been your father. We're going to continue to do everything possible to locate a birth record on you while we try to find him. But we're also beginning the task of sorting through the names of parents throughout the nation whose babies were stolen during that year."

"Would there be a lot?"

"Let's put it this way. In the year you were born, there were reports of 120,000 cases involving the concealment of a child under the age of seventeen and transporting it out of state."

"That many?" she cried in disbelief.

"Not all of them were new babies, of course. But you can understand it's still going to be a huge job sorting it all out."

"We can, however, narrow our search to a window of five, six months," Agent Polk interjected. "In case this Olga was off on her presumption that you were three months old when you arrived at the farm, we'll be looking at names of parents whose babies were born anywhere from March through August."

She looked down at the cards in her hand. "I can't tell you what this means to me."

"If there's a family out there waiting for you to come home, we're anxious to unite you. In the event Antonin was your father, then let's hope he's alive and we can track him down to get answers about your mother. In the meantime, you're free to move about in society."

Free.

"Thank you," she whispered.

"Have fun at the wedding."

They got to their feet and shook her hand. As they left the bakery, Milena was coming through the door. The moment she saw Anna, she motioned her to come out to the car.

"Give me one second," Anna called to her.

Before she left, she had to phone Mr. Markham and thank him for this great gift. The attorney had just presented her with the document she needed to start a new life.

Her cousins had been so good to her, but she'd always felt deep in her heart she wasn't one of them. Since meeting with the agents, that feeling had grown stronger.

But in case she was the daughter of a criminal, she didn't dare allow herself to dream about this fantastic family she belonged to. It was enough to know she could leave the farm and be a legal citizen.

Salt Lake City, Utah
August 12

"MAGGIE? It's Liz."

"Have they found that eight-year-old girl yet?"

"No. The authorities have put out the AMBER Alert, and are asking for more helpers in the search."

"I'll get right on it. Thanks, Liz."

After clicking off, Maggie phoned the person in charge of mobilizing the volunteers. She gave him the necessary information. "One of the newest volunteers is a Mr. Jake Halsey. I'll contact him personally."

Since the kidnapping had prevented her from returning to the firm yesterday, she hadn't heard Jake had dropped by her office until her receptionist had told her that morning. Maggie had a volunteer job for him.

The second they hung up she called her mechanic and told him to get the Cessna 185 ready and towed out to the runway. Then she buzzed her receptionist.

"Beth? Please reschedule my afternoon appointment with Mr. Carlisle for Thursday afternoon. Scott will handle any emergencies. I'm going out on a search. I might have to be gone through Thursday morning."

"Will do. Good luck finding her. I heard the news on the radio. The poor little thing."

"Let's hope we're in time," she said before calling Jake on his cell phone.

In case he wasn't using his work phone, or wasn't there at all, this would be the fastest way to make contact. He picked up on the second ring.

"Maggie?"

His deep voice resonated to her insides, making her feel quivery. "Yes. Do you want to go out on a search with me?"

"When?"

"Right now."

"I'm ready. Shall I walk over to the foundation?"

"No. You're going to need protective clothing and a sleeping bag. I'll come by your apartment in fifteen minutes to pick you up."

"Drive around the back. I'll be waiting."

She wouldn't have had the confidence to call him herself if Beth hadn't told her he'd come by the office to see her. Though he'd probably come on business, she hoped he was starting to be interested in her as a woman.

Twenty minutes later, after she'd changed into khakis and a T-shirt, she drove around to the east side of the old Jordan mansion. Jake walked toward her wearing fatigues and a backpack with a bedroll. When their eyes met, her heart leaped.

He tossed his gear in the back, then climbed in the passenger seat next to her. "Hi."

People said *hi* coming and going all the time, every day. But that two-letter word had never affected her the way this one did coming from Jake.

"You said you were my man. It's reassuring to know I can take you at your word."

"I'm glad to know my application for a volunteer was approved."

"As if there was any doubt. Thanks for being ready. There's no time to lose."

She backed up before driving out the same way she came in. They'd take the short trip down the hill to North Temple, then drive to the airport.

"I turned on the TV when I came home to change. All I heard was that there'd been a kidnapping this morning. No other details."

Maggie's hands tightened on the steering wheel. "An eight-year-old girl was abducted from Yellow Pine campsite at Mirror Lake in the Uintas east of Salt Lake. While her parents were still asleep, she tiptoed out of their tent to take her six-year-old brother to the nearby latrine.

"While she was waiting for him, he could hear a man talking to her. When the boy went outside, she wasn't there. He thought she'd gone back to their camp without him."

"Good Lord." He grimaced. "How far away is it?"

"Two hours by car. Fortunately the park rangers were on the ball and alerted the police. Roadblocks went up hours ago. The fiend who's taken her will have to stay in that area of the mountains to elude capture.

"Unfortunately he could be hiding anywhere in the pine-covered terrain. If he laid in a cache of supplies ahead of time, he could survive long enough to kill her and dispose of her body."

"What's the elevation?"

"A little over ten thousand feet."

Jake whistled. "Then he'll be staying below timberline to keep out of sight."

"Yes, and it's rugged country."

She felt his gaze on her. "How come we're driving west?"

"Because we're going to do a flyover search. You've been relegated to the position of my spotter. When it's dark, we'll search on foot until we're exhausted and need to make camp. If she isn't found by morning, we'll do the whole thing all over again."

Maggie felt instant stillness from Jake.

"The attorney's a pilot, too?"

"Yes. I soloed at fifteen and have been flying ever since."

"How long ago was that?"

A little thrill darted through her body. If he weren't a little attracted to her, he wouldn't have asked the question.

"Fifteen years. If you're nervous about going up with me, tell me now and I'll ask one of the mechanics to drive you home after we reach the small airport."

"You're not going to get rid of me that fast."

Her lips twitched. "I was right about you. You like to live dangerously."

"*You're* still alive," he drawled.

"That's a fact. Just so you know, I intend to stay that way."

He responded with a lazy smile. "I'm overjoyed to hear it."

Despite the seriousness of their mission, she couldn't help but chuckle.

The airport turnoff came up fast. She veered to the right and took the road leading to the McFarland private hangar. To her satisfaction, her white Cessna 185 with the navy trim sat outside all fueled and ready to go.

"Hey, Maggie!" One of the mechanics walked over to her as she and Jake got out of the car. "The Duchesne County sheriff faxed this grid map to you. He'll be on com two."

"Perfect." She studied the information for a moment before folding and stuffing it in her trouser pocket. "I appreciate you getting the plane checked out so fast."

"Pleased to do it, even if it's what you pay me for." He winked.

She turned to Jake. All he was doing was standing there holding his gear, observing everything. But if she could take a picture of him right now and show it to every woman she knew, their knees would buckle the same way hers were doing at the sheer virility of the man.

She relished the thought of flying alone with him. "Come on. We'll store your gear with mine." She headed toward the fuselage and opened the door to the storage area. "If you need anything, take it out now."

He pulled a black case from his backpack.

She looked at him. "I've got binoculars for you in the pouch behind my seat."

Something flickered in the recesses of his eyes. "I've brought a special kind."

She just bet he did.

At this point, nothing surprised her where he was concerned. After he'd stashed the rest of his things, she closed the door. Without her urging, he walked around the passenger side of the single-prop plane and climbed in the copilot's seat.

Maggie took her place at the controls and reached for her headgear. The four-seater plane had a tight-fitting interior. With Jake's arm brushing against hers, the intimacy caused her heart to thud unmercifully fast. "You can stow that case in the pouch behind your seat."

While he complied with her suggestion, she started her preflight check.

"Your headgear is above the window. Put it on first before you fasten your shoulder seat strap."

Every movement of his was so swift and precise, Maggie had the gut feeling he'd done this kind of thing many times before, but he wasn't about to admit it to her. Perhaps before this trip was over, he would reveal a secret or two.

Anxious to be in the air, she ran through the checklist. Conditions were perfect for flying. Ninety degrees out, little wind, one hundred percent visibility. Everything was a go.

"Are you ready?" she asked her passenger.

"What do you think?"

She thought she might turn to mush at the way his gaze traveled over her. With a flick of the wrist, she turned on the key and the motor started up. Like driving a car, she taxied out to the runway.

"Tower? This is Cessna one-eight-five kilo mike, ready for takeoff."

CHAPTER SIX

CRUISING WITH THE UNEXPECTED and extraordinary Maggie McFarland at 13,500 feet produced a high in Jake he hadn't experienced in years. Maybe never. From their unique vantage point up close, the majesty of the rugged Uinta mountains with their towering peaks only added to his wonder.

Below the main ridges, the terrain was divided into numerous alpine basins dotted with crystal-clear lakes and lush meadows. His eyes followed the rivers descending from glacially carved U-shaped canyons.

"That's King's Peak," Maggie pointed out. "It's as high as we are. Glorious, isn't it?"

Glorious didn't begin to express what he was feeling. There were no words to describe his state of euphoria. All this grandeur and Maggie's soft, warm body only inches from his...

"We're approaching the area of the grid to begin our search. It looks like we're the first plane here."

Those few words brought Jake back to reality with a jerk. She handed him the map with coordinates to pinpoint exact locations. "We'll search the area near the timberline level first," she said.

Jake studied the grid in detail. This was just like being in the field, except that instead of another agent for company, he was with a female who drove every thought from his mind but one.

"Better get out that toy you brought along before I make my first sweep. I'll bank to a distance of about two hundred feet above the terrain. When you spot anything moving that looks suspicious, tell me and I'll call it in. The search-and-rescue units will investigate."

While she established radio contact with the ground, Jake started to reach around with his left hand for the case that held his infrared goggles. Damn if his shoulder didn't make it difficult to stretch that far. He made several more attempts, swallowing the curse that almost escaped. Finally he was successful.

"Fancy," she commented when he'd put on the goggles and started making adjustments. "Standard detective issue is it, Mr. Halsey?"

"Nothing gets past you, does it?" He wouldn't say more.

"Let me know when you're ready."

"I'm ready now."

"Okay. I'll cut the speed as much as I dare to give you optimum viewing advantage."

She maneuvered the Cessna as if it were an eagle gracefully swooping toward earth in search of prey. In awe of her expertise, he was able to settle into his job.

Somewhere down there amid the pines was a depraved bastard who'd already had plenty of time to commit the most heinous of crimes. In Jake's mind, to assault an innocent child was the epitome of pure evil.

The goggles' magnification ability picked up every-thing. Their heat-sensing property had already outlined the shape of a moose and several deer. The mountain was alive with nature's creatures who hunted and killed for food with God's permission.

But somewhere down there was another creature more savage than any animal. It killed for an entirely different reason.

Maggie made several more passes, giving him time to cover every inch of terrain. "Any sign of human life?"

"Not so far."

She called in the report over the radio, then said, "I'll take us to area two."

Once again she demonstrated her skill in a graceful downward arc to the midsection of the mountain. After five minutes, he picked up two adults hiking toward a tiny lake.

"Fly over the water one more time. I've spotted a couple of men."

"See anyone else?" she asked after they'd made sev-eral passes.

"No. If they were on the run, they would have noticed us and ducked into some trees by now."

"I'll let the sheriff know anyway."

With painstaking thoroughness they worked their way down the mountain. The lower elevations revealed more hikers, but all of them were adults. No man or men with one child. Maggie related each find to the sheriff.

"The other plane hasn't arrived yet. We've been asked to cover grids four, five and six."

"Let's do it," Jake murmured, keeping his goggles

constantly focused on the breathtaking scenery. They made the same methodical sweeps as before, only they started from the base first and worked their way up to timberline.

Jake had a growing fear that the child had already been killed and was lying in a shallow grave. Some hunter would probably stumble across her remains this fall, or the next. But he kept those thoughts to himself.

Though he was sure Maggie would never admit it, there had to have been times over the years when she'd been plagued by such an image of her own baby sister. *Dear Lord.*

By the time they'd finished searching the last grid, she announced they would have to fly to Evanston, Wyoming, to refuel.

Once they landed, it felt good to get out and stretch, use the restroom, grab a hamburger. But her mood, like Jake's, had become more reflective.

The yawning fear that the girl was dead hovered at the surface of their minds. Neither of them felt like talking, yet Jake was comfortable with her silence. In fact, there wasn't anything about Maggie McFarland he didn't like. It was enough just to be with her.

By the time they were in the air again, the sheriff still had no news. It sent a chill through Jake's body, so he could imagine how Maggie felt. The sheriff indicated the other plane had arrived and was doing a sweep of the next three grids.

Jake put the goggles to his eyes and made an adjustment because of the sun's lower position in the sky. "I'm ready whenever you are."

"Here we go again."

The next two hours were a repeat of their first search. The campgrounds were full, with lots of adults and children nearby. But the higher the elevation of the range of mountains running like a corridor for sixty miles, the fewer the people.

Once again they returned to Evanston for fuel and dinner, then they flew to Duchesne, the closest point where they could land. No services were available, but there was a police unit waiting at the airfield. They'd provided a Jeep for Maggie's use with instructions to search grid twenty-two on foot.

After Jake transferred their gear from the plane to the back seat, they took off for the Mirror Lake road. Soon they passed by the assembly point where the police and search-and-rescue units were parked.

As they drove along, Jake marveled to see at least twelve Dodge Durangos with the words *McFarland Foundation* painted on the doors, parked at quarter-mile intervals. Each one could hold seven people. Though there were a few other cars, it was her volunteers who comprised the majority of the search party.

He turned to her. "You're amazing, Maggie."

"Don't give me any credit. It's at times like this I thank my great-great-grandfather McFarland whose money made all this possible. Tragically, with all the funds available, all the people and technology, we're probably too late to save one child."

Jake swallowed hard. "I read your brochure. It's at times like this you need to think of the seventeen thousand children you have helped save. I don't believe I know another human being who holds that record."

"I needed to hear that about now," she said in a whisper.

A quarter of a mile from the last car, she pulled to the side of the road. He got out and helped her on with her backpack. Like his, the bedroll lay tied across the top. Though they were in a hurry, he savored doing this small favor for her. Anything to help her, touch her. There was a palpable sensual tension between them.

"Th-thank you," she stammered.

"You're welcome."

Forcing himself to remember why they were there, he put on his own backpack. The weight created a little discomfort in his shoulder, but it was inevitable after being unencumbered since the explosion. He guessed this trip would prove how well it had healed.

Right now nothing was more important than finding the little girl, no matter her condition. Her grieving parents would be in excruciating agony until she was recovered.

The faces of Ellen and Reed McFarland flashed before his eyes. The awful tragedy of their lives had carved lines in their faces. Jake had sensed a sadness engrained in their psyches.

Maggie's suffering had produced other telltale signs. Her guard was always up. She was in constant motion, pushing, striving toward some distant mark. It drove her so she couldn't see those who wanted a close relationship with her, be they male or female.

If Jake had his way, he would make a few inroads with her before the night was out.

"When I have another volunteer with me, we usually work apart and keep in touch with each other and the police by cell phone."

"Why don't we stay together this time," he suggested. The thought of her being ambushed by some maniac never left his mind. "These goggles can do the work of half a dozen people trying to cover the same area. Want to take a look?"

A faint smile lurked at the corner of her mouth. "You know I do." She put them to her eyes and trained them on the forested area surrounding them. "Oh Jake—I had no idea."

He chuckled quietly. "It's kind of like looking through a high-powered microscope at a drop of water."

"Every volunteer should have a pair of these." She finally handed them back to him. "I've never seen anything like them at a regular store."

"You never will" was all he was prepared to say for the time being. "Come on. Let's get started."

He could almost hear her brain working it out as they began their search through the pines and heavy underbrush. The sounds of insects, the screech and cry of birds rent the air. When they heard the chatter of squirrels running up and down trees, indignant to be disturbed, Maggie smiled at him. It lit up his world.

Occasionally they came across a family or a group of teens hiking around. Jake stopped each person and alerted them about the kidnapping. Hopefully someone might have information that would help.

She checked in with the sheriff every ten minutes to give their coordinates and find out the latest status. In an hour and a half they'd covered their sector without finding anything suspicious.

"Maggie? It's time to make camp for the night." Evening came early in the mountains, even in summer. Long shadows striped them as they moved between lodgepoles and firs.

She looked around. "How about beneath that clump of pines?"

"You're reading my mind. All those needles will make a nice bed for us."

Bed.

At thirty years of age, Maggie still hadn't been to bed with a man.

She'd dated a lot in college, and occasionally since then. There'd been one or two guys she'd found attractive, but she'd never been able to let herself go.

Though Jake hadn't said it with anything more in mind than a good place to stretch out their sleeping bags, she unexpectedly imagined something else much more intimate. Heat rushed to her cheeks.

A sudden muffled groan coming out of Jake jarred her from her guilty thoughts.

She'd seen the stress in his facial muscles when he'd reached for the goggles case on the plane. Now that he'd relieved himself of his backpack, she knew his shoulder was bothering him. She also knew he wouldn't like it if she said anything about it.

He reminded her a little of her brother Ben. A tough guy who'd go to the greatest lengths not to show weakness.

Deciding she'd better mind her own business, she

pulled out her cell phone and checked in with the sheriff. They talked briefly. Jake watched her hang up.

"I take it there's no news yet."

"Nothing."

She undid her bedroll, then unzipped a side compartment in her pack and reached for her space blanket. Once she spread it out over the needles, she laid her sleeping bag on top of it. Next she removed her boots and socks.

"There. I'm ready for bed." On that note, she climbed inside and sat there.

Jake's low-bellied chuckle rolled on and on.

"What's so funny?"

His brows quirked. "You're not a woman who fusses. I find that a very refreshing trait. Please don't think I was laughing at you."

"I wouldn't mind if you were."

He laid out his bag a few feet from her. "I know. That's what makes you *you*."

Maggie didn't know whether to be pleased with his comment or not. "What are you smiling about now?"

"You've been a surprise from day one," he said as he pulled off his shoes.

"So have you." She rummaged in her backpack. "Here."

The little packet landed at his feet. He picked it up. "Hmm. A strawberry Fruit Roll-Up. How did you know this is exactly what I wanted for dessert?"

Maybe the comic relief was what she needed because it was her turn to laugh.

He shot her a glance she couldn't decipher in the

gathering darkness. "I liked the sound of that. I wonder how long it's been."

"Do I come off that morose?"

"Anything but." After he'd made an adjustment to his goggles, he set them down close by. Next he produced a water bottle. It gave her pleasure just to watch him drink from it.

Maggie's breath caught.

If she could be anywhere else in the world at this moment, she would choose to be right here, right now, with this man.

Tomorrow morning she would still feel the same way. And tomorrow night. *And next week, next month, next year.* The ramifications of that truth shook her to the core.

"Before I bed down, would you like a drink?"

"Thank you, but I have my own bottle if I get thirsty."

She lay back on her arm, content to watch his movements. He eventually climbed inside his bag and stretched out on his back with a low moan. His shoulder was hurting him.

If she were his fiancée or his wife, she wouldn't be afraid to hand him a painkiller. Or give him a massage. What would it be like to really touch him? To be touched by him?

"I heard that sigh," he spoke quietly. "If you need to talk about it, I'm here to listen."

"Actually I'm restless. Why don't you tell me about yourself."

"What do you want to know?"

"Did you love your wife terribly?"

After a pause, he finally said, "I was crazy about her. She was a cute brunette who stood no higher than my heart. We met after I went into the navy as a commissioned officer. She'd already joined. We'd been married two years when she and three others were killed in a freak accident aboard ship."

Maggie clutched the edge of her cover. "Jake—" Tears filled her eyes. "I'm so sorry. I shouldn't have brought it up."

"Why not? It's a perfectly natural question. For a year afterwards, I couldn't talk about it. But it's been nine years and that part of my life seems like a vague memory. I can't even relate to that period of time now."

She could barely make him out as he turned on his side toward her.

"What about your love life, Maggie?"

"It could be summed up in one sentence. I've never met anyone I wanted to marry. You two were lucky to have found each other, even if you only had two years."

"I agree. Maybe that's why it was easier for me to get on with my life after."

"Were you born in San Diego?"

"No. Jacksonville, Florida."

"Is your family still there?"

"I'm afraid not. Both my parents have passed away. Mother died of cancer when I was a boy, so my father raised me. He died of a chest infection a year ago last May."

She bit her lip. "How hard for you, with no siblings."

"I wouldn't know. I was a spoiled, selfish only child and I loved my life."

Maggie chuckled. "You're a very healthy person. I envy you."

He raised himself up on one elbow. "Meaning you're not?"

"Everyone in my family is a workaholic."

"Work keeps the demons away."

"Exactly. But it covers up some fragile psyches. Every time a child is kidnapped, I cringe for the poor families whose lives will never be the same again.

"My brother Ben's marriage almost broke up because of it. It caused their children so much grief. My other brother Cord should have been a rancher. He loves the outdoors so much and loved the time we spent on the family ranch in Colorado. But Mother needed us around, so he stayed here to go to college and started up the shelter.

"Dad went into politics when he should have stayed in Salt Lake to head his business interests and be with Mom. With their baby gone, Mom needed him more than ever—"

Maggie stopped. "Forgive me, Jake. I love my family and don't usually talk about them to anyone."

"I'm flattered. Even the great ones have to vent once in a while."

"Great ones?" she mocked. "I'm a great big idiot. You have my promise I'll go to sleep now. Whoever wakes up first, let the other one know and we'll get going again."

"Fair enough."

She turned on her side away from him. Convinced she wouldn't be able to settle down, it surprised her to awaken much later from a deep sleep. When she looked at her watch, it said three in the morning. Something must have brought her out of her oblivion. Probably the chipmunks she'd heard earlier.

Closing her eyes, she settled down again only to hear a moaning sound too human to be an animal. She shot straight up and looked over at Jake. Not close enough to see him clearly, she crept out of her bag and moved next to him.

He was thrashing around in his bag, muttering something she couldn't understand. She knelt at his side and put a hand to his forehead. It felt hot and clammy. His shallow breathing alarmed her.

"Jake?" She shook his arm gently. "Wake up. You're having a nightmare."

"Is that you, Reiker? Vern's dead. We've got to get the hell out of here! Careful, Reiker— Don't step on that wire! The dump has been mined. Dear God—Reiker! " He screamed in terror.

Maggie couldn't bear to see him in this kind of torture. "Jake—you're having a bad dream. Come on. Wake up!"

"Please God— Please God—don't let him be dead. Don't die on me, Reiker. Don't be dead. Don't be dead."

Jake was in a place where she couldn't reach him. His hands grabbed her and pulled her on top of him. He had no idea of his strength. Those deep sobs reminded her of her father's the other night. Soul-wrenching, gut-wrenching sobs.

He rocked her in his arms. "You can't be dead, too— don't be dead—there's a chopper coming—hold on— don't die on me—"

"Jake." She cupped his wet face in her hands, but the hands clamped around her upper arms felt like bands of steel, trapping her so she couldn't move.

She had no choice but to try to calm him down with tender endearments. "Hush. It's going to be all right." Using her thumbs she smoothed the moisture from his cheeks, then kissed his eyelids and temples.

His body continued to writhe. Maggie smoothed the hair off his forehead and whispered soothing words. Slowly he began to quiet down. Once his breathing sounded more normal, his hands fell away from her arms.

Realizing the nightmare had passed, she hurried back to her sleeping bag. While she lay there wide-awake and trembling, her mind tried to process what she'd just seen and heard.

He'd been talking about a land mine that had exploded. No doubt he'd been caught in it, thus the reason for his shoulder replacement. Putting everything together since she'd first met him, she had an idea he was either a navy SEAL or a special-operations officer for the CIA.

Having spent a lot of time talking to her father about the weaknesses and strengths of the CIA's intelligence-gathering operations, Maggie felt she wasn't far off the mark.

She hadn't really bought the business about him being a police detective from California. Too many things about his story hadn't added up. But she assumed he really could read and write Czech in order to work at the genealogical firm.

Jake had devised a clever cover that would last until

he was healed enough to go back to his secret career in January. He *was* going to leave.

Nothing's permanent, Maggie.

She buried her face in her hands, glad she'd witnessed his gruesome nightmare. Doubly glad she hadn't been able to bring him out of it. This would be *her* secret.

Whenever she was in danger of wanting to get closer to him, she would remember this night. From here on out their relationship would continue on a strictly professional basis.

She'd hired him to find out what he could about the Buric family. So far he'd done a fantastic job because it was his business to pull off the impossible.

But men who could accomplish feats other men only dreamed about didn't stay in one place long.

"COME ON, MERRY SUNSHINE. It's time to get going."

Maggie's eyelids fluttered open. A lavender glow lit up the sky. She could feel Jake's warmth. He'd hunkered down next to her.

In a flash, the unforgettable events of a few hours ago gave her body a jolt. She sat up and smoothed the hair off her forehead, unwilling to meet his intense gaze.

"Good morning. Have you been awake long?"

"About a half hour. I took a little walk around with the goggles."

"You should have wakened me." She climbed out of the bag and got to her feet. He stood up when she did. "I'll be ready to go in a minute."

After putting on her shoes and socks, she dragged her

backpack twenty yards to a clump of bushes. Out of his sight, she could freshen up and brush her hair.

Though August was the hottest time of year, it was always cool in the mountains in the early morning. She found her navy pullover with the hood and slipped it on over her T-shirt. Digging in a side pocket of her pack, she produced some beef jerky and dried fruit packets, enough for both of them.

When she joined him, she discovered he'd rolled up her sleeping bag. The folded space blanket lay on top. His backpack was on. He looked anxious to travel.

"For being such a great helper, I have treats for you." She handed him the snacks.

"Umm. Just what I wanted for breakfast. Thank you." He was oblivious to the fact that he'd had a nightmare last night. She could be thankful for that, at least.

"You're welcome."

While he opened the packets and began devouring his food, she put the blanket away and tied her bedroll to the top of her pack.

"What's the plan?" he asked.

"I'll check in and find out."

There was still no news. She shook her head to let him know. After she clicked off, she said, "They want us to fly over the same grids we did yesterday. They're pretty sure the kidnapper is still in the area. He may have moved to higher ground during the night."

Once again they set off through the forest toward the car. Jake concentrated on scanning the terrain with his goggles.

Now that she had proof of his covert career, he was

fascinating to watch. He functioned with a certain stealth and economy of movement that was automatic to him.

In terms of his being able to take care of her, no woman on the planet could be safer. But emotionally, he had the power to destroy her if she wasn't careful.

By the time she'd finished her snacks, they'd reached the Jeep. On their way to Duchesne they noticed the Durangos still parked on the roadside. More cars had shown up to join in the search.

"I don't suppose you ever have enough volunteers for a manhunt like this."

"Not in these mountains, anyway."

He flicked her a glance. "Are you all right?"

"Honestly?"

Jake nodded.

"I'm heartsick."

"You know what I think?"

"What?"

"You're emotionally exhausted. Maggie McFarland to the rescue. But who takes care of you?"

Don't say things like that, Jake.

Maggie couldn't afford to spend any more time with him, but she had no choice. The parents of that little girl were counting on a miracle. Not everyone had a plane. Now that she was here, to leave without giving it another day would be walking out on the people who depended on her.

Somehow she had to draw on her inner strength and pretend Jake was one of the spotters she usually brought along.

"Flying with you could get to be my addiction," Jake murmured. They'd just reached the Duchesne airfield where the plane was waiting.

"It's the scenery," she mocked.

They stowed their gear and took off for the nearest assigned grids. Jake pointed in the distance. "Clouds are gathering. Come to think of it, there's more wind this morning."

"That's why we're in the 185. It's a tough little workhorse."

His mouth broke into a grin. "And here I was thinking of her as a dainty lady."

Keep it up, Jake, and I won't be able to resist you.

He lifted the goggles off his lap and settled down to the business of finding the proverbial needle in the haystack.

She made pass after pass, flying as close as possible so Jake could canvass the mountain from timberline to the valley. Every human he saw she reported to the sheriff, but the suspect was still on the loose.

"Can't do anymore right now. We're low on fuel."

"I am, too."

"I hear you."

With a sense of déjà vu, they flew to Evanston, filled up and ate a big lunch that would hold them for the rest of the day. They ate fast. With the kidnapping on their minds, neither one of them was in the mood for conversation. After returning to the search area, Maggie spotted two other planes.

"We've got a little more help up here today. You'd think with all these volunteers, we'd find something."

"It's going to happen," Jake stated with confidence.

"I'll hold that thought."

Two hours passed, then they were off to Evanston to refuel for a last go around. Jake bought them a pack of chocolate-chip cookies.

"We need the sugar," was all he said, putting one in her mouth while she was doing her preflight check. The touch of his fingers against her lips sent a current of electricity through her body. She could have been eating sawdust and wouldn't have known the difference.

It was back to grid one, then they'd work their way to three.

Midway up the mountain, Jake made a strange sound in his throat. "I'm picking up two figures moving. One of them is small. Can you do that same sweep again, but get closer?"

Maggie's heart started to race. "I'll do what I can. There's a storm brewing. The wind is buffeting us." She banked the plane and retraced her flight path.

"There— I see a man pulling a young girl through the trees. Tell the sheriff to send some police choppers to grid two while we continue our surveillance."

Absolutely euphoric, Maggie relayed the message while Jake fed her a description.

"How's the fuel?" he demanded.

"We've got thirty more minutes before we have to head for Evanston."

"Radio the sheriff for a backup plane in case the choppers don't get here before we have to turn back. It's vital we don't lose sight of this pervert. As long as we keep bombarding him with low sweeps, the girl is still safe."

Maggie sent the message.

What happened in the next ten minutes was better than any action movie. Two helicopters showed up and several SWAT teams were lowered to the ground.

She could hardly breathe waiting to hear the outcome.

"They've got the girl, Maggie!"

Joy exploded inside the cockpit. It was a good thing Maggie was forced to keep her hands on the controls. Otherwise she'd have thrown her arms around him and all her resolve to keep her distance would have evaporated.

"You found her, Jake."

"We found her. Let's go back to Evanston and celebrate."

Evanston, yes. Celebration, no. If she wanted to survive Jake Halsey, she was going to have to keep their contact strictly professional.

CHAPTER SEVEN

Milwaukee, Wisconsin
August 15

THE STUDENT HOUSING SUPERVISOR unlocked the door for
Anna and gave her the key. "It's good you came today.
This is the last single furnished dorm in the building.
The list of rules is here by the light switch and in the brochure I gave you. Any problem, come see me. If you can
wait until next week, you'll be able to purchase a cell
phone through the university for half the regular price."

"Thank you. I'll do that." Anna shut and locked the
door behind the woman. She lay against it for a moment
with her eyes closed.

Her own room.

She'd never known such luxury in her life. Though
she'd had to pay more for it, she didn't care. For as far
back as she could remember, she'd always had to share
one with someone else.

Thanks to Josef and Milena, who'd driven her to
Milwaukee yesterday, she had completed her enrollment
at the University of Wisconsin-Milwaukee. Better yet,
she had a private room and a bank account.

Petr had transferred her ten thousand dollars in savings to the new account. Twenty-five hundred dollars had already been paid out for tuition and books. Another twenty-five hundred remained to cover her expenses until she found a job. Part of the rest she would spend on a used car as soon as she got her driver's license.

She was still in shock over this new freedom a social-security number had given her. Her excitement growing, she picked up her suitcase and carried it into the tiny bedroom to unpack her things and get settled.

Tomorrow was freshman orientation. In a week, classes would start. That meant seven days to find a job. One that had nothing to do with farming or cooking. Maybe at a hospital.

In her early teens, she'd been sent out to tell one of the older cousins to come to dinner. He was late. When Anna found him, he was lying on the ground in a pool of blood with bee stings all over him.

Horrified, she ran back to the farmhouse to get help. But by the time the others reached him, he was gone. It turned out a swarm had attacked him, causing him to fall off his tractor. He'd cut his head open. The doctor said he'd bled to death.

The experience had been a traumatic one for Anna because she hadn't known what to do for him. Since that terrible day, she'd made up her mind that if she ever got the chance, she'd become a doctor.

No one on the farm ever thought of going to college. They didn't see the need because they were farmers and ran a flourishing enterprise. In that respect, Anna was very different from the rest of them.

Thirteen years ago, the dream to go into medicine had sprung to life. Today it was stronger than ever. If she studied hard, it could become a reality. Though it had been a long time since she'd left the classroom, she'd been a straight-A student in high school and was an avid reader.

The expression "being lonely in a crowd" pretty well described her life. She'd turned to books to shut out the pain of not belonging. If those FBI agents were right and she had been kidnapped, maybe that was why she could never bring herself to embrace the world she'd been raised in.

Even if Antonin Buric, a career criminal, was her birth father, neither he nor her mother had been around to give her an identity.

It was okay. It didn't matter either way. She was in charge of her destiny from here on out. One thing she did know: she would never go back to Skwars Farm to live.

Though Josef and Petr, Julia, Milena—everyone—had told her she would always have a home with them, Anna would never take them up on it. In fact, after being away just one day, she couldn't bear the thought of going back.

Salt Lake City, Utah
August 15

JAKE STOPPED PACING when Maggie breezed into the conference room. Whether in a T-shirt or the stunning peppermint-pink suit she was wearing now, he experienced physical pleasure just looking at her.

"I'm sorry to have kept you waiting. I was deposing a client and it took longer than I expected."

He didn't doubt she was telling the truth, but he knew she'd been avoiding him since they'd flown back to Salt Lake late Wednesday night. His hope they would stay overnight in Evanston, maybe go to a bar and dance, never materialized.

"No problem," he murmured.

"You said you had new information. Please, sit down."

Before Jake could help her, she took her place at the end of the table. Jake preferred to remain standing. He'd left a file for her with all the information he'd accrued to this point.

"It's five-thirty on a Friday, Maggie. Time to call it a day. I'm here to invite you to my apartment. I'll throw some steaks on the grill and we'll talk over dinner."

She flashed him the kind of smile she gave everyone. But he wasn't everyone, and he didn't like it. "I'd love to take you up on it, but I'm due at my brother's place as soon as I can get there."

"Which brother?"

"The one who's on his honeymoon. They're due back soon and I'm going over to help get things ready for them."

Jake had the strongest premonition she was lying about her plans. Something was different about her since she'd wakened on Wednesday morning. Sooner or later he would extract the reason for it, but now wasn't the time to push it. She wasn't going anywhere. Not out of *his* life, anyway.

"Since you're anxious to leave the office, I'll make this quick. In the last two days I've found out the name of Antonin's grandmother. It's Marie Skwars. She married a Jan Buric who was an engraver in New York.

"Their son Vaclav married a woman named Anna, and they had two children, Antonin and Franz, who of course are Tony and Frankie. But the parents died an early death, thus the reason Marie Buric ended up taking care of them.

"Interestingly enough, when I was transcribing a disk of names from a cemetery in Czechoslovakia, I came across the name Vojtech Buric who was born 1871. He married an Anna Molan from Kutna Hora. They had two children, Katrina and Jan. That Jan was the grandfather of Antonin and Franz."

The new revelations brought Maggie to her feet. She looked dazed. "You're a genius," she whispered.

"Hardly. But with this information, we have two places to go for news of Antonin's whereabouts. I've found nothing on Marie in the state of New York. Not even a death record. But I think a visit to the South Bronx where Buric Engravers used to be located would produce a neighbor. Someone who knew her, or of her.

"The other possibility would be to visit Kutna Hora in Bohemia and start inquiring about Antonin. I've already done searches, which have produced nothing. Still, he might have decided to go back to the old country to elude the police. It's all in that file."

She picked it up and clutched it to her chest. "I can't wait to show this to my family. We're indebted to you, Jake. If you'll come out to the reception desk, I'll write you a check for the work you've done so far."

Without waiting for him, she dashed from the conference room and down the hall. He followed slowly. She could write him a check if she wanted. No doubt it was her plan to pay him off and never see him again.

A merciless smile broke the corner of his mouth. He had news for her.

"Here you go," she said a few minutes later.

The check was for ten thousand dollars. His gaze darted to hers. "This has too many zeros." How could she trust him with this kind of money when she had no proof he'd been telling her the truth about anything?

"My father asked me to give you a retainer. There's a standing reward for the person who leads us to her abductor. Once we can prove whether Antonin or Franz or both of them took Kathryn, Dad will give you the rest. He'll insist on it. Of course, no amount of money would be enough to thank you for what you've uncovered so far."

Her beautiful blue eyes glistened with tears. Such faith humbled him. It was the kind that caused her whole family to believe her sister was still alive. That faith made Jake all the more determined to find Kathryn.

He pulled out his wallet and put the check inside before pocketing it again. "How about an invitation to the reception instead? I'd like a chance to meet the kidnapped woman who ended up marrying your brother."

Try to get out of that one, Maggie McFarland.

"I have several in my desk drawer. Just a minute." She returned sooner than that with an envelope in cream parchment.

He took it from her outstretched fingers without opening it. If he wasn't mistaken, her hand was trembling. His plan to get closer to her was working. "Thank you. I'll see myself out."

"AUNT MAGGIE—"

"Katy, darling!" Her little blond, six-year-old niece came running out of the cottage behind the McFarland mansion. Maggie managed to sweep her up in her arms without dropping the shopping bag she was holding. "How long have you been here?"

"Since this afternoon. Brock's making a sign for Uncle Cord."

"I want to see that." She lowered Katy to the ground. Grasping her hand, they walked toward the old French-styled carriage house where her brother would be living with Kit during the weekdays. He had his own home at the top of Alta Canyon forty-five minutes away. But the cottage was more convenient when he had late nights at the shelter.

"Maggie?" her brother called to her. "Come on around the side and see what you think!"

She and Katy walked across the grass and turned the corner. Ben was in cutoffs and tennis shoes, digging up the ground with a shovel.

"Whoa, big brother— What's going on?"

"Clearing out the shrubbery. It's my wedding present to Cord."

"Does he know about it?"

"No. I heard that Kit was hoping to have a little garden of her own, so I thought I'd get this plot ready and save him the trouble."

"That's so sweet of you." Ben was a changed man since he'd dropped the idea of going into politics. These days he was putting his family first. Hallelujah!

She let go of Katy's hand to hug him. "Wooh…"

He'd been in the sun working up a sweat. Laughing, she pulled away from him. "You're going to need a shower."

He grinned. "Tell me about it."

"Where's Julie?"

"In the house helping Brock."

"Now that I'm here, I'll lend a hand."

Ben's smile sobered. "Before you go in, I have to tell you how proud I am to be your brother."

"That's always nice to hear. Whatever did I do to deserve an accolade like that?"

"You know exactly what I'm talking about. You found that eight-year-old girl. The pervert's in custody. You're an angel, Maggie."

"According to Dad, Jake Halsey's the angel. After Wednesday's successful capture, I agree with him. Jake's the one who spotted them." She almost said, "with his goggles." But what Jake did for a living was no one else's business, not even her family's. In fact, she was sure his safety depended on no one finding out.

Ben's speculative gaze traveled over her face. "So besides being a detective and a genealogist, he's decided to be a volunteer, too."

Maggie knew where this conversation was headed and she was going to stop it before Ben dug too deep. "In January he'll return to active duty in San Diego. Until then he's on medical leave, and is bored to tears."

"Your little overnight trip should have solved his problem."

No doubt it *had* for a thirty-six-hour temporary period. But their night in the forest had created a new emotional problem for Maggie that could turn into a lifetime crisis if she spent any more time with him.

A steak dinner. Conversation. At his apartment? Maggie trembled just imagining it.

She eyed her brother steadily. "If it didn't, he's a big boy and can handle it."

"How come he's not married?"

Ben was a shrewd businessman who happened to be her brother. He sensed something was going on between her and Jake. That protective instinct was in full flower.

"His wife died nine years ago. But don't get any ideas about my becoming her replacement. He's never gotten over her."

It was true, but that wasn't the reason Maggie wanted an end to this discussion. She would stake her life on the fact that Jake was married to the CIA. He would probably die a terrible death doing something no one knew about, with no one to mourn his death when he was gone.

She looked down at Katy who'd been hopping around them. "Come on, honey. Let's go find your mommy."

They walked back to the front of the cottage and entered the foyer. Julie and Brock were finishing up painting words on a long piece of butcher paper with red poster paint. It stretched from wall to wall. Brock's dark blond head looked up.

"Hi, Aunt Maggie! Do you like our sign?"

She looked down at it.

Welcome Home Aunt Kit and Uncle Cord!

Not bad at all. "You've done a fabulous job. I love it." She exchanged smiles with Julie. "They'll be so excited when they see it. Where are you going to hang it?"

"Outside across the edge of the roof."

"Guess what?"

"What?" both children asked at the same time.

"I heard rain is forecast for Sunday when they fly in."

"That settles it," her blond sister-in-law declared, getting to her feet. "As soon as this dries, we'll get your father to help us string it here in the foyer."

Brock's head swiveled around. "Yeah. That'll look okay."

"It'll be more of a surprise," Maggie interjected. "While you guys finish up, Katy's going to help me make their bed with these new sheets."

"But it's already got sheets," Katy responded.

"True, but these are a very special soft percale with lace trim. It'll make Kit feel like a bride for a long time to come."

"Uncle Cord doesn't like girl's stuff like that." This was from Brock.

Both Julie and Maggie burst into laughter.

"That was before he met Kit," his mother informed him as Maggie went into the bedroom, the only one in the little house.

"Ooh," Katy said when Maggie shook out the top sheet. She ran her hands over the material. "I want sheets just like this."

"When you get married, I'll buy you some."

Katy helped her make the bed and put the comforter on top. "Aren't you ever going to get married, Aunt Maggie?"

"Yeah, Aunt Maggie." Her good-looking blond brother brought up the trumpet section. He stood in the doorway. Between him and Cord with his handsome features and dark brown hair, she didn't know which one was more attractive.

Jake was something else again. Tough, black-haired, rugged—a force in his own right.

"First I have to meet a man like your daddy."

"But there aren't any daddies like mine. He's the bestest!"

"Thank you, sweetheart."

Maggie smiled at Ben. "There's your answer."

His eyes narrowed. "As I recall, Cord wasn't convinced there was a woman out there for him. Then this irresistible stranger appeared, knocking him sideways and upside down."

Sideways and upside down. What a perfect description for Maggie's emotions since she'd first been introduced to Jake.

"Cord was Kit's first and only love."

"Nine years a widower is long enough for a man to fall madly in love all over again. Don't let his past diminish what's happening now."

"I'm not doing that," she said in a shaken voice.

"Aren't you?"

Maybe she was, a little. Maybe Maggie felt a twinge of jealousy of the woman Jake had been so crazy about. But there was another issue much more important Ben didn't know about. One she couldn't tell him.

"Come on, Katy. Let's see what else there is to do." She hurried out of the room past her brother and headed for the kitchen.

"I've already cleaned the fridge," Julie called to her.

So she had. Maggie shut it. "Tomorrow I'll buy some groceries and stock it with goodies." Speaking of goodies. "Brock, honey?"

"Yeah?"

"Would you come here for a minute?"

He came running. "What is it?"

"Remember when you hid up in the attic?"

An embarrassed look crossed his face before he nodded.

"Will you go up there now and bring down a bottle of wine?"

His eyes grew as round as marbles. "You mean that's what's in those boxes?"

"That's right."

Maggie opened the cupboard and handed him the flashlight. He dashed off to the storeroom. Katy ran after him. They were both back in a shot. He handed Maggie the bottle.

"What's going on?" Ben and Julie had just appeared. The two of them looked so happy again. It took Maggie back to the early days of their marriage when her oldest brother had met Julie skiing in Deer Valley. They'd fallen hard for each other, just like Cord and Kit.

She held up the wine and flashed them a grin. "Some of Great-great-great-grandfather McFarland's special contraband from France for important occasions. We'll leave it on the table with a little note, 'To celebrate the beginning of your life together.' I'd say their marriage is probably the most important thing to happen to this family in a long time."

"But not the last." Ben drove the point home, leaving Maggie in no doubt about what he meant.

Since Ben had decided to take life easier, he was trying to manage her love life instead of the people on his various boards. Two months ago she couldn't have imagined it.

Two months ago she couldn't have imagined a man like Jake Halsey existed.

Dr. and Mrs. Lawrence Talbot
are pleased to announce
the marriage of their daughter
Melissa Kit Aldridge
to
Richard Cordell McFarland
son of Mr. and Mrs. Reed McFarland
July 29, Claremont, California
The pleasure of your company is requested
at a reception to be held at the McFarland Home
Federal Heights, Salt Lake City, Utah
Monday, August 17
7:00 until 10:00 p.m.
Valet parking available

JAKE GLANCED at the invitation, then checked his watch beneath the cuff of his white dress shirt. It was 9:30 p.m. Time to make his move. He put on the jacket of his stone-gray suit. After one more adjustment to his striped tie, he tucked the wedding gift under his arm and left the apartment.

Within five minutes he'd entered Federal Heights. As

he reached the vicinity of the McFarlands' house, he noticed cars lined up bumper to bumper on both sides of the street for several blocks.

Because he intended to be the last guest, he was in no hurry and could afford to wait until someone much closer to the house pulled out, leaving him their parking space.

The rain yesterday had brought down the temperature to about eighty degrees, making it a perfect summer night for an event like this. He got out of his Chevy Tahoe and walked behind a well-dressed couple rushing to get there before it was too late. Most people who'd already attended the reception were returning to their cars.

He heard the sounds of a great dance band before he came in sight of the house and grounds lit up like a magical city hovering in the air. The line of cars was only halfway down the drive now.

A towheaded boy of about ten or eleven, dressed in a tux and already carrying one gift, started toward him. "May I take that wedding present for you, sir?" He had McFarland stamped all over him.

Jake handed it to him with a smile. "Thanks. What's your name?"

"Brock."

"You must be Ben's son."

"Yup."

"How about doing another favor for me?"

The boy blinked. "What is it?"

"Could you show me where I can find your aunt Maggie? The thing is, I want to surprise her."

"Who are you?"

"Jake Halsey."

The boy studied him for a minute. "You were the one who helped her find that girl, huh?"

"Yup."

"That was cool. Okay. Follow me."

Jake didn't care if the other guests were miffed because he was getting special treatment. The end justified the means. He liked Maggie's nephew already.

Brock led him past the line to a private, recessed entrance, a kind of breezeway. It came out on the terrace at the back of the house where half a dozen couples were dancing around the lit rectangular swimming pool.

He noted a dozen candlelit tables on the velvet grass surrounding a fabulous banquet table. The band played beyond the eating area, half-hidden by a sculptured hedge.

"There she is," Brock whispered, but Jake had already spotted her looking sensational in a full-length blue evening gown the same color as the mass of potted hydrangeas lining the terrace.

She stood near a bank of French doors talking to some of the guests.

"Thanks for your help, Brock. I owe you one."

"That's okay. Do you want me to get her and bring her over here?"

"I think I'll wait until there aren't any more guests, but I appreciate the offer."

"Okay. I've got to go. See ya."

Slowly Jake circled the backyard, helping himself to some finger food as he made his way toward the band. "Can you play 'Sunshine of My Life,' Stevie Wonder–style?" he asked the leader. The man nodded.

Dancing was the one legitimate way to get Maggie in his arms, something he'd been wanting to do for a long time.

As the band finished up the song they were currently playing, Jake sauntered toward her from behind. A few feet away now, he could see beyond her to the bride and groom flanked by their parents. There were only a handful of people in the room with them.

The second he heard the first notes of his request, he approached Maggie and slid his hands to her supple waist. The mere contact sent a shock wave of delight through him. "It's time you paid attention to me." He whirled her around, bringing her right up against him.

"Jake—" she whispered. Her eyes blazed with light. He could see the pulse hammering in her throat. It kept time with the thudding of his heart.

"I'm glad to see you still remember my name." Without asking her permission, he began dancing with her. At first she held herself stiff, as if she were afraid to get too close to him.

That was too bad, because the mold of her tall, sylph-like body was made for him. He wanted to feel it. He wanted to feel her. Every square inch of her. Without making an apology, he crushed her to him.

"You cheated me out of a dance in Evanston, so just go with the music and let me breathe in the divine scent of you."

He'd given her no quarter, but it had paid off because he suddenly felt her relax and follow his lead around the terrace.

"You haven't met my brother and his wife yet," she said with a catch in her throat.

Jake rubbed his jaw against her temple, wishing no one was around so he could run his hands through her silky hair.

"I will another time. Right now I want to concentrate on you. If you have a problem with that, too bad because I have no intention of letting you go." Those dynamite legs brushing against his felt so good, he never wanted the music to stop.

"How did you get in without coming through the line?"

"You've got a terrific nephew. I prevailed on him to help me out because I knew if you saw me first, you'd disappear on me."

She almost stumbled, but he held her fast. "That's not true."

"Don't lie to me, Maggie. You've behaved differently towards me since I woke you up Wednesday morning. I want an explanation, and I want it tonight. Either we go to your place or mine to talk. It's your choice."

Though the piece had ended, he continued to spin her around.

"Jake—the music's stopped."

"I'm aware of that. I'll let you go when you give me your answer."

She lowered her head, avoiding his eyes. "You can follow me to my condo. I'll have to get my purse first."

Those were the words he'd been waiting to hear. "We'll leave the same way I came."

When he released her, she looked flushed and out of sorts. "I have to tell someone I'm going."

"Brock's over at the banquet table. We'll ask him to make your excuses. Come on." He grasped her hand and pulled her along. "Hey, sport?"

The boy looked up. "Hi, Jake. Hi, Aunt Maggie."

"Hi, honey. Have you been having a good time?"

"Yeah. This cake is yummy."

"I agree," Jake concurred. "Do us another favor and find your aunt's purse?"

"Where is it?"

Jake turned to her, waiting for her answer.

"I-It's upstairs in my old bedroom on the bed."

"I'll find it."

Jake put a hand on his shoulder. "Meet us at her car."

"Are you guys sneaking out?"

"Yes. After we leave, tell your family so they won't worry about her."

"Okay." He shoved another piece of cake in his mouth, then took off.

Jake slid a hand to the nape of Maggie's neck and guided her down the breezeway passage. "I take it your car is in the garage."

"Yes. Through here." She indicated the second door on the right. He opened it and waited for her to enter first. The garage was deep enough to hold four vehicles.

When Brock returned with Maggie's purse, Jake was ready for him and handed him a five-dollar bill. "You did good work tonight."

"Thanks. I'm saving for a new video game."

Maggie bent down to kiss her nephew. "Don't forget to tell Grandma and Grandpa that I've left."

"I won't."

Once Brock left, Jake climbed in the passenger seat. "My car's about a block and a half away. I'll show you where, then I'll follow you."

She opened the garage door with a remote, then backed down the long drive with the same expertise she flew a plane. Only a few cars remained parked on the street.

He glanced at her lovely profile. "How are the honeymooners, by the way?"

"More in love than ever. Kit has transformed my brother. She's brought him out of himself."

Jake heard the affection for her brother in her voice. The kidnapping had to have forged a special bond between the McFarland children. "The right kind of love has that kind of power."

"Both my brothers are lucky." When they reached the next block, she said, "I see your car. If we get separated in traffic, I live in the McFarland Towers. You enter the underground parking from the west side of the plaza. There are guest stalls next to mine on the first level." She stopped the car so he could step out, but she refused to look at him.

"I'll see you in a minute." He closed the door and got in his car.

This was progress. He was finally going to see inside the place where she lived.

CHAPTER EIGHT

"COME THROUGH TO MY STUDY, Jake."

For days, Maggie had been working nonstop. By nine tonight, she'd been completely exhausted. Her fatigue, combined with the desolation she'd felt because Jake hadn't made an appearance at the reception, had made her seriously consider leaving her brother's party early to go home to bed.

She crossed the room to switch on a lamp, and remembered the sensuous feel of Jake's hands sliding over her hips to her waist to announce his presence. She was frightened to think his electrifying touch had the power to bring her back to life instantly. She'd felt no more fatigue, mental or physical.

Dancing in his strong arms had become much more than a turn around the terrace with an attractive man. It had underlined the sure knowledge that he'd become more important to her than she'd dared dream.

When he went away in January, he wouldn't be back. She didn't want to revel in four months of ecstasy with him, only to have it be over, perhaps forever. She couldn't bear the loss.

Maggie had seen what loss had done to her parents.

To lose someone you loved with your very heart and soul was too horrible, too unbearable to contemplate. Tonight had to be the last time she saw Jake. She would keep their conversation brief.

"From this vantage point, I'm beginning to understand the importance of a penthouse view. What a spectacular panorama."

She stared at him. *He* was the one who was spectacular.

In the soft light of the lamp, his powerful physique standing at the window taking in the downtown lights forged an indelible impression on her mind. In his gray suit, he was the picture of elegant male sophistication. But he could never completely hide the hard-muscled, modern-day warrior beneath.

"May I get you a drink?"

Slowly he turned around. "Where did you go, Maggie?" He'd completely ignored her question. "What happened to you during the night we camped out to make you wake up a different person?"

Until he had answers, Jake wouldn't let this go. If she wanted him to leave her condo and her life, then she'd better tell him as much of the truth as she could.

"Let's just say that those goggles alerted me to the kind of life you must lead—the kind of dangerous job you have."

He moved to within a few feet of her, scrutinizing her through unsmiling eyes. A nerve throbbed near the tiny scar at the corner of his mouth. "Tell me the rest."

Her mouth went dry. "That's all there is."

"No," he whispered. "When I woke up, I thought I'd

smelled the faint scent of your perfume on me, on my bag. What happened during the night?"

"You…had a nightmare."

His lips formed a straight line. "Go on."

"You sounded like you were in agony. You started to scream, so I went over to you to wake you up. But I couldn't bring you out of it." Tears sprang to her eyes.

"Did I mention a name?"

"Yes."

"Kamila?" His hands circled her upper arms and held her tightly.

Who was she?

Maggie shook her head. "No—you screamed out, 'Vern's dead,' and you kept begging God not to let Reiker die, too. It was heart wrenching."

"Damn," he muttered.

"I tried to comfort you. After a while you quieted down enough for me to go back to my bag."

He looked tortured. "Forgive me for putting you through that, Maggie. I thought those nightmares were behind me." He didn't seem to notice he was kneading her shoulders. "You must have been terrified."

"Only for you and your pain."

"Did I hurt you?"

"No, Jake. It was nothing like that. You thought I was Reiker. You clung to me and said you were waiting for the chopper to come. Your sobs haunted me."

A strange sound came from his throat.

"Nothing I tried to do could rouse you from your deep sleep."

A full minute passed before he said, "So what do you think you know?"

"I saw and heard enough of your dreams to understand you weren't with a couple of detectives working a homicide case in San Diego. Unless the criminals nowadays walk into munitions dumps booby-trapped with land mines."

Jake's hands relinquished their hold on her. He turned away, as if he were fighting a war with himself.

"I'll never tell a living soul if that's what you're concerned about."

He swung back around. "You think I don't know that? I'm angry at myself for putting you at risk."

"What risk? Watching you fight your way out of a bad dream?"

Jake lifted a hand to trace her cheek with one finger. "I might have injured you."

"But you didn't."

"You're beautiful, Maggie. So incredibly beautiful. Show me what you did to quiet me down."

It was past time to say good-night.

Though her mind was frantically telling her to do the smart thing, her hands reached out to cup the sides of his head. Unable to resist his compelling entreaty, she began kissing his face. Her lips roved from temple to temple across his closed eyelids where she could feel his other tiny scar.

His breath sounded ragged. "No wonder all the demons went away," he spoke against her lips. She whimpered into his mouth, driven by needs of which she was scarcely aware. Her arms crept around his neck. It didn't seem possible this was finally happening, that he wanted her the way she wanted him.

Jake's kiss was no tentative foray. He kissed her as if he'd hungered for her a very long time. With one hand plunged into her hair at the back of her head, the other clamped around her hips, he crushed her to him. Their bodies formed a seamless line, sending a voluptuous warmth through her system.

So deep was Maggie's rapture, she didn't realize the phone had rung until she heard her mother's voice coming from her answering machine.

"Honey? Where are you? Why haven't you answered your cell phone? If you're there, please pick up. Your father and I are worried sick. After everyone left, we couldn't find you. You looked pale tonight. Are you too ill to answer the phone? This is why we don't like you having a place of your own. If we don't hear from you in the next five minutes, we're coming over."

Maggie let out a little moan of protest as Jake tore his lips from hers.

"Evidently your nephew forgot to give them the message. It's my fault for stealing you away and worrying your mother. You'd better phone her back," he said gruffly.

"For as long as I can remember, Mom has been in a perpetual state of panic if she couldn't find me instantly. This is nothing new. Please don't feel guilty."

He squeezed her hips before letting her go. "Call her, Maggie."

For the first time in her life, she was angered by her mother's intrusion. Maggie's sixth sense told her it had destroyed something fragile and beautiful between her and Jake, something she was afraid they might not get back.

"I'll call her from the bedroom. Help yourself to anything in my fridge. I won't be long." She gave him a brief kiss before darting away. The fact that he didn't pull her back to return it put the fear in her.

"Mom?" she spoke into the phone seconds later.

"Thank heaven! Are you all right?"

No. The man I adore was just kissing the daylights out of me when you interrupted us as only you can. "I'm fine. Brock was supposed to have told you I'd gone home."

"I never saw him. Near the end of the reception Carol called Julie to tell her their dad was sent to the hospital with a heart attack. She thinks it's not serious, but their mother is frantic of course, so Ben made arrangements for them to fly to Colorado Springs on the company jet."

"I could have taken them!" Maggie cried softly.

"Oh, no, you couldn't. What with that last search, and trying to get everything ready for Cord while you've been training Steve, you're exhausted darling. I hope you're in bed."

Maggie's heart was hammering in her chest. "I'm going soon." It all depended on Jake, who was waiting for her in the study. "I've got to go, Mom."

"All right, but I want you to sleep in, then come on up to the house. Steve told me you were taking a couple of days off, so there's no excuse."

"Actually there is. I have to fly down to California to do my recurring flight-safety course." *I'm also going to visit Frankie Burke.*

"Oh no, darling. How long will you be gone?"

"I'll be back late Thursday night. But don't worry, I'll phone you tomorrow evening."

"Maggie—"

"Good night, Mom. It was a fabulous reception, one Kit and Cord will never forget. Give Dad a kiss for me."

She hung up the phone and dashed back to the study. He wasn't there.

"Jake?"

When there was no answer, she hurried into the kitchen. Instead she discovered the reception invitation stuck to the fridge door with one of the bug magnets the kids had given her.

He'd turned it to the back to write a brief message. When she read it, her heart plunged right through the floor.

Maggie? I'll call you when I have any more word on Antonin Buric. Sleep well. Jake.

"DAN?"

"Good grief, Jake. Do you have any idea what time it is?"

"It's two-thirty in the Great Salt Lake Desert."

His boss muttered a couple of expletives. "All right. I'm awake now. What's so important you couldn't have waited three more hours? You know I would have phoned you if I'd had any news about Kamila."

"This isn't about her, Dan."

"Okay. I'm listening."

"Remember when you told me you wanted me to blend in with the salt and the sand?"

After a pause, Dan said, "I guess it was too big of a culture shock. So tell me where you'd like to go. I'll see what I can arrange, but it'll take me a little time."

Jake was standing on his terrace, looking up at the sky. The dark, clear summer night provided the perfect backdrop for the stars and planets flung across the heavens like bits of shattered crystal.

"You've misunderstood me, Dan."

"I what?"

"Just what I said. I've discovered Salt Lake has its attractions."

"You called me at four-thirty in the morning just to tell me that?"

"No. I called to thank you for everything you've done for me over the years."

More silence ensued.

"You sound like you're going somewhere on a long trip and might not be back."

"I hope so."

"Jake—you're starting to make me nervous. What the hell's going on?"

"Are you ready for this? I've decided I want out."

"You know what I think? You're having one of your nightmares. I'll call you tomorrow when I know you're awake."

"Don't hang up on me. I'm not finished."

"If the therapy's not working out, I'll send you to the Mayo."

"My shoulder's coming along. I want you to arrange for my retirement from the agency."

"And what will you do?"

"Genealogy, for one thing."

"Look, Jake—I know you want to find Kamila, but you don't have to go to these extremes to convince me. I've put an extra man there with specific instructions to find her. Just give us a little more time."

"I appreciate that, Dan, but as I said before, Kamila doesn't have anything to do with this decision."

Jake waited for Dan to absorb what he'd said. "You've met a woman."

His hand tightened on his cell phone. "Maggie McFarland. Ex-Senator Reed McFarland's daughter."

"Good grief. How did that happen?"

"It's a long story."

"Okay. You've accomplished your objective. I'm wide-awake. Let's hear it."

"All you need to know is that she's the one."

"How long have you known her?"

"Eleven days."

Jake heard more indecipherable language. "Does she feel the same way?"

"Yes, but there's a problem. There's something that has to happen before I've got her full attention."

"She's engaged to someone else."

"I wish it were that easy."

"Jake—just out with it!"

"Her family's still looking for their kidnapped daughter who disappeared twenty-six years ago."

"That's right. The senator's one of the people responsible for helping get that AMBER Alert bill pushed through the senate."

"Yes. Maggie's on a mission to find her sister. Her

search led her to the genealogical firm. I'm doing all I can to help."

"So *you* find out what happened to the sister and win the hand of the fair maiden."

"If I don't, I'll die trying."

"Good grief. I think you meant that."

"I'm glad we understand each other. Let me know what I have to do."

"Do me a favor and sleep on it for another week."

"I don't need to sleep on it."

"Jake—"

He clicked off and walked back inside the apartment. Having informed Dan, he was free to answer any of Maggie's questions. Now he'd have to wait to see how long it took her to come to him.

And if she doesn't, what will you do then, Halsey?

"EAGLE GATE GENEALOGICAL FIRM, Wendell Smith speaking."

"Good morning, Mr. Smith. It's Maggie McFarland. Has Mr. Halsey come in yet?"

"Yes. He was here when I walked in."

"Does he have a client waiting?"

"Not yet. It's too early."

"In that case, don't bother to tell him I called. I'll be right there."

Maggie left the condo for the short walk to the firm a few blocks away. After she met with Jake, she would go back to her office and spend a full day with Steve. During the time she'd been in California, he'd been closeted in her library going over her cases in more detail.

She'd intended to keep her distance from Jake until he called her. But something she'd learned at the prison in California prompted her to seek him out now. When she entered the firm, Mr. Smith smiled broadly and told her to go on back.

Maggie's pulse rate was already too high to be healthy. The memory of those few minutes in Jake's arms the other night had left her aching for more. It was no wonder her heart leaped when she saw him through his office doorway, deep in concentration at the computer.

Today he was wearing a tan sport shirt. His hair had grown out some since she'd first met him. It had a lot of curl, just as she'd thought.

She knocked on the door.

"More marzipan for me today, Simone?" he asked without looking up. "You're spoiling me."

First Kamila, now Simone.

"If I'd known that was your favorite candy, I'd have brought you some."

He looked up and their gazes locked. "Maggie."

She hurriedly took one of the seats opposite his desk. "Sorry I don't have any treats for you."

"I'm not partial to marzipan," he said in a quiet voice, "but I wouldn't dream of refusing it from my French colleague who works down the hall."

"I don't care for it, either. At one of my birthday parties when I was little, my mother ordered a marzipan cake from a Swedish bakery. I got sick on it and haven't been able to eat it since."

"You don't look sick today." His eyes burned with the

same fire she'd seen in them the other night. "In fact you look good enough to eat."

She'd been thinking the same thing about him. Her cheeks filled with heat. "Speaking of treats, does Kamila work here, too?"

With that question she expected a smile. Instead his expression grew solemn. "Kamila's my stepmother."

"I didn't realize your father had remarried. Was she cruel to you as a child? Is that why you have nightmares about her, too?"

He rubbed his bottom lip with his thumb. "After what I put you through in the Uintas, I can hardly blame you for coming to that conclusion. But the truth is, she's a wonderful person who's been missing, like your sister Kathryn, since my father's funeral fifteen months ago."

"That long?" Maggie said in a hushed cry. "Are you saying she was kidnapped?"

"It's a distinct possibility, but I'll never know anything until I can go after her."

"Wait—" Maggie put her palms up. "You mean all this time while you've been helping me, you've been dealing with your own crisis?"

"Yes."

"Where did she and your father live?"

"Prague."

"The Czech Republic."

He nodded somberly.

There was so much she didn't know about Jake. He only fed her information in bits and pieces. "You must feel helpless being this far away."

"Distance isn't the problem. I could be there tonight.

The booby trap that killed two other agents was an assassination attempt on the three of us. We were betrayed by a person we thought was on our side. My cover's been blown."

"I knew you were with the CIA," she whispered.

Jake eyed her intently. "Those goggles blew my cover with you."

"Thank heaven for them. Because of you, a little girl and her family are going to have years of happiness together. But what about your stepmother? Isn't anyone helping you to find her?"

"Yes, but so far they haven't picked up her trail. I lived there while I attended the University of Prague. I know where she goes, her haunts."

"You went to school there?"

"Four years. My father worked for the Steiner toothpaste company whose headquarters are in Jacksonville. After the Velvet Revolution, Dad went over to help a private firm establish a Steiner branch in Prague. She lived in the same apartment building we did.

"The two of them fell in love and got married. I lived with them and went to school before I joined the navy. I know their friends, their favorite vacation spots. I'm the one who needs to be over there searching for her.

"The double agent who blew my cover knows I have family there. Whoever he takes orders from won't think twice about kidnapping or killing her in retaliation. If she's still alive, I have to get her out. The hell of it is, my superior won't allow me to return to Prague because it'll endanger other operatives in the field."

"And *your* life!"

"I'm not concerned about that. One day soon I'll find a way to infiltrate the city safely. It's the least I can do since I'm the one responsible for putting my father and stepmother in jeopardy in the first place."

"What a horrible worry it must be."

He nodded. "According to my superior, she never reported for work after the funeral. I'd already left to get back to my job and didn't know she was missing until a couple of months ago."

"I'm so sorry, Jake. I don't see how you can function with your stepmother missing. And, you're dealing with your own injury. When did your accident happen?"

"Eight months ago."

She groaned. "You've been a prisoner of your thoughts for a long time."

"Not as long as you have," he replied in a low voice. "But we can talk about that later. Right now I'm working for you. What's brought you to my office?"

"I've just come back from Lompoc prison."

His expression sobered. "I presume Frankie said something crucial that could have a bearing on your sister's case."

"Not without a lot of negotiating. Thanks to you, I had a few surprises for him."

"What leverage did you use?"

"After discussing everything with Agent Kelly, I had a talk with Frankie. I told him we knew the names of his family all the way back to the Burics in Bohemia. When I rattled them off, he didn't bat an eye. Not that I thought he would.

"But then I told him we knew he had an elder brother Antonin who was a criminal, too."

"That must have been a shocker."

She nodded. "I informed him that the police had proof the two of them had worked in the laundry onboard a cruise ship out of San Pedro. I went further and explained that it was the same New Year's cruise my parents took when he and his brother planned the elaborate abduction of their baby who would be born three months later.

"I warned him it was only a matter of time until the authorities caught up to Antonin. Who knew the lies he might tell on Franz to add more years to his life in prison."

"You must be dynamite in the courtroom. How did our Frankie Burke react?"

"Just the way Kit described when she told him she was going to find his grandmother. He got angry and tried to get out of the chair to go back to his cell. To calm him down, I told him I had a proposition for him that could get his sentence reduced by another two years. But he had to promise to sit still and hear me out."

Jake cocked his head. "Two more years lopped off means he would only have four more years before his release from prison. He could be out of there by the age of fifty-two. Obviously he went for it, or you wouldn't be here."

Yes, I would, Jake.

All those lectures she'd given herself about not getting involved with him had gone out the window the night he'd come to the penthouse.

"So don't leave me hanging. What was your proposition that turned the corner for him?"

"I told him that if he would help me to find Antonin before the authorities did, I would make certain he only served two more years in prison. But if he gave me false information, then all bets were off and he would still have six to go."

Jake whistled.

"I explained that we knew his father and grandfather once ran an engraving business in the South Bronx where he and his brother were first arrested. What I wanted from him was particular information. First I needed the address of his grandmother's house. Secondly, if she no longer lived there, I wanted the names of any neighbors or friends who might know what happened to her, where she went or if she died.

"At first I didn't think he was going to respond. When I started to leave, he told me to wait." She opened her purse and handed Jake a piece of paper. "This is the information he finally gave me."

He studied it. "Forty-two East Thirty-third Street, Fordham."

"It's in the Bronx. Frankie only gave me the name of one neighbor. A Mr. Corelli who lived in the house next door on the right."

Jake's dark blue eyes shot to hers. "Let's check it out. What are you doing this weekend?"

She'd been holding her breath, hoping he would say that. "I was about to ask if you would fly to New York with me in the morning. We'll conduct our own investigation and see if we can learn something new. I know it's a long shot, but I have to try."

"If Frankie didn't make up this address, then he gave

you a lot more than you know, Maggie. We can check stores and businesses in the area. There's all kinds of information we may be able to pick up. It's possible Antonin's still hanging around there."

"I hope you're right."

Maggie was already enjoying being with Jake too much. She got up from the chair.

His gaze traveled the length of her body. "When you were down in California, did you do any other sightseeing besides visiting the men's maximum-security facility?"

"Not unless you count my flight-safety recertification in Long Beach. It's an annual thing. Now I have to run. I'll be by for you at six in the morning."

"I'll walk you out."

"Thank you, but it's not necessary."

Maggie rushed away so there'd be no possibility of physical contact. She needed all her powers of concentration to get through her heavy workday.

When she arrived at the law firm, Steve was already doing some research in her private library. She poked her head in the door and said she'd be with him in a minute.

First there was an important phone call to make to Agent Simpson. Maggie had an urgent request.

Eight hours later, she felt confident that Steve could handle any problems if she and Jake ended up having to be gone longer than the weekend.

To her parents' delight, she dropped by the house and ate dinner with them. During dessert she told them her plans to try to find Antonin's grandmother. They were overjoyed.

Her mother's face was awash in tears. "Kit was found alive. I have to believe Kathryn's alive, too. Go with Jake, darling. Find out everything you can."

"He's a brilliant detective, Mom, the kind who won't leave a stone unturned."

"I believe you two have met your match." Her Dad winked at her. "I'm glad you're going with him. He'll keep you safe. He's the kind of man who can take care of himself and anyone else."

It sounded like Agent Simpson had talked to her father. At this point, he probably knew Jake worked for the CIA.

THIS TIME WHEN MAGGIE drove them to the airport on a clear, quiet Saturday morning, a sleek white-and-blue Cessna CJ2 with gold striping had been tugged from the McFarland hangar.

Before they got out of the car, Jake turned to her. "I should have known you're a jet pilot, too. You're spoiling me, Maggie."

"Dad taught me early that if you want to get something done, you need to learn how to do it yourself."

The ex-senator's daughter was in a class of her own and would always intimidate those around her less confident in themselves. That fact, plus the driving inner need to find out what had happened to her sister, had kept her single and preserved for him all this time. Jake had made his mind up about that.

They climbed in behind the pilot's seat. Nice interior. He put their luggage on the banquette at the rear of the plane and strapped them in tight.

Once again he'd be playing copilot. If he had one regret, it was that their seats weren't as close together as in the 185. He'd liked the feel of her arm brushing against his, lighting his fire. But there was always New York. He was living for it in more ways than one.

Closing in on Antonin meant he was a step closer to reining in the elusive Ms. McFarland, who hadn't been the least elusive while she'd kissed him senseless the other night. That was an experience he wanted to repeat for the rest of his life, even if now she was pretending it had never happened.

He loved flying with Maggie. Always full of surprises, she put them down in Detroit.

"There's this great restaurant that serves the best steak sandwiches you ever tasted. I don't know about you but I'm starving."

She was a woman after his own heart.

Later, when they'd been flying for at least an hour, he looked over at her. "Shouldn't we be landing in New York about now?"

"We're not going there yet."

He smiled. It sounded like she had another unexpected treat in store for him. He couldn't wait to find out what it was. "Let me guess. Some place in eastern Canada."

"No. Reykjavik."

Iceland? "Don't tell me they have the best roast salmon you've ever tasted."

"They probably do, but I'm more interested in getting the jet refueled there."

What was going on? "Why Iceland?"

"It's on the way to Prague."

Prague? His thoughts reeled. While he was still speechless, she pulled something out of her pocket and handed it to him.

A U.S. passport. He opened the cover. There was his face. A younger version of himself, when he'd been in the navy.

"Through Agent Simpson's intervention, you've been given a new name. Paul Ames Hillman. Blue eyes. Black hair. I asked her to make you thirty-two instead of thirty-five, along with a few other changes. You're now six foot two instead of three, and 195 pounds though I would guess you're closer to 205. Address, Bountiful, Utah.

"We're flying into Prague under diplomatic immunity of the Kathryn McFarland World Wide Foundation for Missing Children. If anyone asks, we're looking for two women, Kathryn McFarland and Dana Miller, who were kidnapped years ago and probably brought here by Antonin Buric.

"He's a wanted felon from the U.S. The FBI has reason to believe he's living with relatives in the area of Kutna Hora. If we find either woman, the U.S. ambassador to the Czech Republic will meet us at customs to clear one or both of them for flight back to the States.

"If you ask, I'll deny that I know anything about a special favor done for the Czech government by the U.S. in exchange for their cooperation in allowing the women to leave the country."

Wow.

CHAPTER NINE

Manitowoc, Wisconsin
August 21

MILLIONS OF PEOPLE bought cars every day and didn't think about it, but Anna had never owned anything before. The red Nissan Sentra with thirty-eight thousand miles on it she'd bought outright for twenty-four hundred dollars was the most thrilling thing that had ever happened to her.

Classes started on Monday. Before the next week was out, she would hear if she'd gotten the job at the hospital lab. Right now she was glad she had the weekend to take her car on the ferry across Lake Michigan. She'd catch it in Manitowoc, north of Milwaukee, and take it to Ludington. She could drive around there, stay all night and come back tomorrow.

Anna had never been in a rowboat, let alone a ship. She'd never been up in a plane or ridden a train. There was a whole wide world out there to be explored.

When she'd voiced the thought to Josef, he'd slipped her fifteen hundred dollars. "This is my gift to you. Fun money. Spend it on something you want, Anna."

"You mean it?"

He nodded solemnly. "I know you haven't had a lot of fun in your life. Promise you'll do as I say?"

She hugged him. "Thank you. I promise."

Since then, she'd decided she would use the unexpected extra money for a couple of short vacations. One to southern California next summer, where she could lie out on a beach for a week.

The other vacation she would take this winter. After she and Nelly had watched the Salt Lake winter Olympics on their TV in the bakery kitchen, Anna had wanted to go there so badly she could still taste it.

With two hours to wait until she boarded the ferry, she decided to drop in at a travel agency and see what she could arrange. This far away from the holiday season, she might be able to purchase a cheap round-trip airfare.

"There are dozens of ski packages with bargain flights," the employee said a few minutes later. "From the feedback we've gotten, this one in Alta is the best.

"None of the Olympic venues were held in Alta because it would have created too much congestion in the canyon. But the best skiers in the world claim it has the greatest snow on earth."

He handed her a brochure with summer and winter photos of the fabulous mountains. She greedily read the contents.

If you are looking for reasonable ski packages in Utah, look no further than the Alta Peruvian Lodge in Little Cottonwood Canyon, Utah. The Alta Peruvian Lodge is located at the base of the Alta ski resort, giving you the absolute best location for your ski vacation.

The Alta ski resort receives over 500 inches of snow annually. You can ski dry, fluffy powder from November to April, making Alta one of the most incredible resorts around. For more information about ski packages in Utah, the Alta ski resort and the Alta Peruvian Lodge contact us.

"Do they give ski lessons?"

"They have everything, ski rentals, the works. There'll be a shuttle from the Salt Lake International Airport to the resort."

After checking out the price, she said, "Will you book me a flight for December 24 to January 2, and arrange a single room for me at the lodge?"

"Be happy to."

She handed him her new credit card issued to students at the university. Whatever part-time job Anna ended up with, she would make certain she got those days off.

While she waited for him to finish up, she studied the rest of the brochure. One of the pictures showed a high alpine meadow in summer. It was full of wildflowers surrounded by rugged mountains. *Albion Basin,* she mouthed the words. The scene was so glorious, she couldn't believe such a place really existed.

Maybe that's where she'd move after she became a doctor.

Prague, Czech Republic
August 22

"THIS IS THE STREET where we used to live. Pull over to the curb behind that black car and wait for me, Maggie."

She did his bidding without saying anything. Since they'd flown into Prague after their overnight stay in Frankfurt, the tension coming from Jake was palpable.

When he got out, he leaned back inside, searching her face and eyes relentlessly. "So far so good. Customs went without a hitch, but you never know. Lock the car doors after me. I won't be long.

"Kamila's best friend Maria lives in this building. Ours is at the end of the block, but I'm not going near it. If anything frightens you, lean on the horn and I'll come running."

Maggie nodded.

After Jake had disappeared inside the building, she looked around, taking in the beauty of Romanesque, Gothic, baroque and Renaissance architecture more fabulous than anything she'd seen on her other trips to Western Europe.

Jake had explained this was the oldest part of Prague. It was a city of over a million people, built on seven hills, with the Vlatava River running through it. He'd pointed out Prague Castle and the Charles Bridge on their way in from the airport, but she was very aware this wasn't a sightseeing trip.

It killed Maggie because she thought it the most romantic place she'd ever seen. She wished she could be here with Jake enjoying its history and beauty like all the other tourists who'd flocked here for the last month of summer.

With the temperature in the high seventies, she yearned to stroll with him through ancient, picturesque walkways they'd passed in the car. Jake had lived here four years, and knew its many secret delights.

But his choice of career had guaranteed he could never come here again except for a desperate mission like this.

Last night over dinner, before they'd gone to their separate hotel rooms, he'd told her the kind of work he'd been doing when the explosion had occurred.

His job had been to track the sale of Czech munitions to countries supporting terrorist groups in exchange for oil. Once discovered, he blew them up. His work had taken him around the globe. The horrific planned accident that almost cost him his life had happened in the Middle East.

She shivered to think of the dangers he'd faced for close to a decade. It was a miracle he was still alive. After Christmas, he'd be going back to that life. She wished she had the right to beg him not to go anywhere. To stay with her indefinitely.

Her watch said 11:10 a.m., Czech time. He'd been in that apartment close to an hour. Though not normally a person to panic, she was starting to get nervous imagining the secret police lying in wait for Jake at every turn.

When she thought she couldn't stand to sit there another second not knowing what had happened to him, he suddenly emerged from the building. She undid the locks. To her surprise he came around to her side of the car. That meant he wanted to drive.

After moving the seat back as far as it would go in the rental car, she eased herself over the gearshift to the passenger side. He climbed in without a word and started up the motor. In seconds they'd pulled into traffic.

Even though only an hour had passed, he looked older. He didn't speak until they'd joined the E65 headed north on the outskirts of the city.

"If nothing has happened to Kamila, then I think I know where she might be. The day after I left Prague, Kamila told Maria it was too painful to stay at the apartment with my father gone, so she was going to take a little trip. That was the last time anyone saw her.

"When she didn't show up for work the next week, the police paid Maria a visit, wanting to know if she'd seen Kamila. Sensing something could be wrong, Maria, who's a smart lady, told them she hadn't seen or talked to her since the funeral."

Maggie was putting two and two together. "If she's gone into hiding on her own accord, then that means she wasn't kidnapped!"

"Not at that point, anyway," he muttered grimly. "Something tells me that before Dad died, he told her to get away as a precaution because of my undercover work.

"If she'd left the country, I would have heard from her by now through an address where she could have written me. The fact that there's been no word means she didn't dare call attention to herself by trying to cross the border or make contact through the mail."

Maggie shook her head. "Does she have relatives living here?"

"No. She's Polish. Her family's in Warsaw. When we met her, she was working in Prague for the summer with another Polish girlfriend to brush up on her Czech. She speaks excellent English, of course. They worked for a travel agency in Warsaw and wanted to improve their language skills with a view toward promotion.

"Dad was thirty-six when he met Kamila. She was twenty-four, only six years older than me. For obvious reasons, he fought his attraction to her, but she had her heart set on him. I was happy for him and knew he felt the same way about her.

"At the end of the summer, her friend went back to Poland, but she stayed behind. One thing led to another. Dad got her a job at the Steiner company so they could be together all the time. Within the year they were married. I was at the university and gave them as much space as possible because I was doing my own thing in the female department."

Maggie could imagine he'd broken more than one heart. "What does Kamila look like?"

"She's average height with red hair and big brown eyes."

"I wish you had a picture of them."

"Everything's stored in Florida."

With that comment, he went quiet for the next half hour. They were in hilly, lush green countryside now. Everything looked picture perfect, reminding her of the valleys in the lower Alps.

"It's gorgeous here."

"That's why it's called the Bohemian Paradise of the Republic." They'd come to the town of Turnov. "Are you hungry?"

Sensing his urgency to reach his destination she said, "No."

"Neither am I."

He drove on.

"Where are we going?"

"To a guest farmhouse on the outskirts of a little village called Bela. It's about four kilometers from here. Dad and Kamila loved this place so much, they planned to either buy or build a little house after he retired. She may be hiding out here, using her maiden name.

"If I'm wrong, then I don't know where in the hell she could be, and I don't dare stay in the country any longer because your life is already endangered by simply being in my company."

Maggie didn't say anything. She knew it would be fruitless to argue that she didn't care about herself. He wouldn't listen.

Please God—let Kamila be here....

Jake had already lost so much. His mother, his wife, his father. Two colleagues who'd obviously meant a lot to him. He'd been in several hospitals in the last year getting put back together since the explosion. Enough was enough.

"There it is."

The big chaletlike dwelling sat back from the country road on verdant farmland. It looked like something out of a storybook. He drove up to the front entrance.

"Do you want me to wait for you?"

"No. It'll be more normal if we look like a couple of lovers excited to be together. Let me do the talking."

A LITTLE BELL TINKLED when Jake ushered Maggie inside the front office. While he waited for someone to come to the desk, he reached for her and kissed her the way he'd wanted to last night outside her hotel-room door.

Unfortunately it would have been the wrong time to give in to temptation. He'd needed to stay focused, and she was exhausted after their long flight from Salt Lake. Morning would come too soon as it was.

But he wasn't worried about that right now. He needed her kiss like he needed air to breathe. She hadn't seen it coming, but her response after a quick recovery was all he could have asked for.

"Good morning," a woman's voice spoke in Czech. "I'm Sabina."

Reluctantly, Jake tore his lips from Maggie's and turned to the hearty-looking woman with a smile. "Hello," he answered in kind. "I'm Lech Nowach."

"We're looking for my Polish cousin from Warsaw named Kamila. She said she was coming here to rent a place and find work. She has brown eyes, and the last time I saw her, red hair. But she changes it periodically so you never know. She's about this tall." Jake touched his shoulder.

The woman's eyes lit up. "She works for me, but her hair is brown."

Jake's heart jumped. "Where is she?"

"In Bela, delivering eggs to a shop."

"When do you think she'll be back?"

"Any minute. It's time for the little one's nap."

Little one? Maybe Kamila did babysitting for the owner.

"My fiancée and I are on our way to visit Hruba Skala. Would you mind if Kamila goes with us?"

"Of course not. She's never had relatives drop by before. She can take the whole day off."

"That's very kind of you. We'll just wait out in front for her."

He turned to Maggie and started speaking in Polish in case the other woman understood. "Darling? Kamila's here. She'll be back in a few minutes." Once again he surprised her by claiming her mouth.

Maggie played along, not comprehending exactly what he was saying, but obviously understanding that something earthshaking was happening here. When he put his arm around her shoulders to guide her to the door, she slid her arm around his waist and kissed his jaw before they went outside.

"She's here, Maggie," he whispered once they got in the car.

"Oh Jake!" She touched his cheek. He would have kissed her again but he saw movement out of the corner of his eye.

"In fact I think she's in that truck coming toward us. Stay put." He brushed his lips against hers before getting out of the car to stand in the path of the truck.

It forced Kamila to park it next to the car. When she saw who it was, she leaped out of the cab and ran into his arms. He crushed her to him. "Call me Lech, not Jake, and speak to me in Polish, okay?"

"Okay," she said with tears running down her cheeks.

"Thank God I found you in time. No questions now. I'll answer everything later. You're coming with me and Maggie. I've already arranged for you to have the rest of the day off.

"Go inside and give the woman the keys. Remember I'm your cousin Lech Nowach from Warsaw. I'm here on a trip with my fiancée and thought I'd come to see you since I knew you were working here. Then come on out and get in the back seat of the car."

Kamila looked dazed. "First I have to get the baby from the truck. He's in his carryall on the floor."

"She mentioned a little one."

"Yes." Kamila threw her head back, to look him directly in the eye. "It's your half brother, Jared. Your father said he would have called him that if he'd had another son." Her eyes swam in tears. "He looks so much like both of you, it hurts."

Dear God.

"I'll get him while you go inside," Jake said.

Jake hurried around to the passenger side of the truck and opened the door. There on the floor, sound asleep, lay his little half brother who looked to be eight or nine months old. Jake remembered pictures of himself at that age and saw the strong similarity.

Incredible. Tears sprang to his eyes to think his dad never got to see him or hold him. Incredible that Kamila had given birth at the age of forty-one. With trembling hands, he gathered up the carryall and carried him to the car. When Maggie saw him, she jumped out.

"Who's beautiful baby is this?" she exclaimed.

"Maggie McFarland? Meet my half brother, Jared."

"Half brother..." She looked at him in stunned disbelief. "And all this time you didn't know?"

"I do now. Help me strap him in the seat. We've got to get out of here and back to the plane fast!"

By the time they'd secured him as best they could, Kamila had climbed in the seat beside him. For the next hour, the four of them got acquainted while Jake drove. Mostly Kamila sobbed with happiness while she breast-fed the baby, who finally woke up hungry.

He listened while Maggie phoned the embassy to alert them of their imminent arrival at the airport. The ambassador himself was waiting for them in the customs' office.

He smiled at Maggie. "Ms. McFarland? It's an honor to meet the daughter of a good friend. I've informed the authorities that the FBI is waiting to talk to Ms. Miller in New York. Though Antonin Buric is still at large some-where in the Czech Republic, the police commissioner has assured me they'll do everything they can to find him."

The ambassador handled the whole situation with a mastery that made Jake marvel. The customs' officials never said a word.

"On behalf of the foundation and especially my fa-ther, I want to thank you for taking the time from your busy affairs putting yourself out to assist Ms. Miller and her baby," Maggie said.

"It's what I'm here for."

Full of emotion, Jake clasped his hand. "Thank you, sir. We're indebted to you for your service."

The older man eyed Jake with a special gleam. "That works both ways, *Mr. Hillman*."

While Jake digested the thrust of the ambassador's private message, the other man kissed Kamila on both cheeks. "Your horrifying ordeal is now over, my dear. You and that baby have a safe flight back to the States."

Jake didn't dare look at Maggie right then. He was supposed to be a member of the foundation, not her would-be lover. The urge to crush her in his arms was so intense, he felt actual pain having to suppress his emotions.

With her father's connections, plus the help of the State Department, Maggie had pulled off the impossible with that incomparable McFarland flare. He was in awe of her.

"First stop Frankfurt," Maggie announced once she was at the controls of the jet. "As soon as we get to the hotel, we'll do some shopping for you and the baby."

Kamila broke down in tears once more. "I can't believe this has happened. It's a miracle."

"Maggie makes them happen."

"Jake's full of it," she told Kamila before starting her systems check.

"I'll never be able to repay either of you."

He looked over his shoulder at his stepmother. Both mother and baby were fastened securely in their seats. Everyone he cared about in this world was right here inside the plane with him. "You're family, so let's never mention the word *repay* again."

With a sense of contentment he hadn't known in years, Jake put on his headgear and fastened his shoulder strap.

Their second stop would be New York. Maybe another miracle awaited them. Then they'd be winging west for home.

The Bronx, New York
August 25

"I'VE NEVER HEARD of Marie Buric. We bought this house eight years ago from someone named Rozetti. Sorry I'm not any help."

"That's all right," Maggie murmured, trying to hide her disappointment. "What about your next-door neighbor on the right, Mr. Corelli?"

The young mother shook her head. "Mr. and Mrs. Jamison were living there before we moved in. Maybe they remember that name. If not, why don't you try the barbershop around the corner." She gestured in its direction. "My husband gets his hair cut there. I have no idea how long it has been in existence, but it's possible someone could help you."

"Do you remember the name of your Realtor?" When she told Jake he said, "Thanks for your help. We appreciate it."

"I hope you find the person you're looking for."

Maggie nodded. "So do we. Goodbye."

With his hand cupping her elbow, Jake walked them to the Jamisons' where Maggie could see a woman watering her flowers out front.

Jake and Maggie introduced themselves and asked the same question. The woman shook her head. She'd never heard the name Buric or Corelli. They got the same response from everyone they talked to on both sides of the street.

Tears welled in Maggie's eyes. "Frankie was probably laughing his head off when he gave me this address."

"It's early days yet," Jake reminded her. "Come on. Let's find that barbershop."

He took hold of her hand and squeezed it while they walked to the corner. An old-fashioned barber pole caught their attention two doors down. But the barber inside couldn't have been older than thirty, thirty-one. He had a customer draped in the chair.

When Maggie told him what they wanted he said, "Never heard of a Buric or a Corelli. Sorry."

"Thank you, anyway."

She rushed out of the shop ahead of Jake. He'd parked their rental car in front of the house Frankie had said was his grandmother's. Maggie made a beeline for it, hoping she wouldn't burst into sobs in front of Jake before they reached the hotel.

Jake was so happy over his reunion with Kamila and his half brother, Maggie didn't want anything to take away from it. Once she was alone in her room, she could give way to her grief.

"This isn't over yet, Maggie," he said, following her into the suite that adjoined Kamila's. "I'll call that realty company right now and see what I can find out." He moved to the nightstand between the beds and pulled out the directory.

Maggie nodded, and sank back in one of the chairs placed around the table. Suddenly it seemed like all the stuffing had come out of her. He was on the phone quite a while. She closed her eyes while she waited.

The next thing she knew, Jake had picked her up and carried her over to the bed.

"Your shoulder—" She half moaned the words.

"What shoulder?" He removed her shoes and laid the comforter from the other bed over her. "They're going to call me later," he whispered against her lips. "Go to sleep, Maggie. You need it."

Fourteen hours later she awakened, unable to believe it was seven o'clock *in the morning!* She hadn't slept this long since junior high. That's what a fierce case of jet lag did to you.

She sprang out of bed to shower and wash her hair. She was starving. In case no one else was up yet, she rang for room service. The need to know what Jake had found out from the realty firm had her jumping out of her skin.

Once she'd dressed in a clean pair of trousers and a white blouse, she packed her bag so she'd be ready to go. There was a knock on her door. Her breakfast of waffles and sausage had arrived. She needed the calories to keep her alert for the flight home.

A few minutes later she could hear laughter coming from the other room. Jake's deep voice followed by Kamila's lighter one permeated the closed door.

Anxious to talk to him, Maggie opened it. Straight ahead of her, she saw him lying on the bed facedown, playing with Jared who was wide-awake and kicking.

The scene was so beautiful and so touching, Maggie's eyes dimmed for a moment.

"Come on in," Kamila urged. "We're about ready to go. Did you get a good sleep?"

"It was wonderful. I hope you slept well, too, Kamila."

Jake sat up and stared at her. "We all needed a good one."

Maggie waited to hear his news, but nothing was forthcoming.

"Don't fall apart on me yet," his voice grated. "The Realtor said it might take a few days to research."

A few days. Maybe tomorrow. Maybe next week. His words were like a death knell.

CHAPTER TEN

Salt Lake City, Utah
August 26

"THERE! ONE CRIB ASSEMBLED. What else can I do for you?"

"You've done enough," Kamila said while she patted the baby's back. "We haven't even been in Salt Lake a whole day and already you've transformed your guest bedroom into a home for me."

"It'll be your home for as long as you want. When you're ready, I'll help you move to your own condo or house, whatever you want."

She eyed him directly. "You've pampered me enough, Jake. Sabina wouldn't believe it if she could see me now."

"You probably gave her the shock of her life when you called her from Frankfurt and told her you were on your way to the U.S."

"I know I did. When I explained why, she was wonderful about it. I promised to send her some money for any inconvenience I caused by leaving her literally in the lurch without help.

"She shrugged it off, but I'm still going to do it when I can get to the bank and withdraw funds from your father's savings account. I was blessed to be given a job and a place to live. Sabina was marvelous to me when she found out I was expecting. She saved my life, Jake."

"Maybe we can bring her and her husband here for a vacation."

"That would be fantastic. She's never been to the States. For that matter, neither have I." She laughed.

"I'm still trying to absorb all that's happened, so if there's some place else you want to go this evening, please don't let my being here stop you. Jared needs a bath, and then I'll cuddle him in that new rocker you bought for me until he falls asleep."

"There's no place else I'd rather be than right here with my family."

"Liar," she teased with a smile. "You remind me so much of your father, it's uncanny."

"What do you mean?"

"When we first met, he kept his distance from me for a long time. I knew he was interested, but it took him forever to make his move. You're doing the same thing with Maggie."

He flashed her a glance. "Think she's interested in me?"

"You already know the answer to that. Don't do what your father did and force her to wait too long. You never know what can happen." Her voice had gone husky.

Jake closed his eyes for a moment. Robert Halsey had been a great dad and obviously a loving husband.

Thank heaven he'd left her Jared to adore. The little guy had already wrapped himself around Jake's heart.

"Did he know about the baby before he died?"

"No. I never thought I could get pregnant. It just didn't happen. Because your father was older, I stopped worrying about it and simply loved being his wife. I'd only just found out I'd conceived before Robert ended up in the hospital. I was on the verge of telling him our incredible news when he confided in me about your work in the CIA.

"He knew he was going to die. In case you were ever exposed, he was so worried for me being alone without his protection, I promised that if anything happened to him, I'd leave and go to Bela. If I'd told him about the baby, he wouldn't have had any peace."

"He died a happy man, Kamila, all because of you."

"Your dad was already happy when we met. I never saw anyone as proud of a son. You two were so close, I didn't think there was room for anyone else. Please don't let my being here interfere with your plans."

"Don't be absurd. I'm glad you've moved in. I wouldn't want it any other way. This is a big apartment, and it's been like a tomb."

"Just be careful you don't let Maggie think you're shutting her out."

"Except for a few stolen moments, our relationship has been on a more professional basis."

She nodded. "I had those same stolen moments with your father in between long periods of being treated like an acquaintance. It was a very painful experience."

"Maggie's not ready for anything more yet."

"Want to make a bet?"

While he pondered her words, she kissed Jared's neck before laying him down in his bed. "I think your big brother wants us to leave the subject of Maggie McFarland alone. We will for a while. Thank goodness you're too young for me to worry about your love life, little lambkin."

"Kamila?" She raised her head and looked over her shoulder at him. "I love it that you care."

"All your father ever wanted was your happiness. I feel the same way. I miss our old talks. If you need a person to confide in, even if it's the middle of the night, I'm here."

She was here.

She'd brought him a present. A little brother.

For almost two months he'd been living with a hard rock in his gut knowing she'd disappeared. Only now did it dawn on him he didn't have to worry anymore.

Maggie.

It was all because of the magnificent woman who'd dropped them off in her car before heading to her penthouse alone. One day he'd live with her there, or any place else she wanted.

Jake would give her as many children as she wanted.

He'd only had to look at the hunger in her eyes when she'd insisted on tending Jared to know how much she craved to be a mother. Maggie had been so enamored with the baby, she hadn't even noticed how long he and Kamila had taken to shop for the necessities in Frankfurt.

"I'm going to hit the shower, then go to bed. Don't be alarmed if you wake up early and discover I'm not here. I always get a run in before I come back to get ready for work." He kissed their cheeks before leaving the bedroom.

Later, when he climbed in bed, the temptation to phone Maggie and wish her good-night was almost overpowering. But he knew there was only one thing she wanted to hear from him.

Why in the hell hadn't that Realtor called him back yet?

MAGGIE HAD ALWAYS BEEN ABLE to phone Cord at any hour when she needed to talk. But he had a wife now. Kit wouldn't appreciate being disturbed at one in the morning.

Totally wired after all they'd been through, she did something unprecedented and went into the study to watch TV. An old western featuring Hopalong Cassidy was on the movie channel. It was ancient.

Maybe that was what she needed to get her mind off Jake for two seconds.

Ten minutes later she shut it off.

The only time on the trip he'd kissed her had been to put on a performance in front of Sabina. Getting Kamila out of Prague had been his sole objective. With his step-mother and little brother ensconced in his apartment, his pain had vanished.

Other than having to be patient while he continued the therapy for his shoulder, he was free. He could do what-ever he wanted when he wasn't helping Maggie track down Antonin Buric. He could be with anyone he wanted.

She knew he ran up City Creek in the mornings. A lot of women did the same thing. Good-looking women. Ben's warning came back to haunt her.

Nine years a widower is long enough for a man to fall madly in love all over again. Don't let his past diminish what's happening now.

Did she have the guts to run at the same time and hope she bumped into him? Would he leave Kamila and the baby on their first morning in Salt Lake to get in a run before he went to work? Did he even plan to put in time at the office tomorrow?

There was only one way to find out.

She forced herself to go bed. In case she did fall asleep, she set her alarm for six.

At times, other women went to extremes to get in a man's face, but that wasn't something Maggie had ever done. She was too much her mother's daughter and Ben knew it. That was probably why he'd jolted her with a piece of unsolicited advice the other day.

To her surprise she did sleep, but her inner clock must have been attuned to Jake's because she awakened at quarter to six ready to go for a run.

Donning a short-sleeved top and shorts, she hurried to her car and drove around the loop to the small parking area at the entrance to City Creek.

A dozen people at least were jogging up and down the trail. There was no sign of Jake so far. After two miles, she stopped to catch her breath. Filled with disappointment, she decided to return to the car.

"Hi," a male voice called to her. She turned around to discover a blond man staring at her with open interest. He had the build of a tennis player.

"Hi."

Probably any other woman would have been flattered, but they hadn't met Jake or they would understand why no other man could compare.

He smiled. "I hope you're not going back yet."

"Actually I am. I'm due at work shortly."

He blocked her path. "I haven't seen you running up here before."

"This is my first time." It would be her only time. The plan to run into Jake had turned into a fiasco.

"Why don't you come here again tomorrow, same time, and we could go to breakfast after. My name's Jim Peterson."

"I hope that invitation includes me," sounded a deep, familiar voice directly behind her.

Jake.

She spun around. He'd obviously gone up the canyon farther and was on his return run.

"Sorry I'm late, sweetheart." He bounded right up to her and gave her a hard kiss in front of Jim. "You should have waited at the bottom, but I'm glad to know you missed me enough to come all this way."

"Sorry." The other guy hunched his shoulders before continuing his run up the trail.

"You should be," she heard Jake mutter before he flung his arm around her shoulders for the walk back. His possessive tone sent a delicious shiver up her spine.

With their bodies touching from shoulder to thigh, this was better than being in the Cessna 185.

"It's a good thing other people are around or you wouldn't be safe with me."

"That's a great line, Mr. Halsey," she teased, wanting him to mean it, wondering if he did.

In the next breath he led her into some heavy under-brush behind a clump of pines. With his hard body, he forced hers against one of the trunks.

Desire, hot and unmistakable, turned his eyes dark before his head descended. On a little moan, her mouth lifted to meet his. Their deep kiss, like slow burning logs, suddenly burst into flame. She wrapped her arms around his back to bring him closer.

"I could devour you right here," he admitted on a shallow breath. His lips roved relentlessly over her hot cheeks and throat. "If this isn't the reason you came to find me, then don't tell me because I don't want to know."

Maggie remained silent because she refused to lie to him. She'd waded into deep waters. It was a heady new experience. Right now nothing was more important than satisfying her need, which seemed to grow with every hungry kiss.

"Let's go to your apartment," he whispered into her hair.

"I wish we could, but I have to get to the office right away."

"Have dinner with me and Kamila tonight after work. Later we'll go to your place where we can have unin-terrupted time alone."

"All right." Her voice shook.

He pressed his forehead against hers. "I'm glad you agreed, because if you'd said anything else…"

"I wasn't about to."

She felt his body trembling. "Come on. Let's get you back to the parking area before we draw more of a crowd."

Runners were watching them?

With her cheeks hotter than ever, she eased out of his

arms. Jake grasped her hand and pulled her back to the trail. He didn't let her go until they reached the bottom of the canyon.

"See you at six." He helped her into her car, then leaned inside the window and drew another kiss from her before heading for his. They'd reached a level of passion that could only have one outcome because she didn't want to fight what she was feeling for him any longer.

A half hour later, she entered her office. Steve was hard at work. She walked over and put a hand on his shoulder. "Guess who's back?"

"It's good to see you."

"Ditto. Do you remember when you told me I worked too hard? That everyone needed to take time off now and again?"

He grinned. "I remember, and I haven't changed my mind about it."

"Well, I've decided *you* are going to take your own advice. I want you to get out of here and enjoy this beautiful day. I just came back from a run up City Creek. I saw a lot of females about your age beating me by a mile.

"You know what Hollywood says about Utah women. They're the most beautiful in the world. So put on your running shoes. I don't want to see you back here until tomorrow.

"Of course if running up City Creek isn't your thing, ask Cord to take you to his athletic club. He'll introduce you to a couple of attractive CEOs and doctors working out. But if they're not your style, then mosey on up to the U and take advantage of their athletic facilities. A skillion female students hang out there."

"A skillion?"

"That's an old Salt Lake term for a whole bunch."

He got to his feet chuckling. "In other words, you want me out of here."

She winked. "I told you you're brilliant. Since I'm already impressed by the job you've been doing, I want you to enjoy yourself. All work and no play…"

"I'm gone," he quipped before disappearing from her office.

So am I, Steve.

Blown away.

I didn't know I would feel like this when love happened to me.

Milwaukee, Wisconsin
August 27

ANNA HELD HER BREATH WAITING for the doctor who'd operated on her yesterday to make his rounds. The nurses kept her sedated for pain, but the medicine didn't do anything to relieve her anxiety about missing class.

Finally he breezed in the room looking disgustingly healthy and energetic. "Good morning, Anna. How are you feeling?"

"I'll be a lot better when you tell me how soon you'll let me get up on crutches. Yesterday was supposed to be my first day of classes at the university. I can't afford to miss more than a day or two."

His professional gaze studied her speculatively. "Before I operated, you told me you wanted to be able to ski this coming winter."

"I do! In fact I've already made my reservations."

"Then you have to obey my instructions to the letter if you want to heal properly. I understand you don't have anyone to take care of you."

"No, but it's all right."

Actually she had all her Skwars and Buric relatives, but they were the last people she would impose on. Not after all they'd done for her. Not since she'd begun her new life.

"I'm afraid it isn't. You sustained a nasty break in that car accident. For the next week you need to be in bed with your leg elevated. That means someone must wait on you, so I'll arrange for you to be transferred to the hospital's rehabilitation wing in the morning. Your student insurance will cover the cost."

She lifted her head off the pillow. "A whole week?"

"That's not all. You'll need another two weeks with a therapist who'll help you with your crutches."

Hot tears trickled out of her eyes. "Now I'm going to have to withdraw from my college classes."

He smiled at her with compassion. "I know you didn't plan to end up in that collision yesterday, but remember you've still got your life. There's always next semester.

"We'll get an X ray in a week. If everything's fine, I won't need to see you until you're released in three weeks. Take the painkiller and relax. This period will pass. In time you'll be good as new."

"Thank you, Dr. Brewer."

"You're welcome."

The staff didn't give her time to indulge in her grief or the loss of her totaled car. It seemed like someone came in every few minutes to take her vital signs. Before she knew it, they'd brought her a dinner of liquids. The broth turned her stomach. She managed a Popsicle and Sprite.

"Is there anything else I can get you?"

"Could you phone the student housing at the University of Wisconsin-Milwaukee? I need to talk to the supervisor."

"Sure."

The nurse returned a few minutes later and got her on the line. She handed the phone to Anna.

"Hi. This is Anna Buric. I'm in building B, number twenty. Yesterday I was hit by a speeding car that went through a red light. I ended up in Milwaukee West Hospital with a broken leg and won't be coming back to college this semester. Is there some way for my things to be cleared out and brought to the hospital? Then another student will be able to have my room. I'll pay someone to do it."

"I'll take care of it and come by tomorrow to see you. The important thing is for you to get better."

"Thank you so much. Shall I just phone the registrar and cancel my classes?"

"Since it's not too late to drop them, why don't I help you do that when I come over."

"You're very kind."

"That's what I'm here for. We don't want your first days at the university to be blighted by this experience. What a lousy deal."

"It was horrible. The driver of the other car has a broken back."

"Better that person than you, when you were just minding your own business. Don't worry about anything."

"I'll try not to."

It was a lie. Right now Anna was feeling overwhelmed. Tomorrow she would have to call the hospital lab and tell them what had happened. If they were going to give her the job, would they hold it for her?

"That's the spirit. See you in the morning."

When the supervisor hung up, Anna handed the phone back to the nurse with a thank-you.

Three weeks in the hospital before she had to look for another place to live? What an irony to think she'd wanted a job in the lab to get a feel for hospital work.

Who would have dreamed that while she was having a wonderful time on the ferry, tooting around Wisconsin in her new car, she would end up here yesterday on the receiving end of the hospital's services.

Anna knew she should be thankful she hadn't been killed, but tonight the future looked bleak. If the lab job was out, it would be at least a month before she could get another job and start bringing in money. Her skiing trip was definitely out now. Hopefully she'd be able to get some of her money back.

The terrible loneliness that sometimes crept through her was running rampant.

Most people had family to turn to. A relative. But Anna had no idea where she really belonged. The Skwars and Burics had helped raise her, but they were bonded to their own families. She was bonded to no one.

The only thing saving her sanity was the possibility that she'd been kidnapped by Antonin Buric. Ever since her talk with Mr. Markham, she'd been imagining the family she'd been born into.

She had blue eyes—did her parents have blue eyes, too? She was a natural blonde with chin-length hair styled in a casual cut for college. It was lighter in summer as a result of helping in the orchards beneath a full sun. She stood taller, more slender than the women at Skwars farm.

Was her mother tall, or did her height come from her father? How many brothers and sisters did she have, or was she an only child? How terrible for her birth parents if that had been the case.

Anna tried to imagine where they might live. East Coast? West Coast? Somewhere in between? Maybe overseas. In a big city or a small town?

What did her father do for a living? Did her mother work? What were their talents?

Did they have a family pet?

Was Anna the oldest? The youngest?

Were her siblings married? Did she have nieces and nephews?

What was her real name? Was she of English or Scottish stock? Maybe Scandinavian?

Had her father served in the military? Where did her family stand on politics? Did they attend a church? If so, which one?

The questions went on and on until the nurse came in to give her more painkiller and she lost cognizance of her surroundings.

Salt Lake City, Utah
August 27

WITH HIS MIND ON THE EVENING to come, Jake almost collided with Wendell in the hall outside his office.

"There you are, Jake! I just put something on your desk I think you'll be excited about."

"New information on the Buric name?"

"No." He chuckled. "It's the 1746 will of your Halsey ancestor. I printed off a copy for you to keep with your own family records."

Jake had to fight his disappointment. With Kamila and Jared safely under his roof, nothing was more important than finding new evidence on Kathryn's whereabouts. When he saw Maggie tonight, he wanted to bring her something that meant she was a step closer to being united with her sister. He refused to believe Kathryn was no longer alive.

"That's very thoughtful of you Wendell. I really appreciate it."

"I knew you would." He followed Jake inside. "Go ahead and read it out loud."

Jake smiled. Wendell was one of a kind. Resigned to this little task because he liked him so much, Jake picked up the paper and began reading.

"In the name of God, amen. I, Nathanial Halsey of Southampton, in Suffolk County, England, a farmer, being well in health, leave to my son *Recompense?*" Jake's head reared.

Wendell started to chuckle. "Go on."

"I leave to my son Recompense all my houses and

lands at Meacox, and a half of a lot of meadow at—*Accabog in Jumping Neck?*—which I bought off Edward Philips by deed."

Jake darted Wendell a glance. "Are you sure you didn't make this up?" he teased the older man.

"Keep going."

"I leave to my two grandsons, Ananias and Israel Halsey, ten pounds British sterling each." Jake lifted his head. "He sounds as poor as me."

Wendell was loving this.

"I leave to my son Elisha, all my lot of land called the Blank lot. Signed, Abram and Anna Halsey, executors."

Jake eyed his boss. "Doesn't sound like Elisha was in that great a favor with his father."

"He wasn't the first born."

"That had to hurt."

"He didn't want to be a farmer. In fact like you, he heeded the call of the sea at an early age. It turns out Elisha was also an ancestor of Fleet Admiral Halsey." Wendell patted Jake on the shoulder. "Have a good day."

It was already turning out to be the best day of his life so far. Of her own volition, Maggie had sought him out this morning. She'd taken a run up City Creek for no other reason than to be with him. Maggie McFarland just didn't do things like that.

He looked down at the paper in his hand. Even if he didn't have anything new on the Burics, Wendell had given him something priceless to share with her tonight. The end of his workday couldn't come soon enough.

Folding it up, he put the will in his pocket and got busy transcribing off disks. Every day more microfilming of civil, church and cemetery records was being done throughout Eastern Europe. Getting the latest information into the database was a never-ending process.

Until Maggie's advent into his life, he hadn't realized how invaluable genealogy could be in solving past crimes. It was a fascinating business, one he could see himself doing indefinitely.

At two, he checked in with Kamila to find out how she and Jared were getting along. Apparently she'd decided to cook Jake's father's favorite Polish dinner for them tonight to surprise Maggie. Kamila sounded like she was getting along better than fine. Now if only—

The ringing of his cell phone had him grabbing for it. He checked his watch. It was five to three, which meant five to five New York time. Maybe it was the Realtor.

Without looking at the caller ID, he clicked on. "This is Mr. Halsey."

"Jake? It's Maggie."

Didn't she know she only had to say his name and he would always know who she was? But she sounded so upset, he didn't say what he was thinking. "What's wrong?"

"My sister-in-law's father, John Holbrook, passed away at noon. He had a heart attack the other day. It was minor, and they sent him home. But this morning he suffered a massive one and didn't survive."

Jake grimaced. "I'm sorry."

"I am, too. He was only sixty-five. My parents are anxious to be with Julie's mother, so I'm flying them to Colorado Springs right now. We'll stay over at our condo there and come back in the morning. Please tell Kamila I'm sorry. You know how much I wanted to be with you tonight."

Once again Jake was forced to fight his bitter disappointment. Not only because his plans for tonight had just gone up in smoke, but because she hadn't asked him to go with her.

You're not family, Halsey.

They weren't even lovers yet.

"Of course I understand. Your family needs you."

"Thank you, Jake. I'll call you tomorrow when I'm back."

His eyes closed tightly. "I'll be waiting. Please give my condolences to your brother and sister-in-law."

"I will. Talk to you soon."

So much for having a good day.

Jake had hardly hung up when it rang again. He almost broke the chair reaching for it. Maybe she'd changed her mind and didn't want to go without him.

"Maggie?" he said after clicking on.

"No. This is Brett Rosen, the manager of Rosen Realty. I understand from another Realtor you were looking for a Jan and Marie Skwars Buric who used to own a home in Fordham twenty-six years ago."

This time Jake shot to his feet. "That's right. What did you find out?"

"Our company took over Goldman Realty twenty years ago. I checked back in the archives and found the signature of Marie Skwars Buric as the seller."

That meant Franz Buric hadn't been lying! He wanted out of prison enough to turn in his own brother.

"This is great news, Mr. Rosen. Who was the actual agent on the sale?"

"A Michael Geeson."

"Obviously he doesn't work for you."

"No."

"Would you do me one more favor and look up a phone number on him? I'll send you a check for your trouble."

"That's all right. Give me a minute. I'm going to put you on hold."

"Fine." Jake would give him all the time he needed if he could produce the phone number.

Five minutes passed before the Realtor returned to the phone. "Mr. Halsey? I checked with the operator. She did a global search of New York state. Nothing came up with that spelling or a phonetic spelling. I'm sorry."

"Don't be. You've been very helpful. Thank you for getting back to me." They hung up.

Mr. Geeson had to be someplace. Before Jake called the operator to do global searches of the surrounding states, he decided to look up the name in the genealogical database.

Geeson.

Within seconds, several hundred heads of families taken from the 2000 U.S. census appeared on the screen. Gieson, Giesen, Gizon, Geason. Finally he came to a clump of Geesons, all in Ohio except for one in Kansas.

He picked up the phone and asked for Kansas information. The operator did a search and found a couple, but none with the name Michael. Jake jotted down the phone numbers anyway.

Next, he got the Ohio operator on the line. There were two Michaels in Cleveland. He tried the first one. A female answered. "Geeson residence."

Jake said hello and told her what he wanted. When he added that it was a matter of life and death she said, "That would be my father-in-law. While he was in college in New York years ago, he did part-time work for a real-estate agency. I'll give you his cellphone number."

Those were the words Jake had been waiting to hear.

He thanked her, then phoned the other number. When the man answered, Jake once again explained who he was. "You sold a house for a Mrs. Marie Skwars Buric. She had two grandsons, Antonin and Franz."

"Buric...she was the Czech woman. A widow."

Jake's adrenaline was pumping. "That's right. Do you recall meeting her grandsons?"

"No. When she came to the office to sign papers, she was alone."

"Do you remember why she was selling the house, and more importantly, where was she going? Would she have been planning to move to a retirement home by any chance?"

"I...think she might have been going to her brother's, but I'm not positive and I don't remember a name."

Her brother.

He would be a Skwars. That was the next place to search. "You've been more help than you know. Thank you."

"You're welcome. If something else comes to mind, I'll call you."

After their exchange, Jake phoned for a Skwars anywhere in the state of New York. The operator couldn't find it on the global search.

Once again he searched the latest census of names in the computer database. He found close to thirty Skwars who were heads of family, all living in Racine County, Wisconsin.

Wisconsin. He recalled that the largest group of Burics had settled there, too.

Without wasting any time, he phoned the area code for Racine County and asked the operator for Skwars' numbers.

"There are too many of them. Since you don't have a first name, I'll give you the number for Skwars Farm."

Jake wrote it down. After hanging up, he did a search for it on the Internet, curious to know if there was an advertisement. Up popped the home page for Skwars Farm.

Welcome to Bohemian heaven in Wisconsin's fruit belt.

He clicked through the pages listing the fruit market, the bakery, the pick-your-own-fruit program, shipping office, tours of the original homestead, the museum with scheduled classes in egg painting featuring batik, eyelet lace, meadow flowers and painted relief.

It was open year round except for Christmas through New Year's. The flourishing family business started by Jainos Skwars had existed for over sixty years.

What better place for Antonin to be hiding out. Jake whistled. He had a feeling in his bones he was on to something solid at last.

Reaching for the phone, he called Kamila and told her plans had changed.

"The dinner will keep in the fridge until tomorrow night when she's back from Colorado."

It had been so many years, he'd forgotten how nice it was to have family home waiting for him. No one was more pleasant and upbeat than Kamila, even in her pain. Jared didn't know it yet, but he was a lucky boy to have such a terrific mother.

"Thanks for being so great about it. Under the circumstances, why don't I take you and Jared out for an American hamburger? We'll do a little tour of the city at the same time to help you get your bearings."

"We'd love it. Maybe you could show me some places where I could rent a house in a nice residential neighborhood. With the money your father left in that Swiss bank account for me, I can afford it. I don't want Jared to grow up in an apartment. I'm sick of them."

"You can't move out on me yet! You just got here."

"We've always been honest with each other, Jake, so I know you won't take me wrong when I tell you that we both need our own space. I don't want to clutter up your place and then have to move it all out later. I'd rather get on top of things right away."

He smiled. Kamila was a determined woman, and once her mind was made up, there was no turning back. That's how she'd managed to get his father to cave.

"Whatever you say. I'll be home in about an hour, then we'll go house hunting."

"I always could count on you," she said in a choked-up voice. "You're your father's son more than you know. Maggie McFarland and I are the luckiest women in the world."

Jake had no response for that. He was too terrified Antonin might not be where Jake thought he was. If Kathryn's case was never solved, Maggie might not allow him inside her circle of one.

As if just thinking about her had conjured her up, his cell phone rang with her number showing on the caller ID.

His pulse rate tripled. "Maggie?"

"Hi."

Maybe she hadn't gone after all. "Where are you?"

"In Colorado Springs."

"Are you all right?"

"No. Mom's not doing well. She's close to Julie's family and has taken his death very hard. But we all know why her grief is so intense. Dad says she's always better when I'm with her, so he's asked me to stay with them until the funeral's over on Saturday."

And Jake hadn't thought things could get worse.

"I've already called Scott. Between him and Steve, they'll cover for me at the firm. Can we put off dinner until Saturday night?"

"That all depends. When do you think you'll be flying home?"

"The funeral's scheduled for ten-thirty. I'm presuming we'll be back around three in the afternoon, but you never know." Her voice trailed away.

"It'll probably be later, so I have an idea."

"What is it?"

"Why don't you get a good night's sleep on Saturday so you'll be ready to take a trip with me on Sunday."

"Where?" she cried. At least that response sounded eager.

"Racine, Wisconsin."

She was silent for a moment. "What's in Racine?"

"Hopefully Antonin Buric."

"Jake!"

"Don't mention this to anyone else in case this leads to a dead end. I'll tell you all about it when we get in the air."

"After we fly in on Saturday, I'll phone you to touch base. Give my best to Kamila, and a big kiss to that adorable little brother of yours."

"I will. Miss me a little."

CHAPTER ELEVEN

M<small>AGGIE</small> <small>MISSED</small> J<small>AKE</small> so much, the four days away from him were pure torture. But what would have been worse was to come home to no Jake.

It was a good thing she hadn't made plans to be with him Saturday night. By the time Maggie had driven her parents home from the airport, it was past nine. Another ordeal began when her mom begged her to stay at the house instead of going back to her condo.

Four days of togetherness hadn't been enough for Ellen McFarland, not even with all the family and friends who'd come to the Holbrook home both before and after the funeral to talk. Everyone wanted to reminisce about John and what a wonderful man and father he'd been.

Maggie knew her mother's pain was most acute when the whole family was assembled for a major event, whether it be happy or sad. Those gatherings were a reminder that her baby girl was missing, and might always be missing, though she'd never stopped believing Kathryn was alive.

Maggie had envied Brock and Katy, who were able to play quietly with their Colorado cousins. They didn't understand that their grandmother McFarland was suffering because one of her children wasn't there.

Her mom seemed calmest, most serene, when she took a proactive role in foundation business. Then she became a fighter and forgot herself long enough to encourage frantic parents not to give up.

No one could be a more understanding and compassionate person than her mother during someone else's crisis. But no one could comfort her when her heart longed for her baby, except Maggie's father who needed comforting himself.

Jake had accomplished more in the past few weeks than all of the law enforcement agencies working on Kathryn's case put together. He'd given them fresh hope. This latest lead was evidence of his unceasing determination to track down Antonin and find out what he'd done with Kathryn.

Maggie loved him for it. She loved him with a passion she couldn't begin to put into words.

When she drove around the back of his apartment early Sunday morning as arranged, all she could think about was throwing herself in his arms. But he was outside playing with the baby while Kamila looked on. Maggie had to muster all of her self-control to remain composed.

She pulled to a stop next to his car and got out, eager to give the baby a squeeze. Her eyes met Jake's. His intimate gaze traveled over her, bringing her senses alive.

"Could I hold him for a minute?"

"Jared's been waiting for you." He handed the baby over to her.

"Oh you cute little thing." She clutched him to her and kissed his neck before glancing at Kamila. "I swear he's bigger than the last time I saw him."

"It feels like you've been gone a year," Jake said in a low aside.

Jake didn't know the half of it.

Kamila smiled. "He's getting heavier all the time, and hungrier. It's time to feed him his rice cereal. You love that, don't you, lambkin?"

Maggie was forced to relinquish him to his mother. Kamila started up the steps before turning to them. "Have a safe trip. I won't stop praying you find the man responsible."

"Are you going to be all right alone?"

"That's very sweet of you to be concerned, Maggie, but Jared and I have each other, and I've been on the phone nonstop with my family in Poland. They're going to come to the States in October for a visit, so I've got to get my house ready for them."

"What house? You've bought a place already?" Maggie couldn't believe it. She wondered how Jake felt about this.

"It's a rent-to-own plan. I got hold of a Realtor on Wednesday and he showed me dozens of places. Jake approved of the home I picked, so I paid first and last month's rent yesterday. If all goes well, I should be able to move in next week."

"Where is it?"

"Here on the Avenues. Terrace Hills Drive."

"That's a perfect place, so close to the Ensign school and Eleventh Avenue park."

"I'm happy about it."

"So am I." On that note Jake walked over to give Kamila and the baby one more kiss before joining Maggie. "I'll call you and let you know what time we're coming back."

As Maggie climbed in the car, excitement raced through her. With Kamila putting down roots here, no matter how temporarily, how could Jake possibly think of leaving in January to return to that world of covert operations and constant danger?

He loved Jared. The baby was a link to his father. Surely he was having second thoughts at this point about continuing in his former career.

"Stop for a minute," he said when they'd started around the side of the apartment.

She braked before turning to him. "What is it?" He'd put his suitcase in the back, but maybe he'd forgotten something.

"This."

His hand went to the back of her head. The next thing she knew, he'd drawn her close to kiss her. As he increased the pressure, the taste and feel of him blotted out the world.

Her foot slipped off the brake, which caused the engine to die. She didn't care. They kissed feverishly. Maggie strained toward him, but the front seat of the car with a gearshift between them had to be the worst place on earth at a time like this. To add to her frustration, he lifted his mouth from hers way too soon.

"One of my neighbors is behind us," he answered her little cry of protest. "He's been patiently waiting for us to come back to reality."

"Oh, no."

She was in such a daze, her movements were slow as she struggled to recover and start the car.

"You look beautiful," he whispered.

"So do you."

"Maggie—"

"I think we'd better concentrate on the trip ahead of us. You still haven't told me anything. What makes you think Antonin could be in Racine?"

"Not the city itself. On a fruit farm near a little town called Caledonia."

By the time they'd taken off in the jet and had reached cruising speed, he'd apprised her of all the facts. Maggie was so certain Jake's hunch was right, she could hardly contain herself.

"What I want us to do is pretend we're tourists. We'll play it to the hilt. Take the tour, attend a class, pick fruit, buy some fruit at the stands and eat at the bakery.

"As we make the rounds and keep our eyes out for a fifty-year-old man who might faintly resemble his brother Frankie, we'll talk to people, find out if they're a Skwars or a Buric. Sooner or later we're bound to pick up on something crucial."

"What if we don't learn anything?"

"As a last option, I'll revert to speaking Czech and say that I'm looking for Antonin who used to be a friend of mine. If nothing else, it will catch them off guard. I'll be able to tell if they're hiding him or not."

She believed him. That was the kind of thing he did all the time in the CIA. Nobody could do it better. "He's got to be there, Jake."

"If he's not, we'll find out if Marie is still alive and

living in their community. Someone has to know something."

His fierce declaration was what Maggie needed right now to keep her spirits up.

"I wish I didn't have to be back to work tomorrow, but I have an important court case at two o'clock I have to handle myself."

"There's always the next day. Fortunately Wendell has told me to make you my first priority, so I don't have the same problem."

"He's an interesting character."

"You have no idea. Did I tell you he traced my Halsey line back to 1746?"

She smiled. "No. Next you're going to tell me you're related to the famous admiral."

"As a matter of fact I am."

"You're kidding."

"Not according to Wendell. Would you tell me what kind of people name their children Recompense, Ananias, Israel, Abram, Anna, Elisha and Nathanial?"

"Bible-fearing parents. Half of those names were given to some of my ancestors, too."

"Can you imagine Jared being called Recompense?"

Maggie started to laugh. He joined her. It was a welcome relief from the tension of agonizing over what they might or might not find once they reached Wisconsin.

"I have a Scotch-Irish ancestor on my dad's side named Sobriety."

Jake grinned at her. "You made that up."

"I swear I didn't. What's so funny is that her son, John McFarland—"

"The Copper King?" Jake interrupted.

"Yes. During prohibition he kept an ever-flowing stash of French wines and champagne in the attic of the carriage-house cottage behind the mansion.

"In one of his letters to a friend living in Paris he wrote, 'Prohibition makes you want to cry into your beer, and denies you the beer to cry into.' To this day our family laughs about it."

"He was bigger than life, wasn't he?"

He couldn't hold a candle to you, Jake. No man could.

"The only problem with men like that is that they probably did a lot of things I don't want to know about. But I can handle the champagne part. I sent Brock into the attic to bring down a bottle of the good stuff for Kit and Cord to enjoy when they returned from their honeymoon."

"Having been dry since I started therapy, I wouldn't mind going to work on one of those bottles myself."

She flicked him a covert glance. "When we get back to Salt Lake, I'll tell Cord to let you go up in the attic and pick out your favorite year and vintage."

"Only if John's great-great-great-granddaughter will drink some with me. Otherwise it wouldn't be any fun. I forgot. You don't drink."

"On the rare occasion I do."

"Does that mean yes, you will, or no, you won't?" he pushed.

"If you don't know the answer to that by now…"

"I like things spelled out."

Her heart was beating frantically. "I promise that to-morrow night we'll have some at my condo."

"Don't make promises you can't keep" was his gruff response.

"Barring a natural disaster of epic proportions, I intend to hold to my side of the bargain."

"So do I."

The hand that reached out to caress her thigh almost caused her to veer off course. He didn't remove it until they prepared for their descent. Talk about crying into her beer.

Skwars Farm, Wisconsin
August 31

JAKE DROVE THROUGH the open gate with the overhead sign decorated in a Bohemian design. He followed the road a quarter of a mile to the main office located in a farmhouse that looked so much like the one in Bela, Kamila would have to come here and check it out.

There were several dozen cars in the parking lot. Lots of tourists were milling around.

Turning to the quiet woman beside him he said, "Ready?" On the plane Maggie had been relaxed, but once they'd picked up their rental car, he'd felt her tension.

She nodded and undid her seat belt.

"Let's go." He climbed out and went around to help her. Grasping Maggie's hand, they walked past several families with young children. Once inside the farmhouse, Jake escorted her over to the counter.

A fortyish-looking man at the cash register nodded to Jake. "Welcome to Skwars Farm. Have you ever been here before?"

"No, but we've heard about it."

"Let me give you a brochure. It will tell you where to go and what to do."

They both took one.

"My fiancée and I are interested in the complete tour." Jake pulled out his wallet and put two twenty-dollar bills on the counter. The man gave them passes in the shape of a Czech-painted Easter egg to pin on.

Jake studied the front of the brochure for a moment, then looked at him. "Is Jainos Skwars still alive? I'd like to meet the man who started all this."

The other man chuckled. "You're out of luck. He died a long time ago. I'm one of his grandsons, Jiri."

"This is a beautiful place," Maggie commented.

"We love it." The man's eyes lingered on her a lot longer than Jake liked. She was a stunner in her tan jeans and coral top.

"When we were looking up the address, we saw dozens of Skwars in the telephone directory."

Jake's voice recaptured the man's attention. "We're a big family co-op. Probably a hundred cousins, aunts and uncles live here and work the farm."

"It's very impressive." Jake put his arm around Maggie's waist to signal they were leaving.

"You and your fiancée enjoy yourselves."

"I'm sure we will. Thank you."

When they got outside, Jake pulled her closer against his side. "I didn't like the way he was sizing you up."

"Men don't—" She stopped talking, but he knew what she was going to say.

"You think I don't know what they're thinking when they look at you?"

That brought a smile to her lips. "You sounded very possessive just now."

"That's the way I'm feeling." He kissed the side of her neck. "Where shall we start first?"

"Let's begin with the walking tour to the different buildings. There'll be family members at each one to give a lecture. We can cover more ground that way."

"Good idea." They spent the next hour making the rounds. Jake asked the same thing of everyone they met. Was Jainos Skwars alive? Could they meet him?

The answer was always the same, of course. They must have chatted with dozens of Skwarses, both male and female. Jake picked out several men who could have been in their fifties, but none of them answered to the name Antonin.

Finally they met a Buric at the museum. Jake learned there weren't as many of them as there were Skwarses.

It was after one. "I bet you're as hungry as I am. Let's stop at the bakery."

"Actually I don't have an appetite, but I'll buy something anyway because Antonin might be working there in the back where he's not so visible."

"One way or another we'll find out."

A few minutes later, they entered the tiny farmhouse that had been converted into a Czech pastry shop. His mouth watered to see the list of fruit-filled *kolaches* on the menu. It took him back to those days in Prague.

Jake found them a table. Since it was round, he sat right next to Maggie and put his arm across the back of her chair. The feel of her silky hair brushing his arm was tantalizing. He wanted the contact any way he could get it.

Two women in Bohemian costumes worked behind the counter. One of them came out to take their order.

Jake smiled at her. "Everything looks so delicious, it's hard to choose. What do you recommend?"

"The peach."

"Then we'll take two of them and two colas. By the way, is there a restroom?"

"Yes. Go out the door and around the rear of the building."

"Thank you."

When she walked away, Jake whispered in Maggie's ear, "I'll be right back."

He gave her a brief kiss before getting out of the chair. The hope in Maggie's eyes killed him.

When he reached his destination, he discovered three doors. Two with men and women signs. The third had to be the back door. He looked around to see if anyone was watching, then tried the handle. It turned easily.

These were not people who locked their doors.

Without hesitation, he walked right in the back of the bakery. One older woman was busy making pastry. When she saw movement, she let out a little cry of surprise.

"Sorry. I thought this was the restroom. The waitress told me it was around back."

"It's the door next to this one." She followed him out and showed him the right door.

He didn't want to break the bad news to Maggie that he hadn't seen a man who might have been Antonin, but there was no help for it.

Her blue eyes swerved to his when he entered the shop. He shook his head to let her know. She lowered her face.

"We're only halfway through our tour," he reminded her as he began eating.

In a few minutes, their waitress came by. "Can I get you anything else?" She directed her question to Maggie.

"No thank you."

"How do you like the wedding pastry?" The waitress kept staring at her.

"It's very good."

"If we could have our check please."

"Here you go."

He left cash on the table, then accompanied Maggie from the shop. She paused outside the door.

"Jake? Do I have something on my face?"

"Nothing, but I noticed her looking at you, too," he murmured. "That's twice already. If it happens a third time we'll ask why. Let's go pick apples. It says the Jersey Mac and Red Astrachans have come in season."

They followed the directions on the brochure until they reached one of the orchards. A couple with two children told them to take a basket and pick what they wanted.

"We don't allow you to climb the trees. Use the ladders."

Jake turned to the girl who couldn't have been more than ten or eleven. "Will you show us a good tree?"

Her mother nodded her consent.

"Okay. Come with me."

After a couple of rows, she pointed to one laden with fruit. "This has a lot of apples," she said.

"So we see." He turned to Maggie. "Do you want to go up the ladder first?"

"Thank you. Will you steady it for me?"

Oh, Maggie. If she only knew he lived for moments like this. Those long legs were his weakness. So were her eyes, mouth, hair, figure. The list went on and on.

"Do you trust me?"

The girl giggled.

"You know I do," Maggie said.

He handed her the basket. While she got busy, he focused his attention on the girl. "Are you a Buric or a Skwars?"

"A Buric."

Jake felt an adrenaline rush. Now was his chance. "Do you know who told me about this place?"

"No."

"One of your relatives named Antonin."

"I don't know him." She said it so honestly, he believed her.

"I've picked a dozen, Jake. Is that enough?" Maggie called to him.

"Plenty. Come on down. I want to go paint eggs."

He helped her step off the ladder. The girl ran ahead of them to her parents and younger brother. They put the apples in a special bag with the Skwars logo.

Jake got his wallet out and paid the brother. As they were about to walk away, the girl said, "Do we have a relative named Antonin?" He didn't miss the look that passed between her parents.

Deciding to take the initiative, Jake said, "My name's Jake Halsey. This is my fiancée Maggie McFarland. I knew an Antonin Buric a long time ago when I was in the navy. He said something about a family farm in

Wisconsin. I thought this had to be the one so we decided to visit it. I'd surely like to see him again, if only to say hello."

The mother said, "If we're talking about the same Antonin Buric, he's a distant relative, but he's never lived here."

"He had a brother, Franz."

The husband nodded. "We never met him, either."

"Well, I'm glad I asked anyway. It's no wonder he told me about this farm. It's fantastic. Thanks for the apples."

"Sure."

"Just a minute."

He wheeled around. "Yes?"

"Until a few weeks ago his daughter lived here."

The blood pounded in his ears. "He never said anything about a daughter."

The girl's father said, "As far as the family knows, he never acknowledged her or came around."

"Then how did she come to be at the farm?"

"According to my cousin Petr, Great-grandmother Marie brought her from New York when she was just a baby."

"How old is she?"

"Midtwenties."

Maggie didn't realize it, but her nails were digging into the skin of Jake's arm.

"Is the older woman still alive?" Jake asked.

"Oh, no."

"So Antonin's daughter lived here all her life and he never once got in touch with her?"

"It's very sad."

"I agree. You say she just recently left?"

"Yes."

"Do you know where she went? Maybe we could look her up before we have to fly home. I have a few photos of Antonin I could show her."

"After Nelly's wedding, she left to go to college."

"Which one?"

The father scratched his head. "I'm not sure. Josef and Milena would know more about her plans. She's been staying with them for the last few years."

"Where do they live?"

"Give me a brochure and I'll draw it on the map."

Jake's heart had taken off without him.

"What's her name?" he asked when the other man handed it back.

"Anna."

"We'll try to find her. Thanks for the talk and the apples."

"You're welcome. If you see her, tell her Viktor and Lida said hello."

"And me!"

Maggie leaned over the girl. "What's your name, darling?"

"Rickena."

"Did you know Anna well?"

"Yes. She always gave me free *kolaches* and read books to me."

Lida put her arms around her daughter's neck. "Anna was everyone's favorite."

Rickena tugged on her mother's arm.

"What is it, honey?"

"I think she looks like Anna." The girl was staring up at Maggie.

"I agree with you."

The father nodded. "For a minute when I saw you coming, I thought you were Anna."

Maggie's hold threatened to cut off Jake's circulation. "They say everyone has a double somewhere. Thank you for all your help."

Now it was Maggie who started running toward the rental car, pulling Jake after her.

Halfway down the road she dropped the sack of apples and threw her arms around Jake's neck.

"You did it! You found her! Jake—you found my sister! She's alive!"

Half laughing, half sobbing, she clapped her hands on his cheeks. Moisture dripped off her face. "You're the angel Daddy said you were."

The joy in her voice, on her face, would stay with him all the days of his life.

Consumed by emotion, Jake crushed her in his arms. "Let's go find Josef and Milena."

CHAPTER TWELVE

"THIS IS IT, JAKE!"

He pulled up to the front of the farmhouse. "It's a good thing Viktor drew the location for us, otherwise it would have been difficult to know which one it was."

The second he stopped the car, Maggie jumped out and ran up the porch steps. She rang the buzzer. When no one answered, she rang it again.

Jake joined her. "There's no car around. It doesn't appear anyone's home."

"They have to be!"

"I know how you feel. Let's go back to the car. They ought to be coming pretty soon. While we wait I'll call Kamila and tell her we won't be back tonight."

He helped Maggie into the car, then went around and got behind the wheel. She watched him pull out his cell phone.

"I want to call Mom and Dad right this second, but I don't dare until I know exactly where Kathryn is. Once they hear the news, they'll fly out with the family on the company plane. They're going to be so overjoyed! I can't believe this is happening...."

His beautiful smile melted her heart.

This wonderful, brilliant, marvelous man had made the miracle happen. She reached for his free hand and clung to it while he spoke to Kamila.

After a few minutes, he said, "Kamila wants to talk to you."

She took the phone, but almost dropped it she was shaking so hard. "Kamila? Can you believe it? My sister's alive! She's been living on this farm all these years!"

"It's miraculous, Maggie. I'm so very happy for you and your family. When I think of anyone taking my precious Jared from me, I don't know if I could bear to live. Your parents must be strong people to have gone on with their lives."

Tears streamed down Maggie's face. "They never gave up hope. They're remarkable, but so is someone else."

"You mean Jake."

"Yes."

"I see myself in you. I loved his father from the first moment we met. The Halsey men are exceptional."

"I couldn't agree more," she said in a croaky voice.

"I'll let you go now. Jake says you're waiting to meet with the people who can take you to her."

"Thank you, Kamila. Here's Jake again."

She passed the phone to him before breaking down in sobs of joy. In a minute Jake reached across to hold her.

"It's over, Jake," she cried, burying her face against his shoulder. "The hellish nightmare is over. This is going to transform my parents' lives. I saw what happened to the Talbots when they found out Kit was alive.

"My brothers—they're going to feel let out of prison.

It's too incredible. I can hardly believe this day is here. What if you hadn't been working at the genealogical firm? None of this would have been possible."

He kissed the side of her face. "Have you forgotten the part you played in all this? It was no coincidence you came to Wendell's firm. I believe the time had come for you to find your sister. Someone else would have helped you if I hadn't."

"Not the way you have!" As she lifted her head to look at him, she saw a car and truck pull up next to them. "They're here! Oh Jake, I'm so excited, I'm sick."

"The best kind of sickness," he whispered against her lips before they both got out of the car. He came around and gripped her hand.

Three teens jumped down from the truck bed and went into the house. The mom and dad got out of their vehicles and walked over to Maggie and Jake. "Hello. Can we help you?" the man asked.

Maggie felt them studying her, the same way everyone had been doing all day.

Jake squeezed her fingers. "Are you Josef and Milena?" They nodded. "I'm Jake Halsey, a genealogist hired by this woman, Maggie McFarland. We're both from Salt Lake City, Utah. We've been looking for Maggie's sister, Kathryn, who was a one-month-old baby when she was kidnapped from their home twenty-six years ago."

Milena gasped.

"Our search has brought us to Skwars Farm. While we were picking apples a little while ago, we learned a woman named Anna Buric has been living with you. We have reason to believe she's Kathryn."

The couple smiled at Maggie. Josef said, "You and Anna have to be sisters. There couldn't be another explanation for the remarkable likeness. I wish we could tell you she was here."

Maggie was ready to jump out of her skin. "Viktor and Lida told us you know where she is."

Milena nodded. "At the University of Wisconsin-Milwaukee. We drove her there almost two weeks ago. She's living in student housing. We don't know which building or room number. I thought we might have heard from her by now to let us know, but maybe she's been too busy and hasn't purchased a cell phone yet."

"There's a lot we could tell you," Josef inserted, "but it might be better explained if you spoke with Mr. Markham, an immigration attorney in Racine. He's been working with the FBI to help Anna get legal."

Maggie and Jake exchanged glances before she said, "What do you mean?"

"There were no papers on Anna when she came to the farm with her great-grandmother. Everyone always understood she was the daughter of Marie's grandson Antonin. The family waited for him and his wife to show up, but they never did. Which meant there was no birth certificate on Anna, therefore no social-security number.

"Marie died, so her brother's daughter Olga saw to Anna's care. When she passed away unexpectedly, the family took turns looking after Anna. She was with us for the last two years, but she's been unhappy."

"She really has," Milena concurred. "No child can bear to think they were abandoned by their parents. But it's more than that. Anna didn't want to stay on the farm. She has a wonderful mind and craves a higher education, but she couldn't do anything else without having the documentation."

Josef nodded. "My sister Julia put her in touch with Mr. Markham. His first name is Charles. He contacted the FBI who found out Antonin had a police record, and no record of marriage. That raised the possibility that Anna might have been kidnapped. A couple of agents are working on that possibility as we speak.

"If you want to know the truth, I think Anna has been hoping she was abducted because it would mean she has birth parents who love her and have been looking for her."

"They have been!" Maggie cried. "All their lives!"

Milena reached out to hug her. "Josef and I love her, but we realize it's not the same as having your own parents. She and our Nelly roomed together, but Nelly got married a few weeks ago.

"At that point Anna came to Josef and said she wanted to leave. That's when Julia put her on to an attorney who could help her get her life sorted out."

"Thank heaven for you." Maggie hugged Milena, then Josef. "Thank you for taking such wonderful care of her. My parents will be indebted to you forever."

Jake slid his arm around her shoulders. "Come on. Let's go find her." They got in the car.

"Our family will be in touch with you shortly," Maggie said through the open window. She wrote both her cell-phone number and Jake's on one of the foundation brochures she always carried with her and handed it to Josef.

He handed her a business card with their number on it, then looked at the brochure. "Your family set up the Kathryn McFarland Foundation because of her? It will thrill Anna's heart to know she was loved so much."

Copious tears started flowing down Maggie's face once more.

Josef patted her arm. "We'll call Mr. Markham right now and tell him what's happened. He'll probably phone you before the night is over."

"Here." Jake handed her his cell phone as they drove away. "Make that call to your parents. It's the most important one they'll ever receive."

"If I can even talk. Thank you," she cried softly before pressing the digits. "It's five o'clock in Salt Lake. They should both be home."

On the third ring her brother answered. "Hello?"

"Cord?"

"Maggie?"

"I didn't expect you to answer."

"Some wedding gifts came to the house, so Kit and I came over to open them with the folks."

"That sounds fun."

"Hey—what's wrong? Your voice sounds strange."

"Maybe it's the connection. Could I speak to Mom for a minute?"

"You don't want to talk to me?" he teased.

"Of course I do, but—"

"I'll get her. Hang on."

Jake found her free hand and held it tight.

After a minute, her mother came to the phone. "Darling? I'm so glad you called. Where are you? I've been trying to reach you at the condo so you could come over and be with us."

"Jake came across a lead he wanted to check out, so I flew him to Wisconsin. We're outside Racine right now."

"Racine?"

"Yes. Mom? We've got an important question to ask you and Dad. Why don't you put him on another extension?"

"Just a minute."

Within seconds Maggie's father spoke into the phone. "Hi, honey. Your mom and I are both on. What did you want to ask us?"

She fought to compose herself. "Are you ready to hear that the greatest wish of your hearts has come true at last?"

The immediate silence on their end was so eloquent, so poignant, she turned to Jake. "They can't talk," she mouthed the words to him.

"That's how I felt when you announced we were flying to Prague to find Kamila. It's a moment I'll never forget," Jake said.

She bowed her head. "Kathryn's alive and well. Jake and I haven't seen or talked to her yet. She has no idea we know who she is. We've just come from the people who've helped raise her. They know where she is. Kathryn's your angel baby." Maggie choked up. "You should be the ones to see her first."

It was a humbling experience to hear her parents weep with the kind of joy she'd never heard in their voices before.

"Jake found her."

"Bless him forever," her mother cried.

If Maggie had her way, Jake would be in her life forever.

"Bless you forever, darling."

"Mom—" Maggie's voice caught.

"Amen," her father muttered hoarsely.

She tried to clear her throat without success. "We're headed to Milwaukee. That's where she is, attending the University of Wisconsin."

"Your mother and I will get the rest of the family and fly out on the company plane tonight."

Maggie knew that's what he would say. "We'll be there before you, so we'll book rooms for all of us at a hotel with airport limousine service. As soon as I know which one, I'll call you."

Before they hung up, she could hear her mother telling her father they needed to call Ben quick. The happiness in her voice was a revelation. Combined with her dad's yelp of excitement, they both sounded younger.

It was as if some shroud enveloping them had been cast off so they could breathe again.

She turned to Jake. "Mom and Dad said 'bless you forever.' I echo their sentiment."

THE DESK CLERK of the Milwaukee Inn handed Jake the key cards for their two rooms on the fifth floor. The rest of the family's rooms were two floors down. "Enjoy your stay."

"Thank you."

He carried their overnight bags with one arm, and escorted Maggie to the elevator with the other.

If these were different circumstances, he'd have arranged for one room. But not tonight. Not on this redletter night. Kathryn McFarland had been found alive. The news had already transformed her family.

Right now Maggie was in another world. She still wouldn't be able to see Jake clearly until the longawaited reunion had taken place. Jake didn't mind. Maggie's happiness was his, and he wasn't going anywhere.

When they entered her room, she pulled out her cell phone. "Before we call the university, I've got to reach Scott and ask him to go to court for me tomorrow afternoon. I need to call Steve, too."

"Go ahead. I'll be next door taking a shower, then I'll join you."

"Okay. Hurry."

He liked the sound of that, even if she was already dialing.

After he went to his room, he phoned for room service and ordered dinner to be brought to hers. They hadn't had anything to eat since those *kolaches*.

Ten minutes later, dressed in a polo shirt and trousers, he let himself back in her room. She'd showered and changed into denims and a creamy yellow blouse, looking casual yet stylish as only Maggie could pull off without trying.

He found her poring over the phone directory. She lifted her head when she saw him. "Wouldn't you know it's Sunday night?"

"It's always the weekend when you need something vital."

"I phoned the student-housing department, but got a

recording. There won't be a live voice until tomorrow morning at eight."

Just as he was about to make another suggestion, there was a knock on the door.

Maggie looked surprise. "Mom and Dad couldn't be here yet. It's not ten o'clock."

"That will be our dinner."

"Oh. Thank you for ordering it. What would I do without you?"

Jake smiled, having no intention of her ever finding out. "I'll let him in."

The waiter put their trays on the table. Jake tipped him and saw him to the door.

"Come on over here and eat with me. We'll try reaching her through the general-information number."

"That's a good idea." Maggie got up from the bed and carried the directory to the table. While they ate their club sandwiches, she dialed it and a conversation ensued. By the time Maggie hung up, he knew something was wrong.

"The university operator said there's no listing for Anna."

"Maybe she asked not to be put on," he reasoned. "She's only just enrolled. It's possible they haven't had time to update the system."

"I'm sure you're right."

"Try the Wisconsin operator."

"Why didn't I think of that?" But a little research proved there was no listing for Anna there, either.

"Under the circumstances, why don't you phone Mr. Markham in Racine? He'll have her phone number without fail."

Her eyes flashed him a heartfelt thank you. "You're a genius."

Jake tipped his chair back and drank his cola while he waited for her to get the attorney's number from the operator.

"She's connecting me now," Maggie gave him a blow-by-blow account.

He loved it. He loved her. Dear Lord, how he loved her.

No one had a more expressive face than Maggie. He could read it like a book. The sudden fierce frown was not a good sign. She left her name and phone number. After telling him it was an emergency, she clicked off.

"He wasn't there."

"So I gathered."

"We could take a taxi over to the student-housing area and start making inquiries."

"We could, but what if you should run into her? I thought you wanted your parents to be the first."

"I do. Of course I do. I know I'm being impatient."

"Give yourself a break, Maggie. It isn't every day you find your sister who's been missing for twenty-six years."

He got up from the chair and pulled her out of hers. "Come on. You need to relax. After all my therapy, I know how to give a great back rub." He drew her to one of the queen-sized beds. "Lie down on your stomach."

Like a child, she obeyed him without remonstration.

"Close your eyes and think of all the things you're going to say to Kathryn when you have a chance to really talk. The kinds of secrets sisters tell each other."

Jake perched next to her and ran his hands up and down her back, pressing, kneading, massaging those places knotted with tension.

"That feels fantastic. Don't stop," she murmured.

"I had no intention."

This was progress. They were in her hotel room. She was letting him give her a back massage. When he'd first met Maggie, he didn't know if she would ever allow him this much intimacy.

Just when he thought she'd gone to sleep, she raised up. Her eyes were half-veiled as she gazed at him. "Now it's your turn. Lie down on the other bed."

He wasn't going to say no to that.

Afraid to break the enchantment, he did her bidding.

At the first touch of her hands, he didn't think he could refrain from turning over and pulling her into his arms. He'd been burning up with fire for her since they'd met.

But he wanted their first time to be when she didn't have one other thing on her mind or in her heart but him. That day was coming. He could feel it.

Exercising the kind of self-control he didn't know he possessed, he lay there and soaked in the pleasure her fingers gave him as they worked their magic. His mind began to drift. He thought of the years and years of joy ahead of them. Love. Babies.

Their babies would grow up playing with his baby brother. Jared would be an uncle. A very young uncle. Jake smiled as oblivion took over. He knew nothing else until the ringing of a phone brought him awake.

Disoriented, he turned over, surprised to realize he'd

been asleep. There was no Maggie. He reached for the hotel-room phone and put the receiver to his ear.

"Hello?"

"Jake? The family's arrived. We're all in Mom and Dad's suite. Come on down as fast as you can."

"I'll be right there."

CORD STOOD NEXT TO MAGGIE. "Is Jake coming?"

"In a minute."

"I want to shake that man's hand. He's given Mom and Dad back their life."

If the family's elation could be converted to electricity, it would light up a major city. Katy and Brock were acting crazy, running around giggling.

Kit and Julie were seated on one of the beds across from Maggie's mom. The three of them were talking a mile a minute. A light radiated from Ellen's face. She looked more beautiful than Maggie had ever seen her.

Ben and her father had their heads together laughing animatedly like neither of them had done in their lives. The body language of both men was different. Her dad seemed as energized and youthful as his first-born son.

Cord slid his arm around her shoulders. "That's quite a sight isn't it?" he murmured. His voice was full of emotion.

Maggie turned to him and they hugged. "It's too wonderful. I just wish Mr. Markham would call back."

"He will. Even if he doesn't, we'll find her first thing in the morning." Cord rocked her back and forth. "You're the heroine in this family, Maggie. Deny it all you want, but once my wedding was over, you didn't let anything stop you.

"That great brain of yours came up with the idea to hire a genealogist. Without your drive—well, I don't even want to think about it. Your phone call to Mom and Dad changed our lives in an instant. We never have to go back to that dark place again."

"It was dark," she cried softly. "I just didn't realize to what degree until now."

Her brother's body shook with silent sobs. She patted his back. "Let all that guilt go now, Cord. Live the life you were meant to live. Hire someone to run Renaissance House. Become the rancher you always wanted to be. Kit's so in love with you, she would follow you anywhere."

"I know she would, but to tell you the truth, I'm so happy I can't think yet."

"I know what you— Oh, I heard a knock. I'll get it."

She eased away and hurried to the door. It didn't matter how many times she saw Jake's rugged face, that powerful physique, her reaction was the same. When their eyes met, her heart melted.

"Come in, Jake."

The whole family must have realized he'd arrived because they all converged on him at the same time, even the children. Maggie stood apart, watching a group of people trying to convey their gratitude to this extraordinary man responsible for restoring Kathryn to them.

Her mom held on to him, consumed once more in joyous tears. She looked so cute and little compared to the tall men surrounding her, all of whom were broken up, even Jake.

Kit and Julie noticed Maggie and put their arms around her. The three of them clung. It was in this condition Maggie's cell phone rang. She broke free of the girls to pick it up from the table. When she saw Mr. Markham's name, she handed it to her father.

"You talk to him, Dad."

He kissed her cheek. "Thanks, honey."

Everyone found a place to sit. Jake came to stand by her.

Their conversation was surprisingly short. He hung up, then glanced at Maggie's mother. "Mr. Markham doesn't have a phone number for her." Everyone moaned, including Maggie. "She promised to give it to him when she bought a cell phone, but he hasn't heard from her yet. Since he has a lot to tell us, he's going to drive up from Racine right now."

"That's wonderful. I'm dying to talk to him."

"He should be here within a half hour. Why don't we all go downstairs and have something to eat while we wait for him."

"Goody!" Katy cried out in delight.

Jake's gaze swerved to Maggie. "My sentiments exactly. I'm hungriest when I'm happy."

Maggie filed that choice bit of information for future reference. They followed everyone out the door to the elevator. Jake held her back for the next one.

"Quick, before someone sees us." He grasped her shoulders and gave her a long, passion-filled kiss. "That's for leaving me alone."

On a ragged breath she said, "You were sleeping so soundly, I couldn't bring myself to wake you up."

"I'm awake now."

When the elevator doors opened again, Maggie swayed on her way inside. Thankfully Jake had his arm around her waist to hold her up, but he didn't try to kiss her again because there were other hotel guests going down.

The family had found a corner in the dining room where three tables had been put together. Cord motioned Maggie over to his end. Kit beamed at Jake. "When Kathryn meets you and learns what you did, you're going to have a friend for life."

Jake helped to seat Maggie, then sat down. "I was just thinking that after your unique experience, you and Kathryn will have more in common than anyone else. Both of you were denied your birthrights all these years. Who better for her to relate to than you?"

Kit nodded. "She'll love her family on sight, but she'll still need time to process everything." Her gaze traveled to Maggie. "I haven't had a chance until now to thank you for the sheets and the champagne a little elf left at our house."

Maggie grinned. "How about that welcome-home sign?"

"We told Brock we were going to leave it up indefinitely," Cord interjected. "It makes us feel like we're on a constant honeymoon."

"None of us could tell," Maggie ribbed him.

"I thought the stash of Dom Pérignon in the attic might have something to do with that."

Cord flashed Jake a smile. "Living in the cottage has its benefits."

Katy had been listening to everything. "Did you and Kit see the garden Daddy dug?"

"We did, darling," Kit assured her. "It was one of our favorite wedding presents. I can't wait to start planting. Do you want to come with me to pick out daffodil bulbs?"

"I want to come, too!" Brock chimed in.

"You can both help me."

As Jake sent Maggie a secret smile, her father got to his feet to greet the man in a light blue business suit who'd come over to the table. They shook hands before he said, "Family, this is Charles Markham."

The older man nodded and sat down between Maggie's mom and dad. He pulled an envelope from his pocket, then cleared his throat.

"When Anna came to my office last time, she brought two pictures, which I gave to the FBI. These are copies. The first one is Anna's high school graduation picture. The second one is an old photo of Jan and Marie Skwars Buric with their grandsons Antonin and Franz. The back of it indicates they were ten and twelve at the time. I'll pass them around."

Maggie noticed everyone had stopped eating. This was going to be her parents' first glimpse of Kathryn.

"Oh Reed—" her mom cried. "Look! She's the image of Ben and Maggie at that age."

"She's got Cord's nose and your beautiful bone structure, Ellen."

"Genes don't lie, do they?" Mr. Markham commented kindly.

Maggie's eyes dimmed to watch her parents kiss and embrace each other while they rhapsodized over the tangible evidence of their precious daughter's likeness.

Jake's arm had gone around the back of Maggie's chair. He squeezed her shoulder as if he knew how impatient she was to see it. In all honesty, she had to admire the family's restraint while they waited for it to be passed around.

The picture of the Burics reached her first. Together she and Jake studied it. Franz and Antonin didn't look that much alike.

She handed it to Kit who gazed at it for a long time. Cord finally took it from her fingers to study, then he gave it to Ben.

The family had now seen the faces of both Buric brothers responsible for a twenty-six-year-old nightmare.

Mr. Markham got up from his chair. "I've put in a phone call to FBI agents Polk and Davis, letting them know of this miraculous event. They'll be in touch with you tomorrow.

"Never in all my years of practice have I handled a case like this. My heart went out to Anna when she told me her story. She's a strong, courageous and remarkable young woman. I've decided to let her tell it to you. She'll want to talk.

"I have to admit I hoped that if she'd been kidnapped, and her birth family was found, they would be her equal. After meeting you, I realize you're exceptional. She's going to be the happiest girl in the world.

"I'll say good-night, but not goodbye. I'm sure we'll be talking to each other again soon."

While Maggie's parents walked him out, she buried her face against Jake's shoulder. Finally it was their turn to look at Kathryn's picture.

Maggie gasped at the strong likeness to the family.

"No wonder everyone at the farm stared at you today," Jake murmured near her ear. "You could almost be twins."

"It's incredible... Oh Jake—I can't wait for morning to come."

CHAPTER THIRTEEN

"JAKE?"

The frantic tone in Maggie's voice alarmed him. She hadn't said good morning first. He'd been up for an hour waiting to hear from her. In that time he'd had breakfast and had read the paper.

"What's wrong?"

"Kathryn withdrew from her classes at the university over a week ago. She gave up her room at the dorm. No one knows where she is!"

How could this have happened after everything they'd been through? "Where are you now?"

"In Mom and Dad's room. I went downstairs early to be with them when they talked to her for the first time. Dad started phoning at eight and learned the awful news.

"Oh, Jake—my parents are beside themselves. No one Dad talked to in the student housing can recall dealing with her. They suggested he check with the supervisor, but it seems she has the day off to attend a wedding in Ludington. Her cell phone's turned off. We'll have to wait until tomorrow to talk to her."

Hell.

"I can't believe this has happened, Jake. Not now." Her voice shook. He felt it shake him. "I should never have phoned my parents until I'd actually laid eyes on Kathryn," she cried out in pain. "You can't imagine the fragile state they're in."

Actually Jake could, because he knew how *he* felt.

"There has to be a good reason she would do such a thing, Maggie. We just have to find out what it is.

"I've got an idea. Why don't you get your brothers together. We'll go to the building where she was living and talk to every student. Since she looks like you, surely someone she befriended will remember her and tell us where she went."

"I knew you'd come up with something to save the day."

He could only hope.

"Tell you what. I'll meet you downstairs in the lobby, and we'll go over to the campus. This may end up being an all-day thing with students coming and going from classes. Have you eaten yet?"

"Yes. The folks ordered a big breakfast for all of us. It included you when you were ready to come down."

"I've already eaten, and I'm glad you have, too. Let's get going."

"Jake?"

"Yes?" He was waiting to hear her say three little words.

"Thank you from the bottom of my heart. It seems that's all I ever say to you."

He agreed. It was time she said something else. Something he was dying to hear. He'd thought he was getting closer to that supreme moment, but this latest news about Kathryn…

"When we find her, then I'll tell you you're welcome. See you in a minute."

Within five, Maggie and her brothers had joined him out in front of the inn. He groaned inwardly to see the difference in their countenances from the night before.

Their eyes looked haunted, especially Maggie's because he knew she felt responsible for informing her family prematurely about Kathryn. Jake hugged her while Ben found them a taxi. The way she clung to him was the only good thing about the day so far.

When they reached the student housing area, Cord told the driver to take them to building B. "Her room was number twenty."

It turned out there were four floors of ten rooms each. Ben had brought the picture of Kathryn with them. "Cord and I will canvass the two bottom floors."

"Come on, Maggie. We'll cover the top ones." Cupping her elbow, they took the elevator to the third floor and started knocking on doors. Some students were still there. One or two remembered seeing Anna, but no one could shed any light on why she'd moved out.

The fourth floor didn't produce results, either. No students had seen her leave with her things.

Maggie's face looked ashen by the time they met up with her brothers outside the building. If they'd had any good news, they would have called her on their cell phones before now.

"How many doors did you knock on with no response?"

"Half of them," Cord muttered.

Jake nodded. "That was the same for us. Under the

circumstances, why don't we wait out here in the parking lot and question anyone who drives up."

"I was just going to suggest it," Ben commented.

Maggie bit her lip. "I'll phone Josef and Milena. I've got their number. Maybe they've heard from Kathryn in the last eighteen hours."

Jake squeezed the back of her neck gently. "Good idea."

While her brothers vetted students they hadn't talked to before, Jake listened to her conversation with Milena. It ended with tears rolling down Maggie's cheeks. Damn.

She shook her head at Jake. "Milena's in shock. She has absolutely no idea what's happened to Kathryn, but she's going to inform everyone on the farm. If anyone has any news, they'll call us."

He wiped the moisture away with his thumb. "Don't despair, Maggie. We'll find her."

"If I didn't believe that, I'd want to die."

Jake hadn't been expecting that remark. Even if she didn't really mean it, it terrified him.

"I promised Mom and Dad we'd check in." She got on her cell phone once more. In a few seconds, the tears flowed harder than ever. Cord eyed her grimly before his bleak gaze met Jake's in silent misery.

For the next hour they continued to talk to anyone who drove up. Jake kept his arm around Maggie. She'd gone quiet on him.

Another car pulled into the parking area. He watched Ben and Cord approach the driver. Their conversation was just out of earshot. Suddenly they came running.

"She doesn't know why Anna checked out of school.

The last time she saw her, Anna had just bought a used car like that student's Nissan. They chatted about what good cars they were. Then Anna drove off."

"Milena never said anything about Kathryn having a car," Maggie said. "She could be anywhere by now!"

At this point her brothers looked genuinely alarmed. Cord hugged Maggie to him to comfort her.

"I'll call a taxi to take us back to the hotel," Ben muttered.

"While you do that, I've got a call of my own to make." Walking a few steps away from them, Jake phoned Agent Lewis in New York.

"Hey, Jake? What's up?"

"You don't want to know about it."

"Uh-oh. How can I help?"

"We found Anna Buric."

"You mean her body?"

"No, thank God. She's alive and well. At least she was at last count. Now she's disappeared on us again. We've been told she bought a used Nissan sometime in the last two and a half weeks.

"Can you get a person in Wisconsin motor vehicles to give you her license plate number and anything else you can find out? She presumably listed her campus dorm at the University of Wisconsin-Milwaukee as her address. If not, she would have put Skwars Farm, Caledonia, Wisconsin." He spelled it for him.

"This is a life-and-death situation, Lewis. The Mc-Farland family has waited twenty-six hellish years for this moment. They're about to fall apart if they don't lay eyes on their daughter ASAP."

"I'll get right on it and phone you back the second I have the information."

"Thanks."

By the time Jake clicked off, he could see the taxi headed their way.

"How's Kamila?" Maggie asked after he'd climbed in the back seat next to her. Cord sat on her other side and Ben was up front.

"I didn't phone her," he said in a voice for her ears alone. "I'm working on something that should give us answers soon."

Maggie gripped his hand with more strength than she knew. As long as she kept reaching for him, that was all he could ask right now.

When they returned to the McFarlands' suite and related the latest news, Maggie's father thanked them profusely for their help. "The only thing we can do now is wait to talk to that supervisor."

Jake kept his own counsel. He was counting on Lewis to pull through for him.

"Maybe she decided she didn't want to go to school yet and took off on a big trip," Brock theorized.

Ben tousled his hair. "I think you may be right, son."

His comment triggered a new volley of conversation about it being a real possibility. But Maggie didn't contribute. She sat on the love seat next to Jake, still clutching his hand tightly.

Julie ordered lunch for her children and asked if anyone else wanted something. No one did.

"Maggie?" Jake whispered. "I'm going down the hall for a soda. Do you want one?"

"No, thank you."

"I'll be right back."

She lifted tear-drenched eyes to him. "Hurry."

"You won't even have time to miss me." He gave her fingers a little squeeze before leaving the room.

Once outside the door, he phoned Lewis back. The moment the agent answered, Jake blurted, "Can you find out if Anna withdrew a large sum of money from her bank account?"

"Hang on, Jake. I've got another call coming in. This might be what you're looking for."

Perspiration beaded Jake's face as he waited.

"Bingo! She was involved in a serious car accident."

Dear Lord.

"There were ambulances on the scene. The other driver was cited for running a red light. Both drivers were taken to local hospitals in the Milwaukee area."

"Do you know which one?"

"No."

"I'll find out. You do great work. The next time I'm in New York, I'm taking you out for a steak dinner."

"I'm going to hold you to that."

Before Jake told the family anything, he needed to find out the seriousness of Kathryn's condition. And before that, he had to discover which hospital she'd been taken to.

He phoned information and asked for the closest hospital to the university. He'd start there and keep going until he'd found her.

There were two near the campus. His first call produced no results.

On his second, he hit the jackpot. "Ms. Buric is in room W356—that's in the rehabilitation wing." Rehabilitation? "Shall I put you through?"

"No. I'd like the three-west nursing station please."

"One moment and I'll connect you."

"This is three-west. Clerk speaking."

"I'm calling to inquire about the status of Anna Buric's condition."

"Are you a family member?"

I'm going to be.

"Yes. This is Josef Buric, her guardian. I just found out she was in a serious auto accident."

"She was. Her leg was broken in two places, but she's coming along fine."

A broken leg. What beautiful news.

"That's good to hear."

"I'm glad you called. She could use some cheering up. Being new to Milwaukee, she's had no visitors."

She was going to have them now.

"Tell her the family will be coming to see her in the next little while."

"I will."

He clicked off.

Anna Buric was in for the surprise of her life.

The second he knocked on the hotel-room door, Maggie answered it. She noticed his empty hands. "I thought you went to get a soda."

"I lied."

He saw the sudden recognition in her startled eyes before he looked past her to her family.

"Listen up, everybody. I've located Kathryn. She was

in a car accident and is in the Milwaukee West Hospital recovering from a broken leg. I just spoke to the clerk on her floor. She's in W356.

"The only way I could get information out of her was to lie and say that I was her guardian Josef Buric calling. The clerk said Anna hadn't had any visitors. I told her the family would be right over."

The room exploded with their joyous cries, but nothing compared to the feel of Maggie's arms crushing him to death.

A DARK HEAD POKED around the door of Anna's room. "Hi! Are you up for some visitors?"

Anna put down the fascinating book she was reading on Katharine Graham of the *Washington Post,* and stared at the clerk. "Who would want to visit me, Betsy? I don't know anyone here yet."

"These are your Buric relatives."

She blinked. "How did they find out I was here? I didn't want to bother them."

"I don't know, but they've come. There are a whole bunch of them.

Betsy didn't know the half of it. If they'd all arrived en masse, the hospital wouldn't have had room to contain them.

Touched as she was that they'd driven all this way, Anna wished they hadn't. For the whole of her life, the family had been forced to take care of her. Now that she was on her own, she prided herself on being independent.

Josef and Milena must have tried to reach her at student housing and found out what had happened from the supervisor.

"Don't let them in yet. Will you hand me my crutches? I don't want to be in bed."

Betsy brought the crutches over to Anna. Once she had made it to the chair she said, "Would you roll my hospital table over here? I want to brush my hair and put on some lipstick."

She was glad she'd already gotten dressed in her khaki skirt and coffee-toned blouse for her therapy. Until the cast came off, skirts were her salvation.

"There. I'm as ready as I'll ever be while I'm in this cast." *I want the family to see that I'm just fine.* They didn't need to worry about her any longer.

"You look beautiful. If it weren't for that cast, no one would ever know you'd been in an accident."

"Thanks, Betsy."

"I mean it," she said, wheeling the table back to the bed. "Between you and me, you come from an incredibly attractive family." *What?* "They all look alike, and they all look like you."

Anna frowned. "You think I look like them?"

"Are you blind, girl? I'll tell them they can come in."

"Wait—will you hand me my book, please?" Anna didn't want them to think she lay around all day feeling sorry for herself.

"Here you go. Enjoy your visit."

To her surprise, Agent Polk and Agent Davis came in first. "Hi." They smiled at her.

"Hi. The clerk didn't tell me you were out there, too."

"We didn't tell her."

Anna checked them out. She supposed they were attractive for men in their fifties, but they certainly didn't resemble her. What on earth had Betsy been babbling about?

"I hope you didn't influence Josef and Milena to stop by to see me."

They both drew up a chair and sat down. "Josef and Milena aren't the ones out in the hall dying to come in."

Something about their demeanor raised the hairs on the back of her neck. "You found my birth parents?" Her voice wobbled.

"Yes."

Anna averted her eyes. "I—I don't know if I want to see them. He's a criminal. They never once came to see me at the farm." She shook her head. "My parents abandoned me. Now I'm not ready to see them."

"They didn't abandon you," Agent Polk replied. "You were stolen from them by Antonin Buric."

The blood pounded in her ears. "You mean I was really kidnapped?"

"For a reason we still don't know, he took you clear across the country to his grandmother's house in New York and left you with her. The woman who was with him could have been his wife, but it was probably a girlfriend."

Her thoughts were reeling. "When you say clear across the country—"

"You were born in Salt Lake City, Utah, on April second, twenty-six years ago," Agent Davis broke in. "You're the daughter of Reed and Ellen McFarland. You have a brother Ben who's thirty-five and married with two children. You also have a brother Cord, thirty-three, who just recently married, and you have an unmarried sister, Maggie, who's four years older than you."

Anna started to tremble and couldn't stop. It was too much to comprehend. "What's my real name?"

"Kathryn Cordell McFarland. K-a-t-h-r-y-n."

"Kathryn?" she mouthed her name incredulously.

"Your great-great-great-grandfather John McFarland was Utah's Copper King, the famous mining magnate. He was one of the wealthiest men in America.

"Reed McFarland, your father, now holds that distinction. Until recently he was a four-term U.S. senator. You may have heard of him."

Senator McFarland was her father? Anna's eyes rounded in astonishment.

"You were born in a French-styled mansion on South Temple John had built for his wife. It was one of four homes he owned in London, Paris and Rome. Today it's a shelter for homeless women called Renaissance House, which is your brother Cord's brainchild."

Agent Polk leaned forward and handed her a brochure. "If you have any doubt at all that your birth parents haven't grieved for you, then this should dispel it."

She took the brochure from him and began reading.

Welcome to the Kathryn McFarland
National Foundation
Located in the McFarland Plaza on South Temple
in Salt Lake City, Utah.
This Web site is updated daily
May 3 marks the twenty-sixth anniversary of the ab-

duction of our fourth child, Kathryn McFarland, from the McFarland home in Salt Lake City, Utah. Born April 2, she'd only been a month old at the time she was taken.

Soon after the kidnapping and community search, the Kathryn McFarland Foundation was founded and now honors Kathryn's memory by finding missing children and preventing others from going missing in the first place.

When Kathryn was kidnapped, our community and many others joined together to help us find her because there was an immediate recognition that she was everyone's child and—

The words started blurring together. Anna couldn't read for the tears. She wiped them away madly, trying to make out the rest.

All too often it is only a matter of hours before a kidnapper commits an act of violence against the child. That is why we're pleased that the U.S. Senate has acted to pass legislation creating a national AMBER Alert system, which galvanizes entire communities to assist law enforcement in the timely search for and safe return of child victims.

Since its inception, the foundation has assisted approximately 17,000 families, as well as law-enforcement agencies in their searches. We have seen over 85% of those children returned home safely. This is what continues to give us hope.

Her gaze dropped to the picture. She studied each face hungrily. No wonder Betsy had said what she did.

Euphoric, Anna cried out, *"That's my family!"*

"Yes." The agents nodded. Their eyes were wet. "Are you all right?"

"Y-Yes," she said between sobs. "It's just so much to absorb."

"That's why we told your family we'd prepare you first."

"I want to see them!"

"We're right here, darling girl."

Anna's head swiveled around. Her mother and father came rushing toward her with tears streaming down their faces, just the way she'd always fantasized in her dreams.

It dawned on her then that what Helen Keller had once said was true. *The best and most beautiful things in the world cannot be seen or even touched. They must be felt with the heart.*

In Anna's heart, she'd always known them. Now they had faces and bodies that looked like hers.

When their arms closed around her, she felt at rest. She knew she'd come home.

"Our precious baby." Her mother wept.

Her father's arms encircled both of them while he sobbed.

Anna sobbed with them. With each heave of her body, she felt the years of pain, loneliness…the heartache, wash away.

"I belong to you. I can't believe it. I always longed for my mother and father."

"You've got us forever, honey." Her father kissed her repeatedly.

Her mother cupped her face so she could really look at her. "Do you want us to call you Anna?"

"No—" she blurted without hesitation. "That's not my name. I want the name you gave me."

"Kathryn, darling," her mother cried. "You've come home to us. I've ached for you all these years. There's always been a hole in my heart. My dear little baby. You've grown up to be so beautiful."

"That's the truth."

Her parents made way for her blond brother to embrace her. "I'm Ben. Welcome home, little sister. Haven't seen you for a long time."

His remark made her laugh in spite of her tears. Soon her brown-haired brother had joined them.

"I'm Cord, and you're a sight for sore eyes. How come you had to go and break your leg at a time like this?"

She laughed and broke down all over again, so happy and excited she couldn't formulate words.

"You've got a sister, too," her father said. "Come here, Maggie."

The one member of the family who looked the most like Kathryn moved from behind their brothers and reached for her. "Thank God you're home at last," Maggie said in a voice full of emotion.

Anna squeezed her around the neck. "That's what I'm doing. Thanking Him and thanking Him."

"I've missed you, Kathryn. When I was little and had tea parties, I'd always save a place for you."

Kathryn hugged her harder. "I used to pretend I had a younger sister, and I would read her stories for hours and hours."

They laughed and cried once more until Maggie said, "The rest of the family is waiting to meet you." She kissed Kathryn's cheek before backing away.

Another lovely blond woman took Maggie's place. "I'm Julie, Ben's wife." She put her arms around her and whispered, "He was nine when you were taken, just old enough to feel guilty he didn't hear anyone come in the mansion and take you from your crib.

"You have no idea what this day means to him—to all of us. I've never been so happy in my life, either." She sniffed. "Brock? Katy? Come here. Meet your aunt Kathryn."

Kathryn watched her blond niece and nephew move closer. They were darling. "The clerk told me my family looked like each other, and that I looked like them. It's really true. Can I have a hug?"

Without hesitation, their young arms went around her neck.

"Does your leg hurt?" Katy asked.

"It did at first, but not now."

Brock studied her intently. "Did you know you were kidnapped?"

"Not until a few minutes ago."

"Whoa. Do you feel funny?"

"I should, but I don't."

"That's what Aunt Kit said."

"Kit?"

"I'm Kit, Cord's wife," said the attractive brunette woman standing behind the children. "Twenty-six years ago, I was kidnapped by the same men who kidnapped you. I know how you're feeling right now, because I was only united with my birth parents two months ago."

"You, too?" she whispered.

The children nodded.

Kathryn looked at Katy. "All my life I've dreamed that I had this fabulous, wonderful family out there somewhere who missed me and loved me. But for some reason they didn't know where I was. I prayed and prayed they'd find me."

Tears choked her up once more. "Today my prayers came true." She put her hand over her heart. "In here, it all feels right."

Katy held on to Kathryn's hand. "You're pretty like Aunt Maggie."

"And you're beautiful just like your mom."

Her little face broke out in a huge smile. "Have you got a boyfriend?"

"Not yet."

"How soon can you come home with us?"

"Today!" her father declared. "Just as soon as we can find the doctor to release her."

"You'll love living with Grandma and Grandpa," Brock confided. "They have a pool. When you get your cast off, we'll come over and swim with you."

"I'd love that."

Katy cocked her head. "Do you like ant farms?"

Kathryn chuckled. "I lived on a giant one."

Both children's eyes rounded. "You did?"

Maggie's amused glance met Kathryn's. "Your aunt was raised on a fruit farm near here."

"What kind of fruit?"

"Apples, pears, cherries, peaches, strawberries. People from all over Wisconsin come there to buy produce. A lot of families pick their own."

Katy looked at her mother. "I wish we could do that."

"Could you eat all you wanted?" Brock asked.

Kathryn couldn't help laughing. "I could, but I wouldn't have felt very well. You see my job on the farm was to cook fruit pastry we sold at the bakery."

"You worked in a bakery?" Brock cried. "So did Aunt Kit! She used to bake cakes in hotels and decorate them."

Kathryn glanced at Kit. "Sounds like you and I have a lot in common already."

Her sister-in-law smiled. "Probably more than we know. Some day when we have time, we'll have to compare notes."

"Will you make that pastry for us?" Katy asked.

"I'd love to."

"Can we help?" Brock wanted to know.

"When Kathryn's cast comes off, we'll all help," Kathryn's mother chimed in. She bent over and kissed her again. "Until then, we're going to wait on her."

"Is it pie? My daddy loves pie." Katy's thoughts were still on food. She was adorable.

"Kind of. In the Czech Republic it's served at wedding feasts."

"Where's that?"

The whole family chuckled

"That's a country in Europe. The people who raised me are called Czechs."

Brock's mind was working it out. "What language do they speak?"

"Czech."

"What's their name?"

"The immigrant who started the farm was called Jainos Skwars."

Both children frowned at the odd sound of it.

"Marie Skwars, his sister, was the one who took me to the farm after I was kidnapped by her grandson. Her last name was Buric."

"Do you speak that language?"

"Yes."

"Say something."

Maggie put her hands on their shoulders. "If you children want to hear a conversation in Czech, then we need Jake to jump in here." Kathryn watched her glance at the rugged, dark-haired male standing in the background.

"Kathryn? Meet Jake Halsey, the man who found you," her voice trembled. "Without him, this day might never have happened. Come here, Jake."

Kathryn studied both of them. They had the look of a couple deeply in love, like Nelly and Miki. The signs were unmistakable.

"*Dobre den,* Jake."

"*Dobre jitro. Tesi me,* Kathryn. *Vitame vas.*"

"*Dekuji.*"

Continuing in Czech, Jake said, "I guess you don't have to be told how overjoyed your family is to have you restored to them."

"I'm the one who's overjoyed. How can I ever thank you for making all our dreams come true?"

"You already have with your smiling eyes and face. Though you're going to hear this from the others, I'm going to tell you something now. It was Maggie who came to the genealogical firm where I work for help in solving your case. Like the rest of the family, her whole life has been devoted to finding you.

"I'm in awe of their great strength and unwavering faith. They always believed you were alive. Now that I've met you and learned a little about your courage and determination, I can see that you're made from the same great McFarland mold. It's a pleasure and a privilege to meet you at last. Do you mind if I give you a hug?"

"If it weren't for this leg, I'd have hugged you first."

He bent down and put his arms around her. "As you're going to find out, you belong to the greatest family there is."

"Whoa, Jake. What were you and Aunt Kathryn saying? That sounded cool."

He stood up and ruffled Brock's hair. "Stuff."

Kathryn took pity on her nephew. "It takes longer to say things in Czech," she teased. "What Jake told me was that I'm the luckiest person in the world to belong to this family, but I already know that."

"Great news," her father said, breezing back in the room with an illuminating smile. "You've been released to our care, Kathryn. We can go home." He rushed to her side. "How does that sound to you, honey?"

She looked from her dad to her mom, who'd taken hold of her hand. "I've been ready to go back for twenty-six years. Can we get a plane reservation this fast?"

"We have our own plane," Katy piped up.

Their own plane…

She belonged to a family who had their own plane? None of it had sunk in yet. Not really.

"I've never been on one before."

"You're kidding!" the children exclaimed.

"Nope. I've never done a lot of things."

"Like what?"

"Go to the ocean."

"You've never seen it?" Brock was incredulous.

"It's hard to believe, isn't it? I only took my first ferry ride across Lake Michigan a week ago."

"I've never done that," he said quietly.

"What do you want to do the very mostest?"

She hugged Katy around the waist. "Learn how to ski."

Ben flashed her a grin. "You're our sister, all right."

"Uncle Cord will teach you," Brock informed her. "His house is in Alta."

Kathryn's gaze flew to her brother's in shock. "You live in *Alta?*" Her voice came out more like a squeak.

He eyed her curiously. "That's right. At the top of Little Cottonwood Canyon in the Albion Basin, the most beautiful spot in the world. Our great-great-great-grandfather must have thought so, too, because he bought the land the second he saw it."

An anxious look crossed over her mother's face. "Darling—what's wrong? I felt you shiver just now."

Suddenly the whole family was staring at Kathryn with concern.

"You're not going to believe me when I tell you."

CHAPTER FOURTEEN

"KAMILA?" JAKE CALLED OUT quietly in case the baby was asleep. "I'm home."

She walked in the kitchen to greet him. "I'm so glad you're back."

He gave her a hug. "Me, too. Where's my little brother?"

"I put him down about twenty minutes ago. I thought you'd bring Maggie in with you."

"I would have, but the whole family will be arriving on the company plane any minute now. Her mother asked her to hurry to the house and get the bedroom on the main floor ready for Kathryn."

"Why didn't you go with her and help?"

He grimaced. "She didn't ask me."

"Did you offer?"

"No. Their family just got Kathryn back. Maggie's in as much of a daze as the rest of them."

Kamila shook her head. "You're the one who's in the daze, Jake. Why are you being so stubborn? What are you afraid of?"

His jaw hardened. "I'd rather not talk about it."

"That was a Robert Halsey remark if I ever heard one, and I'm not going to let you get away with it."

He couldn't handle the kind of conversation Kamila had in mind right now. Picking up his suitcase, he walked through the house to his bedroom. En route he passed the study.

She'd left on the TV. There was a picture of Maggie's parents on the screen.

"Good grief—it's made the news already. No doubt the hospital couldn't resist leaking it to the press."

"It's huge news, Jake. Since five o'clock, Kathryn's story has been on every channel. They've shown footage from twenty-six years ago. It would have broken your heart to watch."

"The media can't leave it alone."

"That's the kind of world we live in. You sound exhausted. Why don't you take a shower while I fix you something to eat."

"I'm not hungry."

By the time he reached his room, he realized he'd taken out his foul mood on Kamila. Dumping his suitcase on the bed, he retraced his steps to the study.

"Kamila? Forgive me for being rude just now. There's no excuse."

She eyed him from the couch. "A Halsey in a state of undeclared love is worse than a woman scorned."

He shut off the TV with the remote and sank down in the chair next to the coffee table. "The McFarland family is an exclusive club."

"You think you're not welcome?"

"No. That's not the problem. It's Maggie. Her instinct to sacrifice herself for them puts distance between us, a distance she doesn't see."

"In other words you're hurt that you're not the whole focus of her life."

"I didn't say that."

"You didn't have to. If you weren't in so much pain, you'd see the irony here and laugh."

"What do you mean?"

"In the past you've always run a mile from women who needed you to validate their existence. Don't you know you're a man who comes across as bigger than life? It's possible Maggie is afraid she doesn't measure up."

"Maggie?" he cried out. "You have to be joking."

"Not at all. Does she know you were married to Barb for two years?"

"Yes. What does that have to do with anything?"

"Possibly everything."

"You've lost me."

"In Maggie's eyes, a bigger-than-life guy had to be married to a bigger-than-life woman, right? That's what I thought after I met your father."

"You did?"

"Oh, Jake. Let me explain this from a woman's point of view. My point of view at least. I assumed that any man as attractive as he was, who'd remained a widower all those years, had to still be in love with his wife's memory."

Kamila had just grabbed his attention.

"But unlike aggressive me, who has never known loss of any kind until your father died," she continued, "Maggie's family history has made her emotionally cautious to the extreme. She needs help. What have you done for her in that department?"

He stared at Kamila. Her insight into human nature staggered him.

His mind flashed back to a certain conversation that night in the Uintas when Maggie had asked him if he'd loved his wife terribly. When he remembered his honest answer to her, he shot to his feet and smacked his palm with his fist.

Instead of reassuring her that he was eager to know that kind of love again and build a new life with someone else, he'd rolled away from her so he wouldn't be tempted to get physical with her before she was ready.

"Your father played hot and cold with me until I almost began to believe he was the kind who would always enjoy the chase, but not the kill."

"How did you bring him to his knees?"

"I called him at Steiner's to say goodbye. He didn't know it was from Mrs. Strom's apartment across the hall. I told him I'd decided to go back to Warsaw with Rayna, and we were getting ready to call for a taxi.

"She'd already left for the airport of course, but I didn't tell him that. Without giving him a chance to say anything, I hung up. That began the waiting game from the crack in Mrs. Strom's door. If he didn't come to the apartment to stop me, then I'd determined to leave Prague with Rayna."

Jake began to chuckle.

"My heart almost failed me when he suddenly came running down the hall and beat on our door. When no one answered, I heard some amazing new words come out of him. Finally I took pity on him and said, 'Just kidding.'

"When he turned around and saw me, he was angry.

But his eyes said something else. That's when I knew I had him."

"You had him all right. When I got home from class that day he was whistling like crazy."

She smiled. "That was the day we worked everything out. So what I'm trying to say is, why don't you let this be the night *you* work everything out with Maggie."

"This is their family's night, Kamila."

"So? Go barge in. Why do you think the notion of the knight on the white horse coming to rescue the fair damsel has persisted through the ages? Beneath all those layers that make Maggie McFarland such a fascinating woman, lives a very vulnerable female who needs reassurance.

"Let her know she's the bigger-than-life woman in your life now. Don't leave her in any doubt. A woman likes to know a man will walk through fire for her."

"Like breaching the walls of the McFarland battlements," he murmured.

Her eyes lit up. "Exactly."

Jake liked the idea of that picture a lot.

"Thanks for helping me get my head on straight, Kamila. I'm going to take a shower."

"And then?"

She must have driven his father nuts. "And then I'm going to do what I've been wanting to do for a long time."

MAGGIE DASHED UPSTAIRS for the floor lamp in her childhood bedroom. It would be the perfect height for Kathryn when she wanted to sit in a chair to read.

She pulled the plug from the socket, then picked up

the lamp and started across the room with it. But to her surprise she was met by both brothers before she reached the door. Even more puzzling was the fact that they'd closed it behind them.

"What are you guys doing up here?"

"We thought this would be the best place to talk in private." Ben took the lamp from her and set it by the wall.

"But Kathryn—"

"Kathryn's busy looking at her baby book with Mom and Dad," Cord informed her. "And once she's finished with that, they've got a ton of scrapbooks to pore over. They're in heaven and don't know anyone else exists right now. Everyone else is in the pool."

"Then what's wrong?"

"Plenty," Ben muttered, "and you know it. Sit down, Maggie. You're like a squirrel running up and down a tree, always in motion."

She chose to remain standing. "I seem to recall a time not too long ago when you were guilty of the same thing."

"You're right, and it almost cost me my family. But I wised up before it was too late."

"Too late? What are you talking about?"

"Jake," Cord stated baldly. "Where is he?"

"At his apartment."

"Whose idea was that?"

"It wasn't an idea. I dropped him off on the way home from the airport."

Ben folded his arms. "Why didn't you bring him to the house?"

"I didn't think he wanted to come. On the flight home

he talked a lot about Kamila and his little brother. I knew he was anxious to see them and make certain everything was all right while he'd been gone."

"You could have waited for him to touch base, and then brought him over here."

"He didn't try to make plans with me, so I assumed he was glad to be back with his family."

"The man's got it bad for you."

"Not that bad, Cord. I've given him chances to make his move."

"When?" Ben demanded.

"When we slept over in the mountains, and when we were in the hotel room in Milwaukee."

"Both times you were on a mission," came his shrewd observation. "A man wants to know he's not going to be disturbed. Now that there's no more mission, what are you going to do about it?"

She stiffened. "I'm not going to do anything. He's leaving in January."

Cord frowned. "So you can't go with him?"

Maggie averted her eyes. "No."

"Why not? Mom's got her baby back. You're free."

"But Jake isn't."

"Bull," Ben blurted. "His wife's been gone too long for him to still be grieving."

"I wasn't talking about his wife."

"His career then," Cord suggested. "You're afraid he'll get killed in the line of duty."

"Yes."

"That's bull, too. Ben and I figured out a long time ago he's no police detective from San Diego. The guy's a lethal weapon with contacts only a few elite people have access to."

Maggie's heart started to race.

"Be assured his secret is safe with us."

She stuck out her McFarland chin. "In that case you'll understand why there's no point to this conversation."

"Tell him you want him to give it up. Maybe all he's waiting for is to hear the words."

"Don't you think I want to beg him to stay in Salt Lake?" she cried.

"Why don't you then?"

"I'm afraid."

"Where's the faith that kept you believing our sister was alive?"

"That was different."

"The hell it is," Ben protested. "You didn't know what the outcome would be, but you never gave up."

"Ben's right," Cord declared. "You've got to fight for your love the same way you fought to find Kathryn."

"But—"

"Now you're sounding like Mom used to sound. No buts, Maggie." Ben had never been so fierce. "Get on the phone and ask Jake to come over for a swim."

"I'm scared."

"We know." Cord smiled before pulling out his cell phone. "What's his number?"

Her brothers weren't about to let her get out of this. "Oh, all right. I'll do it."

"Good." He handed it to her.

Taking a shaky breath, she punched the digits. Her heart was beating so fast, she would probably expire before he answered. When all she got was his voice mail, her disappointment was too great to leave a message.

"He's not answering."

"Maybe he's in the shower. He'll get back to me when he sees my caller ID. You keep the phone. Want to bet he'll be calling within the next five minutes?"

"Cord and I will rustle up some swim trunks for Jake while you change. Meet you at the pool." Ben grabbed the lamp and the two of them disappeared out the door.

Convinced Jake had gone to bed or was watching TV and didn't want to be disturbed, she had no other choice but to join the rest of the family. This was Kathryn's homecoming. Maggie had no desire to spoil it for her.

Quickly she changed into her suit and slipped on a beach robe. Before long, she walked out to the pool where everyone had congregated. Even Steve was here, and he waved to her from the pool. Kit must have called him to come over and meet Kathryn. Though it was only ten-fifteen, the night was still balmy, a perfect time to swim.

Her parents had helped Kathryn onto a lounge chair to support her cast. She could watch the family, and go through picture albums at the same time.

Ten minutes had passed and no phone call. Maggie put Cord's cell phone on the patio table heaped with sandwiches, chips and drinks. He'd lost the bet.

"Come on in, Aunt Maggie!" the children shouted with excitement.

Her brothers had already joined Julie and Kit.

She removed her robe and dove in the deep end. When she surfaced, Brock said, "I'll race you five laps."

"You're on." Her nephew didn't know it but she needed some physical activity to channel the feelings rioting inside her body. Everyone moved to the sides to make room for them.

As Maggie kicked off for the last lap, someone with a steel-like grip caught her by the ankles. It was probably Ben, who'd wanted to give his son the advantage.

She twisted around determined to dunk him. But that wasn't possible because the man holding her fast had hunkered down at the edge of the pool. Since their flight, he'd changed into light gray trousers and a black silk shirt.

"Jake—"

His slow white smile turned her heart over. He still held on to her legs, forcing her to tread water with her arms.

"Hope you don't mind me crashing the party."

"I used Cord's phone to call you to come over, but you didn't answer."

"I saw his caller ID. Since I was on my way here, I figured I'd catch up to him."

Jake had come to the house of his own volition.

"My brothers will lend you a suit."

"They already handed me one. I'll change and be right back."

She watched his powerful frame until he disappeared inside the cabana. When she became cognizant of her surroundings, her brothers shot her a glance that said "We told you so."

"How come you're wearing a T-shirt?"

Trust Katy to ask that question the second Jake reappeared wearing plaid trunks. He had a spectacular physique.

"I had some surgery a while ago, Katy. The scars are still healing."

"Ooh. Do they hurt?"

"Not at all."

"Who's up for a game of water polo?" Cord shouted.

Everyone responded in the affirmative.

"I wish I could play with you," Kathryn called out.

"Don't worry. Your day will come, little sister. Okay, Jake? Why don't you, Steve, Maggie and Brock stand the rest of us."

For the next twenty minutes it was a battle. Maggie had never had so much fun in her life. Jake went at it like a naval destroyer, blowing away the competition. Her brothers put up a mighty struggle, but in the end they were solidly beaten.

When they laughingly called it quits, Maggie swam over to him. "I'm afraid your shoulder's going to be in pain."

His black hair, slicked back by the water, made him look dangerous. And gorgeous. "Actually it was good for me. The more exercise I get, the better it feels. I needed this after the flight."

"So did I." She was winded, but not because of the polo game. "How are Kamila and the baby?"

His dark blue eyes wandered over her facial features. "They're fine."

Maggie clung to the side of the pool. "That's good. If she hadn't been waiting for you, I would have asked you to come home with me."

"They've gone to bed. You can ask me now."

He'd deliberately misconstrued what she'd meant.

The old Maggie would have let it pass, but tonight she needed an answer to a certain question. Before she lost her nerve, she said, "Why don't we both change and leave."

"Your family won't mind?"

She looked beyond him to the patio. "Mom and Dad have already taken Kathryn inside. Things are winding down."

"Then I'll follow you home." He levered himself to the deck and headed for the cabana. Maggie couldn't take her eyes off of him. In a little while they were going to be alone with no possibility of anything or -one disturbing them.

A voluptuous shiver enveloped her body. She swam to the steps and got out of the pool. Everyone had clustered around the table to eat. As she slipped on her beach robe, her eyes met her brothers' questioning glances.

They loved her. She knew that. It was the reason why she flashed them a mysterious smile on her way into the house.

THE CABANA HAD A SHOWER ROOM with every kind of toiletry. Jake took advantage of what was offered. When he'd dressed and emerged minutes later, he felt totally alive and eager to join Maggie. For the first time in their relationship, she'd provided an opening inside that tight circle she'd drawn around herself.

He nodded good-night to the family and strode through the breezeway to his car at the bottom of the drive. Soon her car was backing down to the street. Their eyes met in passing.

Within five minutes they'd reached the plaza and he'd followed her inside her condo. As far as he was concerned, the click of the lock closing out the world had symbolic significance.

One lamp lit her study. She didn't bother to add more light. Her hair was still damp from her shower. She smelled sweet and feminine. In fact, she looked like a bride in her lacy white dress that flounced around her knees. It was the kind bought by tourists in Mexico. Only a tall woman like Maggie should wear one.

She slipped off her sandals and sat on one end of the couch with her golden legs tucked beneath her.

He sat down in the chair closest to her. "Today your lives changed forever," he began.

"Because of you," she whispered.

"Let's agree we both had something to do with finding Kathryn. How does it feel?"

"There aren't any words."

"Tomorrow when you wake up, you're going to wonder what to do with the rest of your life. Have you thought about that?"

She nodded slowly. "I've been doing a lot of thinking. Especially about you."

His heart began to thud. "In what regard?"

"When you came to Salt Lake, you must have wondered how you were going to handle a desk job while you waited to get back to your career. It must have seemed like a penance."

"I won't lie. It did. But all that changed when Wendell introduced me to Margaret McFarland. Because of you, I've discovered there are aspects to genealogy more exciting than hunting for illegal weapons and disposing of them."

She lowered her head so he couldn't quite see her face. "Not every genealogical search could be as challenging as my sister's. Now that it's over—"

"It's far from over," he broke in. "We've still got to track down Antonin Buric and put him behind bars. I'm going to need your help more than ever."

"Then I hope we find him before you have to leave in January."

"I won't be going anywhere as long as he's still on the loose."

She sat forward. "I thought January was an absolute deadline for you."

"It is if I want to stay in the CIA. But I've been toying with an idea I haven't even talked to Wendell about yet."

Her gaze searched his. "What idea?"

"To remain a genealogist who assists in criminal investigations. I don't know if there is such an animal, but that's what I've been doing for you and I've discovered I like it."

"Enough to do it as a lifetime career?" The shock in her question gave him immense pleasure.

"Why not? It only makes sense. Kamila has already rented a home here she can buy. It's a great place to raise Jared. I intend to keep the promise I made to my father to look after her.

"Of course, there's another factor to consider. The most important one. Part of this new job would entail flying around the country to check out leads. I'd need my own private pilot I could call on when it became necessary. Can you think of anyone who might be willing to go into partnership with me?"

"Be serious, Jake." Her voice sounded unsteady.

"You're my first choice." He kept speaking as if she hadn't said anything. "But it would mean you'd have to cut down on your caseload at the firm.

"I was thinking if you hired another attorney to handle the bulk, and you only took a certain percentage of new clients, it would free you to keep up with your foundation work and still fly me around. I, in turn, would continue to volunteer my services to the foundation to help in searches."

More silence. Another gratifying sound while she turned over his proposition in her mind. That was good.

While he had her at an advantage, Jake reached in his pocket for his wallet. After opening it, he pulled out the check she'd written him.

"Here." He tore it up and put the pieces in her hand. She looked at them, then shot him a disbelieving glance. "Write Wendell a check for ten thousand dollars for his firm's services. Without his willingness to let your case be my top priority, it wouldn't have been solved as quickly. He won't be expecting it, but no one deserves it more.

"Next, I'm going to buy a house in the area. Nothing huge or ostentatious. Just a home with maybe four bedrooms, three baths, a two-car garage. There would have to be a family room as well as a dining and living room. A fireplace of course. You know the kind of house I mean. Something charming and cozy for a family of four or five people. I haven't lived in one since Dad and I left Florida for the Czech Republic.

"My wife and I had planned to buy one when we both got out of the navy. That dream got lost in the years that followed, but it has been resurrected since I came to Salt Lake. A home is the perfect place for two people to start out their life together."

She scrambled off the couch. He shot out of the chair and grabbed her upper arms.

Gathering her against him he said, "I'm hoping you'll go house hunting with me. You see I'm getting married in a month's time and want the place ready for my bride.

"You have such impeccable taste. Besides, I'll need a good attorney to help me with the earnest money offer and final transaction. Who better than the woman I love with every atom of my being," he whispered against the soft skin of her neck.

"I'm madly in love with you, Maggie McFarland. I won't be able to handle it if you turn me down...so don't."

CHAPTER FIFTEEN

FOR THE SECOND TIME today, Maggie knew an epiphany of joy that transcended all other earthly experiences.

"If you'd said anything else…"

"Is that a yes?"

The vulnerability in his voice was a revelation. The Jake Halseys of this world just weren't like that, but she'd been given living proof she was wrong in that assumption. It was something to treasure in her heart and remember.

Maggie turned in his arms. She put her hands on his chest and slid them all the way to the back of his neck. When she looked into his eyes, she saw that a trace of uncertainty still remained.

"That's right, darling. You like everything spelled out. Well how about this?"

She sought his mouth with uninhibited desire, no longer afraid to show him how she felt. He was waiting for her. They swayed under the sheer explosion of their long-suppressed needs.

"My answer is yes, yes, yes," she cried when he finally allowed her breath. "I've wanted to be Mrs. Jake Halsey for a shamefully long time."

His lips roved over her face and throat, thrilling her with every kiss. "How shamefully?"

She smiled. "Since the moment Wendell started telling you about my Scotch-Irish ancestor. Your gaze trapped mine and that was it."

He kissed away her smile until they were both trembling. "I'm afraid I was even more shameful. The first thing I noticed was a stunning pair of legs.

"When my eyes traveled up the rest of you and saw that you didn't wear a wedding ring, I determined then and there I was going to have you no matter how long it took. If you were involved or engaged to someone else, I would find a way to break it up so you could belong to me."

She crushed him tighter. "I was already yours before I left your office."

His expression sobered. "No, sweetheart, you weren't." He gave her another long, hard kiss, as if he were afraid she might disappear on him. "In fact with everything that's happened today, I'm not sure you know your own mind yet."

She knew it, but it seemed this marvelous man needed more convincing.

"Come with me." Grabbing his hand, she pulled him over to the side table where she kept her house phone and answering machine. Without explanation, she phoned her parents.

"Who are you calling this time of night?" His surprised expression was priceless.

"Darling?" sounded her mother's voice. It resonated throughout the study.

Maggie smiled at the man she adored. "Hi, Mom. Are you and Dad still talking to Kathryn?"

"No. She's gone to bed. Thank you for getting everything ready for her. The poor darling was exhausted and fell asleep the second her head touched the pillow. Your dad's just locking up the house."

For the rest of their lives Maggie's father would view that as a grave responsibility.

Clearing her throat she said, "I know you're the two happiest parents on the planet tonight. I hope you can stand a little more happiness because I have something to tell you that can't wait. Could you tell Dad to get on another extension?"

"Maggie—" Jake had clamped her against him. She felt his lips caressing her nape. She was melting fast.

"Of course, darling. Just a minute."

While Maggie waited, she turned to meet Jake's mouth. Once again he swept her away to a rapturous place.

"Hi, honey. I'm on with your mother. We've been waiting for your call."

His reply astonished Maggie. She tore her lips from Jake's.

"You have?"

Her dad started to laugh. It was the full-bodied kind that began in the belly. "The family's been taking bets on when Jake would propose. Your brothers figured tonight was the night. How soon are we going to put on another wedding around here?"

"Why not make it sooner than later, darling," her mother chimed in. "Your poor father about killed himself off getting the yard ready for Cord's reception.

While it's still looking its best, let's take advantage of it."

Maggie's parents had turned into different people.

Delighted, she lifted her gaze to Jake's. "They want us to pick a date now. Since you need to keep a low profile, we'll make it small. Just family and a few close friends. No formal invitations."

A new light radiated from his eyes. "Two weeks? I'd rather elope with you tonight, but I think your family needs that long at least to prepare. Maybe in that amount of time, Kamila's family can make arrangements to fly over for it."

Maggie heard her father's voice in her ear. She'd almost forgotten she was on the phone with her parents.

"Is that Jake I can hear in the background?"

"Yes, Dad."

"Put him on."

"I'm right here." Jake put his arm around her shoulders and pulled her close. "Your daughter has made me a happy man. I hope I have your blessing."

"You can ask that after what you've done for this family?" Her father's voice rang out with pure emotion. "It was evident from the first you were the one she wanted for her husband. You've made us very happy parents."

"You have!" her mom cried. "We love you, Jake. Welcome to the family."

Maggie knew there was one question her parents were holding back. "Mom? Dad? Jake's not going back to San Diego. We're going to buy a home here and he's going to continue to work at the genealogical firm."

With that news, her parents dissolved in fresh tears. "Our cup just ran over, Maggie honey."

"Come on up to the house in the morning, darling. We'll plan the wedding. Getting your sister involved will be the best thing that could happen to her while she's convalescing."

The second Maggie heard the click, her world tilted. She found herself in Jake's arms being carried to the couch. He followed her body down.

"This is where I've wanted to be for a very long time. Hold me, Maggie. Love me."

She needed no urging, not when the communion of their mouths and bodies brought her such ecstasy. Deep in the throes of passion, her phone rang. They let her machine pick up the message. It was Cord.

"Hey, Maggie— Way to go! Mom and Dad just phoned. Kit and I are overjoyed. If you're there, Jake, just want you to know we couldn't be happier. Until I met you, I never thought any man could be good enough for my sister. Looks like we'll be bringing down another bottle of bubbly from the attic to celebrate. Congratulations! See you in the morning."

"Did you hear that?" she whispered.

Jake didn't stop covering her face with kisses. "I heard, and it's very gratifying, but right now I have other things on my mind."

The phone rang again. Jake's body heaved in reaction to the interruption. Again, they didn't pick up.

"Maggie?" It was Ben. "Your news has brought me as much happiness as finding Kathryn. You've sacrificed your whole life for this family. When the rest of us were overcome with sadness, you never let it dominate you.

"You're the strongest woman I've ever known. I love you, and I thank God a man like Jake came along. As Brock said tonight, 'He's a super-cool dude.' Amen to that.

"It's time you grabbed hold of your happiness with both hands. Jake's the person to make all your dreams come true. If you're within hearing distance, Jake, I just want to say Julie and I are thrilled there's going to be another brother in the family. We'll all be there in the morning to congratulate you. If there's anything we can do to help expedite your wedding plans, you can count on us."

First Cord, now Ben.

Telltale tears trickled from the corners of Maggie's eyes. She couldn't help it after their touching words.

Jake must have tasted the moisture on her face. With a quiet groan, he rose up and pulled her onto his lap. "I think your brothers were trying to tell me something."

"That they love you."

"That, too." His lips twitched. "But they knew you and I were together. It was their not-so-subtle hint to go slow and easy with their precious sister."

"No, darling—they wouldn't do that."

"The hell they wouldn't."

She blinked. "Don't pay any attention."

"I'm glad they did." He kissed her hair. "They've let me know you're a prize. I already knew it, but their brotherly concern is going to keep me honest until our wedding night."

"No, Jake. I'm not a teenager. I've waited my whole life for you."

"That's the point, sweetheart. You *have* waited. Since I'm going to be your one and only lover, I want to do this right and be your husband first."

He reached in his pocket and pulled something out. She felt him grasp her left hand. "This was the engagement ring my father bought for my mother when he was only eighteen. Dad gave it to me before he died. He told me he was twice lucky in love, and hoped I would be, too."

Jake looked deep into her eyes. "Maggie McFarland, will you wear my mother's ring?"

"Oh Jake—" She helped him slide it on her ring finger. It was a perfect fit. "I'll treasure it forever."

He rocked her in his arms. "It's a tiny diamond," he said.

"It represented your father's love, and now it represents yours. If you think I care about possessions…"

"I know you don't! You're a living miracle, Maggie. I need you so badly in my life. Morning, noon, night and every second in between."

Jake didn't know the half of it.

WHILE KATHRYN WAITED for Maggie to finish talking to Cheryl Cummings, who ran the volunteer desk, she walked around the foundation headquarters on her crutches.

After a week at home with the family waiting on her hand and foot, it was a relief when the doctor at North Avenues Hospital told her she could start moving around on her own. She knew those words had to be liberating for her parents as well.

Seven days after arriving in Salt Lake, she felt like the true McFarland she was. There was no strangeness.

She couldn't understand it. In fact if anything made her nervous, it was the absence of struggle. Just this morning when Milena had phoned to see how she was getting along, she'd called her Anna. Kathryn had trouble relating to her old name.

Long talks with Kit, who'd been born Melissa, had revealed she'd been able to embrace her birth family wholeheartedly, too. But she still lived with a certain amount of sorrow that the woman who'd raised her all those years had lied to her about being her mother.

The Skwarses and the Burics had never lied to Kathryn. In that regard, she would always love them for their goodness to her.

As Kathryn looked around, it struck her how amazing it was that neither she nor Kit had been murdered. Whatever the Buric brothers' criminal activities, they hadn't taken that final, evil step.

According to Agent Simpson, they'd never been arrested for killing anyone, yet it was a threat to kill that had earned Franz his prison sentence for armed robbery. Poor Kit's mother had come close to death when Franz had used a knife to force her to drive him away from the bank the day he kidnapped Kit. Kathryn shivered to think Antonin was still at large and might be doing that to someone else.

The history behind their two kidnappings was incredible.

Kathryn's eyes blurred with tears to see that everything the foundation stood for had its nascence with her abduction. By the time she'd toured the room with all its displays, she felt a burning need to get involved.

Now that Maggie was getting married, Kathryn intended to take her own place on the board with the rest of the family and relieve her sister of some of her responsibilities.

Maggie had been running a law firm and helping to run the foundation for a long time. Kathryn could do the same thing while she attended the University of Utah next January. Between now and then she could give full-time to the foundation.

"Sorry I took so long," Maggie said a few minutes later. "If you're not too tired, I'll show you around my office before Jake drives us up the canyon."

"I'm anything but tired. Lead the way."

This was what Kathryn had been waiting for. Ever since the travel agent had shown her the brochure of the Albion Basin, she'd dreamed of seeing it in full flower, just like in the photograph.

Saturday evening was finally here. Cord and Kit were fixing a barbecue for the family, a sort of combined dinner and wedding shower at their home in Alta.

Maggie could have set up her law firm anywhere, but she'd chosen to live and work at the heart of the foundation. Kathryn's admiration for her sister continued to grow as they entered her impressive suite.

"In here is the conference room." Kathryn poked her head inside. "And right down here is my office." When Maggie opened the door, Kathryn glimpsed Kit's brother Steven Talbot.

She'd met him a week ago at the pool. The third-year law student was incredibly attractive whether he was playing water polo like a professional or working in his shirt sleeves.

He looked up from the desk. Though he said hi to Maggie, his blue eyes, so identical to Kit's, fastened on Kathryn and lingered. He stood up. "Hello again."

"Hi, Steve."

"For you to be out and about means you're healing fast."

"That's what the doctor said. I asked Maggie to show me around."

Her sister sorted through some files on her desk, eyeing the latest notations. "I thought you'd already left for Alta, Steve."

"After talking to Jake, we decided you'd drive up with him and I'd take Kathryn with me. The Altima has more leg room in the front to accommodate her cast. If that's all right with both of you."

But he was asking Kathryn. Her heart did a little extra skip.

"Of course. That's very thoughtful of you."

"Good. Then let's get going. Why don't you two go out to the front of the plaza by the statue. I'll bring the car around and meet you. Jake's meeting you there as well, Maggie."

"We'll be waiting."

His glance swerved to Kathryn. "I'll see you in a minute. My car is metallic blue—you can't miss it."

After he left, she and Maggie walked through the office to the main doors. Maggie set the lock with her remote and they started across the plaza courtyard.

"I didn't realize Steve was invited."

Maggie eyed her speculatively. "Would you rather ride with Jake and me? All you have to do is say the word."

"No. It's not that. I'm just surprised."

"I'm not. Last week he couldn't take his eyes off you while you were telling everyone about your life on the farm. Is that what's bothering you? The fact that he's interested and you're not? You can tell me the truth. We're sisters."

"We are! It's so wonderful, I still feel like I'm dreaming."

Maggie hugged her. "I'm floating off the ground myself these days. So?" she persisted.

Kathryn chuckled. "Steven Talbot's one good-looking guy, but—I don't know. I can't explain it exactly. He's just right there invading your space, you know?"

"Not exactly like the quiet-spoken Skwars/Buric men you grew up around?"

"You noticed that with one visit?" Maggie was amazing.

"I did, and Kit's brother is nothing like them."

"You can say that again."

"Let me tell you something. There aren't too many men like him period. Don't forget he's born and bred Southern Californian. He's got it all. Kit's mother confided to me he's been a heartbreaker from the time he was in third grade. Girls have always flocked to him. But I can guarantee he's never met a woman like you."

"That's because I'm the missing McFarland child. No doubt the fascination will wear off shortly."

"His sister was the missing Talbot child. I don't think that's the reason he's attracted. There's his car coming around the corner."

It upset Kathryn that her pulse started to quicken

without her volition. She watched him pull up to the curb and jump out of the car. He went around to open the front passenger door and adjusted the seat for her.

Once he'd relieved her of her crutches and put them in the back seat, he steadied her while she got in. Then he hunkered down and carefully supported her cast before placing it on the floor.

He'd done what anyone would have done who was attempting to help her. But somehow with him, it seemed too intimate. "Thank you."

His gaze was still on eye level with hers. "You're welcome."

Steve Talbot had a killer smile.

Just before he shut the door, she heard Maggie cry out Jake's name. Apparently he'd driven up behind them. Theirs was the kind of love Kathryn wanted to have one day with the man she married.

"I'll take care of Kathryn, Maggie. See you in Alta." Steve got behind the wheel and they took off. "Are you nervous to drive in a car since your accident?"

"Not really."

"I wouldn't blame you if you were."

"My eagerness to be in the mountains is probably the reason why." She told him about the plans she'd made to ski in Alta this winter.

"That sounds like more than a coincidence."

"It did to me, too. To think that one of the places I'd dreamed of going would end up being Cord's backyard."

"What's the other place?"

"The beach in Southern California. I've never seen the ocean."

He glanced at her. "Now you've given me chills."

"Why?"

"Our family has a place at Laguna Beach. In fact, my parents are going to be at the party tonight so you can meet them. They bought a beach house years ago. You walk out the glass doors right on to the sand. When you come down with Kit and Cord, I'll teach you how to surf. It's more exciting than snow skiing."

Too exciting.

"That'll have to be next summer, I'm afraid."

"I'll take you to a lot of beaches. They all have their own personality."

"Can a law student take off that kind of time?"

He grinned. "This law student can, and will! What are you going to study at the U?"

"I have to get my undergraduate work done first. Before everything happened, I thought medicine. Now I'm not so sure."

"Why?"

"The FBI agents who were working on my case were very kind to me. When I look back on my experience, I can see what a vital role they played in helping me to deal with a very difficult situation both before and after I found out I was kidnapped.

"Agent Simpson came to the house the other day. We had a long talk. I learned how instrumental she was in helping solve your sister's case. I was very impressed with her knowledge and her dedication."

"So you think you might like to become an agent?"

"I don't know. It's a thought. When I see how involved my family is helping other people, I marvel."

"Maybe that instinct is in the McFarland genes, which would explain why you thought of becoming a doctor long before you knew who you were."

"Maybe."

They were almost to the top of the canyon now. She looked all around her in wonder. "It's spectacular up here."

"Just wait till you see Cord's place. We're almost there."

Between the man sitting next to her and the scenery, she experienced an exhilaration she'd never felt before. They rounded a bend on the mountain road, then she saw the meadow filled with wildflowers, and the jutting peaks behind it. The last rays of the sun gilded everything.

She gasped. "Oh, Steve, this couldn't be real—"

"That's how I felt the first time I saw this place. There are bits of heaven on earth. This is one of them."

NIGHT HAD COME to the Albion Basin. Jake stood behind Maggie on the deck of Cord's home with his arms around her. They'd eaten and they'd opened gifts. The Talbots had offered the use of their beach house for the honeymoon. Jake was living for it.

Because the evening had been so magical, he'd held back vital information he'd learned over the past couple of days. But he couldn't keep it to himself any longer.

Maggie turned in his arms and lifted concerned eyes to him. "What was that deep sigh for?"

She was so attuned to him, it was uncanny the way she could read him and his moods.

"I have a present to give both families. I'm just not sure if tonight's the time to break the news."

She let out a small cry. *"You found Antonin!"*

"Let's just say I pursued a few ideas and the FBI did the rest. Agent Simpson knew our wedding was getting close so she left it up to me to decide when to tell everyone."

"I don't care how sobering it is. We all need closure to get on with our lives. Come on. Let's not put this off another second."

"If you're sure."

She held his face between her hands. "As long as Antonin was still on the loose after violating our family, I don't think anyone has felt entirely safe. Oh yes, darling. This is the perfect time to put all our fears to rest."

Jake knew it.

There was a part deep inside Maggie that had feared Antonin might come after them again. It was the supreme moment for Jake to know he could give her the one gift that would ensure their total happiness. He lowered his head and kissed the lips he would always hunger for, always crave.

Her response made him tremble. Though it was only a matter of days now, their honeymoon couldn't come soon enough.

Reluctantly he broke off their kiss. Sliding his hand to her nape, he guided her back inside to the living room of the rustic home. It was as magnificent as the mountains towering over it.

"Ah. There they are," Maggie's mother said. At her comment, everyone's heads lifted in their direction.

"Jake and I want to thank you for this fabulous party.

I've never been so happy. Before we leave, he has something important he wants to tell all of you."

He looked around the crowd of loved ones assembled. Kamila held Jared in her arms. She flashed him a quiet smile. His stepmother knew what he was about to reveal.

"Two days ago Antonin Buric was arrested in Alaska for kidnapping."

An explosion of cries resounded in the room.

"Going on a hunch that he was always on the run and had worked on a ship before, I talked it over with Agent Kelly in California. Together we systematically phoned every port on the Pacific Coast from Mexico to Alaska to get names of all commercial shipping lines. Those companies gave us the lists of their crews. Sure enough, Tony Burk's name came up as part of a salmon fishing boat outfit. The rest was easy, and the FBI picked him up."

Reed shook his head. "That was an incredible piece of detective work, Jake."

"The person who's really incredible is Agent Kelly. He played a trick on Antonin by telling him they were arresting him for the kidnapping of Melissa Talbot and Kathryn McFarland.

"It worked because he spewed venom against his brother Franz for telling on him about the McFarland kidnapping. That was the proof Agent Kelly had been looking for, that Antonin had been directly involved.

"Once in custody, he went into a rage about how his younger brother had mental problems and had always copied him, how he'd ended up bungling the bank robbery because he'd decided to kidnap the baby of someone with no money. They'd already planned the kidnapping of the McFarland baby who would be worth millions once it was born."

Both the Talbots and Maggie's parents stared at each other in shock.

"So he got Franz to dump the Talbot baby on his girlfriend Rena Harris. Right before they left for Salt Lake he not only forced Franz to tell her it was the McFarland baby, he made him threaten her that if she and the baby didn't want to die, she'd better shut up about it.

"If she didn't, then Rena would be the one blamed for the McFarland kidnapping and she'd be given the death penalty for stealing the child of someone so wealthy and famous. Apparently the threat worked. Rena kept quiet, never knowing it was the Talbot baby she was raising."

"Poor Rena," Kit burst into tears before burying her face against Cord. "At least she didn't have anything to do with the kidnapping."

"She withheld evidence,' Kit's mother murmured, "but we have to be thankful that in the end she found the courage to tell you the truth. If it weren't for Rena, none of us would be here tonight."

Jake didn't even want to think about that. It meant he would have never met Maggie. That was something he couldn't comprehend.

"She was only eighteen and an orphan. Franz had to have terrified her into keeping quiet. It seems Antonin got Franz to drive to Salt Lake and together they planned the break-in of the mansion. They watched the grounds and noticed the milkman came every morning very early in his truck."

"The milkman!" Ellen cried out.

"The police interrogated ours!" Reed exclaimed before shaking his head.

"You were up against professionals. Franz agreed to steal a milk truck parked at your dairy during the night when it wouldn't be noticed. Antonin hid inside.

"They drove to the rear entrance where Antonin, masquerading as a milkman, hid on your porch. In the middle of the night he sneaked up the stairs to the nursery and stole Kathryn."

Maggie's sister had gone white. "This is unbelievable." Reed put his arm around her.

"I agree, Kathryn. Then he went back to his hiding place on the porch. Franz drove up early in the morning, and Antonin got inside with the baby. When your milk came at the regular delivery time, no one was the wiser. They made it to a prearranged location where they'd parked their car. Antonin followed Franz back to the dairy where he put the truck back under the noses of everyone.

"Once that was accomplished, they began their trek across the country to New York where Antonin planned to tell his grandmother he needed a place for him and his wife and child to stay. From there he would write the ransom note.

"Franz got nervous and didn't want to face his grandmother, so he ditched his brother. Antonin called on an old girlfriend to pose as his wife and help him take care of the baby. For cash she was willing. But she got nervous when she saw him writing the note.

"The McFarland kidnapping had been all over the news. She figured something screwy was going on so she took off. Antonin was afraid she'd go to the police. He decided to put off sending the note for a while and just cool his heels until the fervor died down.

"When he finally went back to his grandmother's apartment, he found out she'd gone to her family in Wisconsin and taken the baby with her. That changed everything, so he gave up the idea of getting a ransom.

"At that point he turned to other types of crimes and subsisted until the feds picked him up."

In the stunned quiet that followed, Maggie turned to him with an awed look in her eyes. "You *are* an angel. I never believed in them before."

THE POUNDING OF THE SURF, the pounding of Maggie's heart.

It was all one as she reached for her husband in the middle of the night and began kissing the scars that covered a portion of his shoulder and chest.

Until they'd made love on their first night as man and wife, over a week ago, she hadn't realized the extent of his wounds caused by the explosion. He could have been killed. Unknowingly, she let out a little sob.

"Sweetheart?" he murmured, pulling her on top of him. "What's the matter?"

"I love you so much, Jake. Every time I think of what my life would be like if you hadn't come in to it, I can't bear it."

"I feel the same about you." He kissed a certain favorite spot. "But we did meet. We've got each other forever, and right now there's only one thing I want to do. Come closer," he begged in an aching voice.

She moaned her need as their bodies entwined. His mouth and hands brought her such exquisite pleasure, she could hardly breathe. He started making love to her with a refined savagery. It went on until long after the sun had risen above the horizon.

When she opened her eyes, she discovered Jake's head propped in his hand studying her. "How long have you been awake?"

"For a little while. You have no idea how beautiful you are," he said in a husky voice. "I lusted after you the second we met. I still lust after you. I don't ever want to leave this beach house or this bed."

"I'm so glad you said that, because I've decided to keep you here all day and wait on you. Maybe I'll let you go out on the beach for a walk with me this evening."

She felt his low chuckle invade her bones.

"If Steve could see me now, he'd be totally shocked."

His smile faded. "What about him?"

"On the night of Cord's wedding, he asked if I'd like to come down here to the beach house for a few days' vacation."

"So I *was* right," Jake muttered. "He did have a thing for you."

"No, darling. It wasn't like that between us. Anyway, I told him I was too busy. He couldn't believe I wouldn't want to lie on the sand with nothing more to do than listen to the surf. My answer to him was that it would be pure torture.

"Little did I know then that one day I would be lying here with a man my dreams couldn't even conjure." Her eyes filled. "At the altar when the pastor asked me if I took you to be my lawfully wedded husband, I wanted to blurt that I'd already made those vows in my heart."

Jake pulled her tightly against him. "When, Maggie?"

"That night in the mountains while you were thrashing about in your sleeping bag. It happened while I was trying to comfort you. I knew then, I would be there for you always, if you would have me."

"If I would have you!" he cried out.

She kissed the tiny scar at the corner of his mouth. "I hoped."

"Oh Maggie." He crushed her against him. "I'm still haunted by that night and what I might have done to you without realizing it. Tell me the truth. Have I had any more nightmares?"

"Not one, darling."

He looked down at her. "That's because of you, my love."

Maggie smiled up at him. "Isn't love wonderful? I never knew how wonderful. I want to shout my happiness to the world. I want your babies. I'm hoping you've given me one already. It's possible. I've even got a name picked out if it's a boy."

"Anything you want sweetheart except... Recompense."

"Oh, but we have to!" she cried. "I thought Robert Recompense Halsey."

Jake grinned. "He'll never forgive us."

"True."

Suddenly she flung her arms around his neck, because a Jake who was grinning, laughing or chuckling, was more than her heart could resist.

"Let's discuss more names, but let's talk about them later. First there's something I want to do. I *have* to do." She drew his head down to her, leaving him in no doubt she was his for the taking.

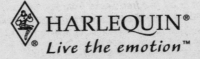